The Retrieval Artist

The Retrieval Artist
and Other Stories

51598

Kristine Kathryn Rusch

Five Star • Waterville, Maine

Five Star First Edition Science Fiction and Fantasy Series.

Published in 2002 in conjunction with Tekno-Books and Ed Gorman.

Cover illustration by Ken Barr.

Set in 11 pt. Plantin by Elena Picard.

Printed in the United States on permanent paper.

Library of Congress Cataloging-in-Publication Data

Rusch, Kristine Kathryn.
    The retrieval artist, and other stories /
Kristine Kathryn Rusch.
        p. cm.—(Five Star first edition science fiction and fantasy series)
        ISBN 0-7862-4330-9 (hc : alk. paper)
        1. Science fiction, American. I. Title. II. Series.
    PS3568.U7 R48 2002
        813'.54—dc21   2002067511

This book is dedicated to
the entire staff at Tekno-Books,
who keep me thinking and help me stretch.

Table of Contents

Introduction

When I turned forty, I embarked on a life-long dream: I started taking piano lessons. I'd been fiddling with pianos my entire life. I knew music very well. In fact, anyone who met me in high school and later discovered that I'd spent my life in the arts would have guessed that I had become a musician, not a writer.

It's one thing to learn an instrument when you're ten and your parents force you to practice. It's another to learn when you're an adult, and all the responsibility lies with you. I don't give recitals or participate in my teacher's student concerts. I'm learning the piano just for me.

Since I already had a music background, I didn't have to learn a new language. I had to learn a new way to communicate the notes I found on the page. And it wasn't easy. A flute player, which I was, plays one note at a time; a pianist can play at least ten, sometimes more. Each finger becomes an instrument in itself.

The biggest problem I had, however, was my own imagination. Because of my musical background, I could look at a sheet of music and know how it should sound. But my fingers didn't have the capability my mind had. My fingers were thick and clumsy, and didn't want to work alone. Never mind adding my feet into the mix—at first I had to ignore the pedals entirely.

Because I got lost in the notes, sometimes remaining on one measure for a week at a time, I found myself thinking about technique. Not piano playing technique—I couldn't master the notes, let alone attempt expression—but composition techniques.

I noticed that each composer had a recognizable style within each composition, a signature if you will. Sometimes it was a certain combination of notes. Sometimes it was just the key signature—some composers seemed to favor the key of G for example, while others preferred the key of C. Sometimes it was the way the notes fell together, something about the piece that was so clearly Mozart instead of Tchaikovsky or Bach instead of Beethoven.

I also learned that musical notation could be deceptive. A musical piece that looked easy might be a lot more difficult than something with measures of sixteenth notes and huge crashing chords. I never knew until I got inside the music what I would find.

The more I played, the more I realized how similar the arts were. Writers who start becoming serious about their craft in their thirties or forties feel the same frustration I felt as a beginning piano player: they could imagine the story in their head, but they couldn't put it down on the page.

Because I started writing so young (I finished my first story at seven), I never thought about my own process until I spent frustrating hours with the piano. Many other writers outline or write character notes, but I couldn't be bothered. I always figured that was because I was an organic writer. I wrote a quick first draft, and then shaped the story to be what I wanted it to be.

Often my short stories would turn into novels. I would

10

finish the short story, then realize I wasn't done with the world or the characters, and start all over again—this time as a novel.

I simply figured that this was how I worked—and if I thought about it (which I didn't), I would have guessed this was how everyone worked.

It isn't. Each writer has a different process, but I might not have noticed that without the music. You see, composers often explored something in the short form—a prelude, perhaps—and then explored the same musical idea in a longer form—let's say a sonata.

I remember noticing, when I was stuck in the middle of some pieces Tchaikovsky wrote for children, that he explored some of the same themes in those that he examined in his famous *Nutcracker*—and not all of them were musical themes. Dolls, for example, are very important to both. (My favorite sequence in the children's book was "The Sick Doll," "The Doll's Funeral," and "The New Doll.")

Even though the themes explored were similar—or often laid the groundwork for the other pieces—the resulting music was different. No one would ever confuse "The New Doll" with *The Nutcracker*, although an attentive listener would hear the signature and know both were by Tchaikovsky.

I tend to explore similar ideas and themes in both the long and short form. In my case, the short form always comes first. I rarely go from novel to short story (and then only because someone has asked me to do so). But I often go from short story to novel.

The process works like this: I explore the idea in the short story and then realize that I have a lot more to say. In some cases, I write several additional short stories. In others, I turn immediately to a novel.

11

There are examples of both types of short stories in this volume, as well as stand-alone short fiction. For example, three stories have become novels. "The Retrieval Artist," which was nominated for a Hugo award for Best Novella, marks the first time I dealt with the world of Miles Flint. As I wrote the novella, I realized I had a lot more stories to tell in this world. I've just finished the first novel, *The Disappeared*, which will be published in July by Roc. I'm going to start the second novel at the end of this month, and it'll be published in early 2003.

The other two stories, "Dancers Like Children" and "Alien Influences," formed the basis for my Arthur C. Clarke-nominated novel *Alien Influences*. It wasn't until I wrote the second story that I realized this alien world wasn't going to let me go until I explored it fully.

A few of the others stories will become novels some day. I know that the character of Geneva from "Without End" hasn't let me go, and I wrote that story ten years ago. I just don't know where she'll take me.

"The One That Got Away," is part of a series of short stories that I have written over the past ten years, all set in Seavy Village. My novel, *Façade*, is set in Seavy Village as well. Things go awry in Seavy Village, and I'm sure it'll turn up in other stories—and other novels—as the years go by.

The remaining stories in this collection have their links—in my mind—to novels yet unwritten. But I'm not sure how they'll factor in, whether as chapters, or missing pieces, or simply character studies. But rest assured, they'll appear somewhere.

You see, like the composers I'm studying, I happen to like some key signatures too. Not all of my stories are written in those keys, but many of them are. Those keys are my settings. The combination of notes that recur over and over again in my fiction are characters who simply won't let go.

After two years, I'm still at the piano. My fingers aren't as hesitant, and I don't spend a month on a measure any more. But I'm not making music yet either—at least, music as I define it.

Thank heavens for writing. At least here, my process is set and my brain and fingers work together. There no longer is a gap between the story I imagine and the story I put on paper.

I will never be a concert pianist. I don't have the time or the patience for it.

But I love being a writer, and I love sharing stories. Here are nine of my best. Enjoy.

—Kristine Kathryn Rusch
February 18, 2002

The Retrieval Artist

1

I had just come off a difficult case, and the last thing I wanted was another client. To be honest, not wanting another client is a constant state for me. Miles Flint, the reluctant Retrieval Artist. I work harder than anyone else in the business at discouraging my clients from seeking out the Disappeared. Sometimes the discouragement fails and I get paid a lot of money for putting a lot of lives in danger, and maybe, just maybe, bringing someone home who wants to come. Those are the moments I live for, the moments when it becomes clear to a Disappeared that home is a safe place once more.

Usually though, my clients and their lost ones are more trouble than they're worth. Usually, I won't take their cases for any price, no matter how high.

I do everything I can to prevent client contact from the start. The clients who approach me are the courageous ones or the really desperate ones or the ones who want to use me to further their own ends.

I try not to take my cases personally. My clients and their lost ones depend on my objectivity. But every once in

15

a while, a case slips under my defenses—and never in the way I expect.

This was one of those cases. And it haunts me still.

II

My office is one of the ugliest dives on the Moon. I found an original building still made of colonial permaplastic in the oldest section of Armstrong, the Moon's oldest colony. The dome here is also made of permaplastic, the clear kind, although time and wear have turned it opaque. Dirt covers the dome near the street level. The filtration system tries to clean as best it can, but ever since some well-meaning dome governor pulled the permaplastic flooring and forgot to replace it, this part of Armstrong Dome has had a dust problem. The filtration systems have been upgraded twice in my lifetime, and rebuilt at least three times since the original settlement, but they still function at one-tenth the level of the state-of-the-art systems in colonies like Gagarin Dome and Glenn Station. Terrans newly off the shuttle rarely come to this part of Armstrong; the high-speed trains don't run here, and the unpaved streets strike most Terrans as unsanitary, which they probably are.

The building that houses my office had been the original retail center of Armstrong, or so says the bronze plaque that someone had attached to the plastic between my door and the rent-a-lawyer's beside me. We are an historic building, not that anyone seems to care, and the rent-a-lawyer once talked to me about getting the designation changed so that we could upgrade the facilities.

I didn't tell him that if the designation changed, I would move.

You see, I like the seedy look, the way my door hangs slightly crooked in its frame. It's deceptive. A careless Tracker would think I'm broke, or equally careless. Most folks don't guess that the security in my little eight-by-eight cube is state of the art. They walk in, and they see permaplastic, and a desk that cants slightly to the right, and only one chair behind it. They don't see the recessed doors that hide my storage in the wall between the rent-a-lawyer's cube and my own, and they don't see the electronics because they aren't looking for them.

I like to keep the office empty. I own an apartment in one of Armstrong's better neighborhoods. There I keep all the things I don't care about. Things I do care about stay in my ship, a customized space yacht named *The Emmeline*. She's my only friend and I treat her like a lover. She's saved my life more times than I care to think about, and for that (and a few other things), she deserves only the best.

I can afford to give her the best, and I don't need any more work although, as I said, I sometimes take it. The cases that catch me are usually the ones that catch me in my Sir Galahad fantasy—the one where I see myself as a rescuer of all things worthy of rescue—although I've been known to take cases for other reasons.

But, as I'd said, I'd just come off a difficult case, and the last thing I needed was another client. Especially one as young and innocent as this one appeared to be.

She showed up at my door wearing a dress, which no one wears in this part of Armstrong any more, and regular shoes, which had to have been painful to walk in. She also had a personal items bag around her wrist, which, in this part of town, was like wearing a giant *Mug Me!* sign. The bags were issued on shuttles and only to passengers who had no idea about the luggage limitations.

She was tall and raw-boned, but slender, as if diet and exercise had reduced her natural tendency toward lushness. Her dress, an open and inexpensive weave, accented her figure in an almost unconscious way. Her features were strong and bold, her eyes dark, and her hair even darker.

My alarm system warned me she was outside, staring at the door or the plaque or both. A small screen popped up on my desk revealing her and the street beyond. I shut off the door alarm, and waited until she knocked. Her clutched fist, adorned with computer and security enhancements that winked like diamonds in the dome's fake daylight, rapped softly on the permaplastic. The daintiness of the movement startled me. I wouldn't have thought her a dainty woman.

I had been cleaning up the final reports, notations and billings from the last case. I closed the file and the keyboard (I never use voice commands for work in my office—too easily overheard) folded itself into the desk. Then I leaned back in the chair, and waited.

She knocked three times, before she tried the door. It opened, just like it had been programmed to do in instances like this.

"Mr. Flint?" Her voice was soft, her English tinted with a faintly Northern European accent.

I still didn't say anything. She had the right building and the right name. I would wait to see if she was the right kind of client.

She squinted at me. I was never what clients expected. They expected a man as seedy as the office, maybe one or two unrepaired scars, a face toughened by a hard life and space travel. Even though I was thirty-five, I still had a look some cultures called angelic: blond curls, blue eyes, a round and cherubic face. A client once told me I looked like the pre-Raphaelite paintings of Cupid. I had smiled at him and said, *Only when I want to.*

"Are you Mr. Flint?" The girl stepped inside, then slapped her left hand over the enhancements on her right. She looked faintly startled, as if someone had shouted in her ear.

Actually, my security system had cut in. Those enhancements linked her to someone or something outside herself, and my system automatically severed such links, even if they had been billed as unseverable.

"You want to stay in here," I said, "you stay in here alone. No recording, no viewing, and no off-site monitoring."

She swallowed, and took another step inside. She was playing at being timid. The real timid ones, severed from their security blankets, bolt.

"What do you want?" I asked.

She flinched, and took another step forward. "I understand that you—find—people."

"Where did you hear that?"

"I was told in New York." One more step and she was standing in front of my desk. She smelled faintly of lavender soap mixed with nervous sweat. She must have come here directly from the shuttle. A woman with a mission, then.

"New York?" I asked as if I'd never heard of it.

"New York City."

I had several contacts in New York, and a handful of former clients. Anyone could have told her, although none were supposed to. They always did though; they always saw their own desperation in another's eyes, figured it was time

19

to help, time to give back whatever it was they felt they had gained.

I sighed. "Close the door."

She licked her lips—the dye on them was either water-proof or permanent—and then walked back to the door. She looked into the street as if she would find help there, then gently pushed the door closed.

I felt a faint hum through my wrist as my computer notified me that it had turned the door security back on.

"What do you want?" I asked before she turned around.

"My mother," she said. "She's—"

"That's enough." I kept my tone harsh, and I didn't stand. I didn't want this girl/woman to be too comfortable. It was always best to keep potential clients off balance.

Children, young adults, and the elderly were the obvious choices of someone trying to use my system for the wrong purposes, and yet they were the ones most likely to contact me. They never seemed to understand the hostility I had to show clients, the insistence I put on identity checks, and they always balked at the cost. *It feels as if I'm on trial, Mr. Flint,* they would say, and I wouldn't respond. They were. They had to be. I always had to be sure they were only acting on their own interests. It was too easy for a Tracker to hire someone to play off a Retrieval Artist's sympathies, and initiate a search that would get the Disappeared killed—or worse.

The girl turned. Her body was so rigid that it looked as if I could break her in half.

"I don't find people," I said. "I uncover them. There's a vast difference. If you don't understand that, then you don't belong here."

That line usually caused half my potential clients to exit. The next line usually made most of the remaining fifty percent excuse themselves, never to darken my door again.

"I charge a minimum of two million credits, Moon issue, not Earth issue—" which meant that they were worth triple what she was used to paying—"and I can charge as much as ten million or more. There is no upper limit on my costs nor is there one on my charges. I charge by the day, with expenses added in. Some investigations take a week, some take five years. You would be my exclusive employer for the period of time it takes to find your—mother—or whomever I'd be looking for. I have a contract. Several of my former clients have tried to have the courts nullify it. It holds up beautifully. I do not take charity cases, no matter what your sob story is, and I do not allow anyone to defer payment. The minute the money stops, so do I."

She threaded her fingers together. Her personal items bag bumped against her hip as she did so. "I'd heard about your financial requirements." Which meant that one of my former clients had recommended me to her. Dammit. "I have limited funds, but I can afford a minor investigation."

I stood. "We're done talking. Sorry I can't help you." I walked past her and pulled open the door. Security didn't mind if I did that. It would have minded if she had.

"Can't you do a limited search, Mr. Flint?" Her eyes were wide and brown. If she was twenty, she was older than I thought. I checked for tears. There were none. She could be legit, and for that I was sorry.

I closed the door so hard the plastic office shook. "Here's what you're asking me," I said. "If the money runs out, I quit searching, which is no skin off my nose. But I'll have dug a trail up to that particular point, and your mother—or whomever I'm looking for—"

She flinched again as I said that. A tender one. Or a good actress.

21

"—would be at more of a risk than she is now. Right now, she's simply disappeared. And since you've come to me, you've done enough research to know that one of six government programs—or one of fifteen private corporations—have gone to considerable expense to give her a new life somewhere else. If the cover on that existence gets blown, your mother dies. It's that simple. And maybe, just maybe, the people who helped her will die too, or the people who are now important to her, or the people who were hidden with her, for whatever reason. Half an investigation is a death sentence. Hell, sometimes a full investigation is a death sentence. So I don't do this work on whim, and I certainly don't do it in a limited fashion. Are we clear?"

She nodded, just once, a rabbit-like movement that let me know I'd connected.

"Good," I said and pulled the door back open. "Now get out."

She scurried past me as if she thought I might physically assault her, and then she hurried down the street. The moon dust rose around her, clinging to her legs and her impractical dress, leaving a trail behind her that was so visible, it looked as if someone were marking her as a future target.

I closed the door, had the security system take her prints and DNA sample off the jamb just in case I needed to identify her someday, and then tried not to think of her again.

It wouldn't be easy. Clients were rare and, if they were legit, they always had an agenda. By the time they found me, they were desperate, and there was still a part of me that was human enough to feel sympathy for that.

Sympathy is rare among Retrieval Artists. Most Retrieval Artists got into this line of work because they owed a favor to the Disty, a group of aliens who'd more or less taken over

Mars. Others got into it because they had discovered, by accident, that they were good at it, usually making that discovery in their jobs for human corporations or human crime syndicates.

I got in through a different kind of accident. Once I'd been a space cop assigned to Moon Sector. A lot of the Disappeared come through here on their way to new lives, and over time, I found myself working against a clock, trying to save people I'd never met from the people they were hiding from. The space police frowned on the work—the Disappeared are often reformed criminals and not worth the time, at least according to the Moon Sector—and so, after one of the most horrible incidents of my life, I went into business on my own.

I'm at the top of my profession, rich beyond all measure, and usually content with that. I chose not to have a spouse or children, and my family is long dead, which I actually consider to be a good thing. Families in this business are a liability. So are close friends. Anyone who can be broken to force you to talk. I don't mind being alone.

But I do hate to be manipulated, and I hate even more to take revenge, mine or anyone else's. I vigilantly protect myself against both of those things.

And this was the first time I failed.

III

After the girl left, I stayed away from the office for two days. Sometimes snubbed clients come back. They tell me their stories, the reasons they're searching for their parent/child/spouse, and they expect me to understand.

Sometimes they claim they've found more money. Sometimes they simply try to cry on my shoulder, believing I will sympathize.

Once upon a time maybe I would have. But Sir Galahad has calluses growing on his heart. I am beginning to hate the individuals. They always take a level of judgment that drains me. The lawyers trying to find a long-lost soul to meet the terms of a will; the insurance agents, required by law to find the beneficiaries, forced by the government to search "as far as humanly possible without spending the benefits"; the detective, using government funds to find the one person who could put a career criminal, serial killer, or child molester, away for life; these people are the clients I like the most. Almost all are repeat customers. I still have to do background checks, but I have my gut to rely on as well. With individuals, I can never go by gut, and even armed with information, I've been burned.

I've gotten to the point where coldness is the way of the game for me, at least at first. Once I sign on, I become the most intense defender of the Disappeared. The object of my search also becomes the person I protect and care about the most. It takes a lot of effort to maintain that caring, and even more to manage the protection.

Sometimes I'll go to extremes.

Sometimes I have no other choice.

On the third day, I went back to my office, and of course, the girl was waiting. This time she was dress appropriately, a pair of boots, cargo pants that cinched at the ankles, and a shirt the color of sand. Her personal items bag was gone—obviously someone, probably the maitre d' at the exclusive hotel she was most likely staying at, told her it made her a mark for pickpockets and other thieves. Thin mesh gloves covered her enhancements. Only her long hair marked her as a newcomer. If she stayed longer than a month, she'd cut it off just like the rest of us rather than worry about keeping it clean.

She was leaning against my locked door, her booted feet sticking into the street. In that outfit, she looked strong and healthy, as if she were hiring me to take her on one of those expeditions outside the dome. The rent-a-lawyer next door, newly out of Armstrong Law, was eyeing her out of his scarred plastic window, a sour expression on his thin face. He probably thought she was scaring away business.

I stopped in the middle of the street. It was hot and airless as usual. There was no wind in the dome, of course, and the recycled air got stale real fast. Half the equipment in this part of town had been on the fritz for the last week, and the air here wasn't just stale, it was thin and damn near rancid. I hated breathing bad air. The shallow breaths, and the increased heartbeat made me feel as if there was danger around when there probably wasn't. If the air got any thinner, I'd have to start worrying about my clarity of thought.

She saw me when I was still several meters from the place. She stood, brushed the dust off her pants, and watched me. I pretended as if I were undecided about my next move, even though I knew I'd have to confront her sooner or later. Her kind only went away when chased.

"I'm sorry," she said as I approached. "I was told that you expected negotiation, so I—"

"Lied about the money, did you?" I asked, knowing she was lying now too. If she knew enough to find me, she also knew that I didn't negotiate. All the lie proved was that she had an ego big enough to believe that the rules were different for her.

I shoved past her to use my palm to unlock the door. I

only used a palm scan when someone else was present. It let us in, but initiated a higher level of security monitoring.

She started to follow me, but I slammed the door in her face. Then I went to my desk, and switched on my own automatic air. It was illegal, and it wouldn't be enough, but I wasn't planning to stay long. I would finish the reports from the last case, get the final fees, and then maybe I'd take a vacation. I had never taken one before. It was past time.

I wish, now, that I had listened to my gut and gone. But there was just enough of Sir Galahad left in me to make me watch the door. And of course, it opened just like I expected it to.

She came inside, a little downtrodden but not defeated. Her kind seldom were. "My name is Anetka Sobol," she said as if I should know it. I didn't. "I really do need your help."

"You should have thought of that before," I said. "This isn't a game."

"I'm not trying to play one."

"So what was that attempt at negotiation?"

She shook her head. "My source—"

"Who is your source?"

"He said I wasn't—"

"Who is it?"

Again she licked that lower lip just like she had the day before, a movement that was too unconscious to be planned. The nervousness, then, wasn't feigned. "Norris Gonnot."

Gonnot. Sobol was the third client he'd sent to me in the last year. The other two checked out, and both cases had been easy to solve. But he was making himself too visible, and I would have to deal with that, even though I hated to do so. He was extremely grateful that I had found his daughter and granddaughter alive (although they hadn't appreciated it), and he'd been even more grateful when I was able to prove that the Disty were no longer looking for them.

"And how did you find him?"

She frowned. "Does it matter?"

I leaned back in my chair. It squeaked and the sound made her jump ever so slightly. "Either you're up front with me now or the conversation ends."

The frown grew deeper, and she clutched her left wrist with her right hand, holding the whole mess against her stomach. The gesture looked calculated. "Do you treat everyone like this?"

"Nope. Some people I treat worse."

"Then how do you get any work?"

I shrugged. "Just lucky."

She stared at me for a moment. Then she glanced at the door. Was she letting her thoughts be that visible on purpose or was she again acting for my benefit? I wasn't sure.

"A cop told me about him. Norris, that is." She sounded reluctant. "I wasn't supposed to tell you."

"Of course not. Gonnot wasn't supposed to talk to anyone. This cop, was he a rent-a-cop, a real cop, a Federal cop, or with the Earth Force?"

"She," she said.

"Okay," I said. "Was she a—"

"She was a New York City police officer who had her own detective agency."

"That's illegal in New York."

She shrugged. "So?"

I closed my eyes. Ethics had disappeared everywhere. "You hired her?"

"She was my fifth private detective. Most would work for

a week and then quit when they realized that searching for an interstellar Disappeared is a lot harder than finding a missing person."

I waited. I'd heard that sob story before. Most detectives kept the case and simply came to someone like me.

"Of course," she said, "my father's looming presence doesn't help either."

"Your father?"

She was staring at me as if I had just asked her what God was.

"I'm Anetka Sobol," she said as if that clarified everything.

"And I'm Miles Flint. My name doesn't tell you a damn thing about my father."

"My father is the founding partner of the Third Dynasty."

I had to work to hide my surprise. I knew what the Third Dynasty was, but I didn't know the names of its founders. The Dynasty itself was a formidable presence all over the galaxy. It was a megacorp with its fingers in a lot of pies, mostly to do with space exploration, establishing colonies in mineral rich areas, and exploitation of new resources. My contacts with the Third Dynasty weren't on the exploration level, but within its narrow interior holdings. The Third Dynasty was the parent company for Privacy Unlimited, one of the services which helped people disappear.

Privacy Unlimited had been developed, as so many of the corporate disappearance programs had, when humans discovered the Disty, and realized that in some alien cultures, there was no such word as forgiveness. The Disty were the harshest of our allies. The Revs, the Wygnin, and the Fuetrer also targeted certain humans, and our treaties with these groups allowed the targeting if the aliens could show cause.

The balance was a delicate one, allowing them their cultural traditions while protecting our own. Showing cause had to happen before one of eighteen multicultural tribunals, and if one of those tribunals ruled in the aliens' favor, the humans involved were as good as dead. We looked the other way most of the time. Most of the lives involved were, according to our government, trivial ones. But of course, those people whose lives had been deemed trivial didn't feel that way, and that was when the disappearance services cropped up. If a person disappeared and could not be found, most alien groups kept an outstanding warrant, but stopped searching.

The Disty never did.

And since much of the Third Dynasty's business was conducted in Disty territory, its disappearance service, Privacy Unlimited had to be one of the best in the galaxy.

Something in my face must have given my knowledge away, because she said, "Now do you understand my problem?"

"Frankly, no," I said. "You're the daughter of the big kahuna. Go to Privacy Unlimited and have them help you. It's usually not too hard to retrace steps."

She shook her head. "My mother didn't go to Privacy Unlimited. She used another service."

"You're sure?"

"Yes." She brushed a hand alongside her head, to move the long hair. "It's my father she's running from."

A domestic situation. I never get involved in those. Too messy and too complicated. Never a clear line. "Then she didn't need a service at all. She probably took a shuttle here, then a transport for parts unknown."

Anetka Sobol crossed her arms. "You don't seem to understand, Mr. Flint. My father could have found her with his own service if she had done something like that. It's simple enough. My detectives should have been able to find her. They can't."

"Let me see if I can understand this," I said. "Are you looking for her or is your father?"

"I am."

"As a front for him?"

Color flooded her face. "No."

"Then why?"

"I want to meet her."

I snorted. "You're going to a lot of expense for a 'hello, how are you.' Aren't you afraid Daddy will find out?"

"I have my own money."

"Really? Money Daddy doesn't know about? Money Daddy doesn't monitor?"

She straightened. "He doesn't monitor me."

I nodded. "That's why the mesh gloves. Fashion statement?"

She glanced at her enhancements. "I got them. They have nothing to do with my father."

My smile was small. "Your father has incredible resources. You don't think he'd do something as simple as hack into your enhancement files. Believe me, one of those pretty baubles is being used to track you, and if my security weren't as good as it is, another would have been monitoring this conversation."

She put her left hand over her right as if covering the enhancements would make me forget them. All it did was remind me that this time, she didn't react when my security shut down her links. This was one smart girl, and one I didn't entirely understand.

"Go home," I said. "Deal with Daddy. If you want family ties, get married, have children, hire someone to play your mother. If you need genetic information or disease history, see your family doctors. I suspect they'll have all the records you need and probably some you don't. If you want Daddy to leave you alone, I'd ask him first before I go to any more expense. He might just do what you want. And if you're trying to make him angry, I'll bet you've gone far enough. You'll probably be hearing from him very soon."

Her eyes narrowed. "You're so sure of yourself, Mr. Flint."

"It's about the only thing I am sure of," I said, and waited for her to leave.

She didn't. She stared at me for a long moment, and in her eyes, I saw a coldness, a hardness I hadn't expected. It was as if she were evaluating me and finding me lacking.

I let her stare. I didn't care what she thought one way or another. I did wish she would get to the point so that I could kick her out of my office.

Finally she sighed and pursed her lips as if she had eaten something sour. She looked around, probably searching for some place to sit down. She didn't find one. I don't like my clients to sit. I don't want them to be comfortable in my presence.

"All right," she said, and her voice was somehow different. Stronger, a little more powerful. I knew the timidity had been an act. "I came to you because you seem to be the only one who can do this job."

My smile was crooked and insincere. "Flattery."

"Truth," she said.

I shook my head. "There are dozens of people who do this job, and most are cheaper." I let my smile grow colder. "They also have chairs in their offices."

31

"They value their clients," she said.

"Probably at the expense of the people they're searching out."

"Ethics," she said. "That's why I've come here. You're the only one in your profession who seems to have any."

"You have need of ethics?" Somehow I had trouble believing the woman with that powerful voice had need of anyone with ethics. "Or is this simply another attempt at manipulation?"

To my surprise, she smiled. The expression was stunning. It brought life to her eyes, and somehow seemed to make her even taller than she had been a moment before.

"Manipulation got me to you," she said. "Your Mr. Gonnot seems to have a soft spot for people who are missing family."

"Everyone who's missing is a member of a family," I said, but more to the absent Gonnot than to her. I could see how he could be manipulated, and that made it more important than ever to stop him from sending customers my way.

She shrugged at my comment, then she sat on the edge of my desk. I'd never had anyone do that, not in all my years in the business. "I do have need of ethics," she said. "If you breathe a single word of what I'm going to tell you . . ."

She didn't finish the sentence, on purpose of course, probably figuring that whatever I could imagine would be worse than what she could come up with.

I sighed. This girl—this woman—liked games.

"If you want the sanctity of a confessional," I said, "see a priest. If you want a profession that requires its practitioners to practice confidentiality as a matter of course, see a psychiatrist. I'll keep confidential whatever I deem worthy of confidentiality."

She folded her slender hands on her lap. "You enjoy judging your clients, don't you?"

I stared at her—up at her—which actually put me at a disadvantage. She was good at intimidation skills, even better than she had been as an actress. It made me uncomfortable, but somehow it seemed more logical for the daughter of the man who ran the Third Dynasty.

"I have to," I said. "A lot of lives depend on my judgments."

She shook her head slightly. It was as if my earlier answer stymied her, prevented her from continuing. She had to learn that we would do this on my terms or we wouldn't do it at all.

I waited. I could wait all day if I had to. Most people didn't have that kind of patience no matter what sort of will they had.

She clearly didn't. After a few moments, she brushed her pants, adjusted the flap on one of the pockets, and sighed again. She must have needed me badly.

Finally, she closed her eyes, as if summoning strength. When she opened them, she was looking at me directly. "I am a clone, Mr. Flint."

Whatever I had thought she was going to say, it wasn't that. I worked very hard at keeping the surprise off my face.

"And my father is dying." She paused, as if she were testing me.

I knew the answer, and the problem. When her father died, she couldn't inherit. Clones were barred from familial inheritance by interstellar law. The law had been adapted universally after several cases where clones created by a non-family member and raised far from the original (wealthy) family inherited vast estates. The basis of the inheritance was a shared biology that anyone could create. Rather than letting large fortunes get leached off to whomever was smart enough to steal a hair from a hairbrush and use it to create a copy of a human being, legislators finally decided to create the law. The courts upheld it. It was rigid.

"Your father could change his will," I said, knowing that she had probably broached this with him already.

"It's too late," she said. "He's been ill for a while. The change could easily be disputed in court."

"So you're not an only child?" I had to work to keep from asking if she were an only copy.

"I am the only clone," she said. "My father had me made, and he raised me himself. I am, for all intents and purposes, his daughter."

"Then he should have changed his will long ago."

She waved a hand, as if the very idea were a silly one. And it probably was. A clone had to come from somewhere. So either she was the copy of a real child or a copy of the woman she wanted me to find. Perhaps the will was unchanged because the original person was still out there.

"My mother vanished with the real heir," she said.

I waited.

"My father always expected to find them. My sister is the one who inherits."

I hated clone terminology. "Sister" was such an inaccurate term, even though clones saw themselves as twins. They weren't. They weren't raised that way or thought of that way. The Original stood to inherit. The clone before me did not.

"So you, out of the goodness of your heart, are searching for your missing family." I laid the sarcasm on thick. I've handled similar cases before. Where money was involved, people were rarely altruistic.

"No," she said, and her bluntness surprised me. "My father owns 51% of the Third Dynasty. When he dies, it goes into the corporation itself, and can be bought by other shareholders. I am not a shareholder, but I have been raised from birth to run the Dynasty. The idea was that I would share my knowledge with my sister, and that we would run the business together."

This made more sense.

"So I need to find her, Mr. Flint, before the shares go back into the corporation. I need to find her so that I can live the kind of life I was raised to live."

I hated cases like this. She was right. I did judge my clients. And if I found them the least bit suspicious, I didn't take on the case. If I believed that what they would do would jeopardize the Disappeared, I wouldn't take the case either. But if the reason for the disappearance was gone, or if the reason for finding the missing person benefited or did not harm the Disappeared, then I would take the case.

I saw benefit here, in the inheritance, and in the fact that the reason for the disappearance was dying.

"Your father willed his entire fortune to his missing child?"

She nodded.

"Then why isn't he searching for her?"

"He figured she would come back when she heard of his death."

Possible, depending on where she had disappeared to, but not entirely probable. The girl might not even know who she was.

"If I find your mother," I said, "then will your father try to harm her?"

"No," she said. "He couldn't if he wanted to. He's too sick. I can forward the medical records to you."

One more thing to check. And check I would. I guess I was taking this case, no matter how messily she started it. I was intrigued, just enough.

"Your father doesn't have to be healthy enough to act on his own," I said. "With his money, he could hire someone."

"I suppose," she said. "But I control almost all of his business dealings right now. The request would have to go through me."

I still didn't like it, but superficially, it sounded fine. I would, of course, check it out. "Where's your clone mark?"

She frowned at me. It was a rude question, but one I needed the answer to before I started.

She pulled her hair back, revealing a small number eight at the spot where her skull met her neck. The fine hairs had grown away from it, and the damage to the skin had been done at the cellular level. If she tried to have the eight removed, it would grow back.

"What happened to the other seven?" I asked.

She let her hair fall. "Failed."

Failed clones were unusual. Anything unusual in a case like this was suspect.

"My mother," she said, as if she could hear my thoughts, "was pregnant when she disappeared. I was cloned from sloughed cells found in the amnio."

"Hers or the baby's?"

"The baby's. They tested. But they used a lot of cells to find one that worked. It took a while before they got me."

Sounded plausible, but I was no expert. More information to check.

"Your father must have wanted you badly."

She nodded.

"Seems strange that he didn't alter his will for you."

Her shoulders slumped. "He was afraid any changes he made wouldn't have been lawyer-proof. He was convinced I'd lose everything because of lawsuits if he did that."

"So he arranged for you to lose everything on his own."

She shook her head. "He wanted the family together. He wanted me to work with my sister to—"

"So he said."

"So he says." She ran a hand through her hair. "I think he hopes that my sister will cede the company to me. For a percentage, of course."

There it was. The only loophole in the law. A clone could receive an inheritance if it came directly from the person whose genetic material the clone shared, provided that the Original couldn't die under suspicious circumstances. Of course, a living person could, in Anetka's words, "cede" that ownership as well, although it was a bit more difficult.

"You're looking for her for money," I said in my last ditch effort to get out of the case.

"You won't believe love," she said.

She was right. I wouldn't have.

"Besides," she said. "I have my own money. More than enough to keep me comfortable for the rest of my life. Whatever else you may think of my father, he has provided that. I'm searching for her for the corporation. I want to keep it in the family. I want to work it like I was trained. And this seems to be the only way."

It wasn't a very pretty reason, and I'd learned over the years, it was usually the ugly reasons that were the truth. Not, of course, that I could go by gut. I wouldn't.

"My retainer is two million credits," I said. "If you're lucky, that's all this investigation will cost you. I have a con-

37

tract that I'll send to you or your personal representative, but let me give you the short version verbally."

She nodded.

I continued, reciting, as I always did, the essential terms so that no client could ever say I'd lied to her. "I have the right to terminate at any time for any reason. You may not terminate until the Disappeared is found, or I have concluded that the Disappeared is gone for good. You are legally liable for any lawsuits that arise from any crimes committed by third parties as a result of this investigation. I am not. You will pay me my rate plus expenses whenever I bill you. If your money stops, the investigation stops, but if I find you've been withholding funds to prevent me from digging farther, I am entitled to a minimum of ten million credits. I will begin my investigation by investigating you. Should I decide you are unworthy as a client before I begin searching for the Disappeared, I will refund half of your initial retainer. There's more but those are the salient points. Is all of that clear?"

"Perfectly."

"I'll begin as soon as I get the retainer."

"Give me your numbers and I'll have the money placed in your account immediately."

I handed her my single printed card with my escrow account embedded into it. The account was a front for several other accounts, but she didn't need to know that. Even my money went through channels. Someone who is good at finding the Disappeared is also good at making other things disappear.

"Should you need to reach me in an emergency," I said, "place 673 credits into this account."

"Strange number," she said.

I nodded. The number varied from client to client, a

random pattern. Sometimes, past clients sent me their old amounts as a way to contact me about something new. I kept the system clear.

"I'll respond to the depositing computer from wherever I am, as soon as I can. This is not something you should do frivolously nor is it something to be done to check up on me. It's only for an emergency. If you want to track the progress of the investigation, you can wait for my weekly updates."

"And if I have questions?"

"Save them for later."

"What if I think I can help?"

"Leave me mail." I stood. She was watching me, that hard edge in her eyes again. "I've got work to do now. I'll contact you when I'm ready to begin my search."

"How long will this investigation of me take?"

"I have no idea," I said. "It depends on how much you're hiding."

IV

Clients never tell the truth. No matter how much I instruct them to, they never do. It seems to be human nature to lie about something, even if it's something small. I had a hunch, given Anetka Sobol's background, she had lied about a lot. The catch was to find out how much of what she had lied about was relevant to the job she had hired me for. Finding out required research.

I do a lot of my research through public accounts, using fake ID. It is precautionary, particularly in the beginning, because so many cases don't pan out. If a Disappeared still has a Tracker after her, repeated searches from me will be flagged. Searches from public accounts—especially different public accounts—will not. Often the Disappeared are already famous or become famous when they vanish, and are often the subject of anything from vidspec to school reports.

My favorite search site is a bar not too far from my office. I love the place because it serves some of the best food in Armstrong, in some of the largest quantities. The large quantities are required, given the place's name. The Brownie Bar serves the only marijuana in the area, baked into specially marked goods, particularly the aforementioned brownies. Imbibers get the munchies, and proceed to spend hundreds of credits on food. The place turns quite a profit, and it's also comfortable; marijuana users seem to like their creature comforts more than most other recreational drug types.

Recreational drugs are legal on the Moon, as are most things. The first settlers came in search of something they called "freedom from oppression" which usually meant freedom to pursue an alternative lifestyle. Some of those lifestyles have since become illegal or simply died out, but others remain. The only illegal drugs these days, at least in Armstrong, are those that interfere with the free flow of air. Everything from nicotine to opium is legal—as long as its user doesn't smoke it.

The Brownie Bar caters to the casual user as well as the hard-core and, unlike some drug bars, doesn't mind the non-user customer. The interior is large, with several sections. One section, the party wing, favors the bigger groups, the ones who usually arrive in numbers larger than ten, spend hours eating and giggling, and often get quite obnoxiously wacky. In the main section, soft booths with tables shield clients from each other. Usually the people sitting

there are couples or groups of four. If one group gets particularly loud, a curtain drops over the open section of the
booth, and their riotous laughter fades into nearly nothing.

My section caters to the hard-core, who sometimes stop
for a quick fix in the middle of the business day, or who like
a brownie before dinner to calm the stress of a hectic afternoon. Many of these people have only one, and continued
work while they're sitting at their solitary tables. It's quiet
as a church in this section, and many of the patrons are
plugged into the free client ports that allow them access to
the Net.

The access ports are free, but the information is not.
Particular servers charge by the hour in the public areas,
but have the benefit of allowing me to troll using the server
or the bar's identicodes. I like that; it usually makes my preliminary searches impossible to trace.

That afternoon, I took my usual table in the very back.
It's small, made of high-grade plastic designed to look like
wood—and it fools most people. It never fooled me, partly
because I knew the Brownie Bar couldn't afford to import,
and partly because I knew they'd never risk something that
valuable on a restaurant designed for stoners. I sat cross-
legged on the thick pillow on the floor, ordered some turkey
stew—made here with real meat—and plugged in.

The screen was tabletop, and had a keyboard so that the
user could have complete privacy. I'd heard other patrons
complain that using the Brownie Bar's system required
them to read, but it was one of the features I liked.

I started with Anetka, and decided to work my way backwards through the Sobol family. I found her quickly
enough; her life was well covered by the tabs, which made
no mention of her clone status. She was twenty-seven, ten
to twelve years older than she looked. She'd apparently had

those youthful looks placed in stasis surgically. She'd look girlish until she died.

Another good fact to know. If there was an original, she might not look like Anetka. Not any more.

Anetka had been working in her father's corporation since she was twelve. Her IQ was off the charts—surgically enhanced as well, at least according to most of the vidspec programs—and she breezed through Harvard and then Cambridge. She did postdoc work at the Interstellar Business School in Islamabad, and was out of school by the time she was twenty-five. For the last two years, she'd been on the corporate fast-track, starting in lower management and working her way to the top of the corporate ladder.

She was, according to the latest feeds, her father's main assistant.

So I had already found Possible Lie Number One: She wasn't here for herself. She was, as I had suspected, a front for her father. Not to find the wife, but to find the real heir.

I wasn't sure how I'd feel if that were true. I needed to find out if, indeed, the Original was the one who'd inherit. If she wasn't, I wouldn't take the case. There'd be no point.

But I wasn't ready to make judgements yet. I had a long way to go. I looked up Anetka's father, and discovered that Carson Sobol had never remarried, although he'd been seen with a bevy of beautiful women over the years. All were close to his age. He never dated women younger than he was. Most had their own fortunes, and many their own companies. He spent several years as the companion to an acclaimed Broadway actress, even funding some of her more famous plays. That relationship, like the others, had ended amicably.

Which lead to Possible Lie Number Two: a man who terrorized his wife so badly that she had to run away from him also terrorized his later girlfriends. And while a man could keep something like that quiet for a few years, eventually the pattern would become evident. Eventually one of the women would talk.

There was no evidence of terrorizing in the stuff I found. Perhaps the incidences weren't reported. Or perhaps there was nothing to report. I would vote for the latter. It seemed, from the vidspec I'd read, everyone knew that the wife had left him because of his cruelty. My experience with vidspec reporters made me confident that they'd be on the lookout for more proof of Carson Sobol's nasty character. And if they found it, they'd report it.

No one had.

I didn't know if that meant Sobol had learned his lesson when the wife ran off, or perhaps Sobol had learned that mistreatment of women was bad for business. I couldn't believe that a man could terrify everyone into silence. If that were his methodology, there would be a few leaks that were quickly hushed up, and one or two dead bodies floating around, bodies belonging to folks who hadn't listened. Also, there would be rumors, and there were none.

Granted, I was making assumptions on a very small amount of information. Most of the reports I found about Sobol weren't about his family or his love life, but about the Third Dynasty as it expanded in that period to new worlds, places that human businesses had never been before.

The Third Dynasty had been the first to do business with the Fuetrers, the HDs, and the chichers. It opened plants on Korsve, then closed them when it realized that the Wygnins, the dominant lifeforms on Korsve, did not—and apparently could not—understand the way that humans did business.

I shuddered at the mention of Korsve. If a client approached me because a family member had been taken by the Wygnins, I refused the case. The Wygnin took individuals to pay off debt, and then those individuals became part of a particular Wygnin family. For particularly heinous crimes, the Wygnin took firstborns, but usually, the Wygnin just took babies—from any place in the family structure—at the time of birth, and then raised them. Occasionally they'd take an older child or an adult. Sometimes they'd take an entire group of adults from offending businesses. The adults were subject to mind control, and personality destruction as the Wygnin tried to remake them to fit into Wygnin life.

All of that left me with no good options. Children raised by the Wygnin considered themselves Wygnin and couldn't adapt to human cultures. Adults who were taken by the Wygnin were so broken that they were almost unrecognizable. Humans raised by the Wygnin did not want to return. Adults who were broken always wanted to return, and when they did, they signed a death warrant for their entire family—or worse, doomed an entire new generation to kidnap by the Wygnin.

But Wygnin custom didn't seem relevant here. Despite the plant closings, the Third Dynasty had managed to avoid paying a traditional Wygnin price. Or perhaps someone had paid, down the line, and that information was classified.

There were other possibles in the files. The Third Dynasty seemed to have touched every difficult alien race in the galaxy. The corporation had an entire division set aside for dealing with new cultures. Not that the division was infallible. Sometimes there were unavoidable errors.

Sylvy Sobol's disappearance had been one of those. It had caused all sorts of problems for both Sobol and the Third Dynasty. The vidspecs, tabs, and other media had

had a field day when she had disappeared. The news led to problems with some of the alien races, particularly the Altaden. The Altaden valued non-violence above all else, and the accusations of domestic violence at the top levels of the Third Dynasty nearly cost the corporation its Altade holdings.

The thing was, no one expected the disappearance—or the marriage, for that matter. Sylvy Sobol had been a European socialite, better known for her charitable works and her incredible beauty than her interest in business. She belonged to an old family with ties to several still existing monarchies. It was thought that her marriage would be to someone else from the accepted circle.

It had caused quite a scandal when she had chosen Carson Sobol, not only because of his mixed background and uncertain lineage, but also because some of his business practices had taken large fortunes from the countries she was tied to and spent them in space instead.

He was controversial; the marriage was controversial; and it looked like, from the vids I watched, that the two of them had been deeply in love.

I felt a hand on my shoulder. A waitress stood behind me, holding a large ceramic bowl filled with turkey stew. She smiled at me.

"Didn't want to set it on your work."

"It's fine," I said, indicating an empty spot near the screen. She set my utensils down, and then the bowl. The stew smelled rich and fine, black beans and yogurt adding to the aroma. My stomach growled.

The waitress tapped one of the moving images. "I remember that," she said. "I was living in Vienna. The Viennese thought that marriage was an abomination."

I looked up. She was older than I was, without the funds

to prevent the natural aging process. Laugh lines crinkled around her eyes, and her lips—unpainted and untouched— were a faint rose. She smiled.

"Guess it turned out that way, huh? The wife running off like that? Leaving that message?"

"Message?" I asked. I hadn't gotten that far.

"I don't remember exactly what it was. Something like 'The long arm of the Third Dynasty is impossible to fight. I am going where you can't find me. Maybe then I'll have the chance to live out my entire life.' I guess he nearly beat her to death." The waitress laughed, a little embarrassed. "In those days I had nothing better to do than study the lives of more interesting people."

"And now?" I asked.

She shrugged. "I figured out that everybody's inter- esting. I mean, you've got to try. You've got to live. And if you do, you've done something fascinating."

I nodded. People like her were one of the reasons I liked this place.

"You want something to drink?" she asked.

"Bottled water."

"Got it," she said as she left.

By the time she brought my bottled water, I had indeed found the note. It had been sent to all the broadcast media, along with a grainy video, taken from a hidden camera, of one of the most brutal domestic beatings I'd ever seen. The images were sometimes blurred and indistinct, but the ac- tions were clear. The man had beat the woman senseless.

There was no mention of the pregnancy in any of this. There was, however, notification of Anetka's birth six months before her mother had disappeared.

Which lead me to Possible Lie Number Three. Anetka had said her mother traveled pregnant. Perhaps she hadn't.

Or, more chillingly, someone had altered the record either before or after the clones were brought to term. There had to be an explanation of Anetka in the media or she wouldn't be accepted. If that explanation had been planted before, something else was going on. If it were planted afterwards, Sobol's spokespeople could have simply said that reporters had overlooked her in their rush to other stories.

I checked the other media reports and found the same story. It was time to go beneath those stories and see what else I could find. Then I would confront Anetka about the lies before I began the search for her mother.

V

I contacted her and we met, not at my office, but at her hotel. She was staying in Armstrong's newest district, an addition onto the dome that caused a terrible controversy before it was built. Folks in my section believe the reason for the thinner air is that the new addition has stretched resources. I know they aren't right—with the addition came more air and all the other regulation equipment—but it was one of those arguments that made an emotional kind of sense.

I thought of those arguments, though, as I walked among the new buildings, made from a beige material not even conceived of thirty years before, a material that's supposed to be attractive (it isn't) and more resistant to decay that permaplastic. This entire section of Armstrong smelt new, from the recycled air to the buildings rising around me. They were four stories high and had large windows on the dome side, obviously built with a view in mind.

This part of the dome is self-cleaning and see-through. Dust does not slowly creep up the sides as it does in the other parts of Armstrong. The view is barren and stark, just like the rest of the Moon, but there's a beauty in the starkness that I don't see anywhere else in the universe.

The hotel was another large four-story building. Most of its windows were glazed dark, so no one could see in, but the patrons could see out. It was part of a chain whose parent company was, I had learned the day before, the Third Dynasty. Anetka was doing very little to hide her search from her father.

Inside, the lobby was wide, and had an old-fashioned feel. The walls changed images slowly, showing the famous sites from various parts of the galaxy where the hotels were located. I had read before the hotel opened that the constantly changing scenery took eight weeks to repeat an image. I wondered what it was like working in a place where the view shifted constantly, and then decided I didn't want to know.

The lobby furniture was soft and a comforting shade of dove gray. Piano music, equally soft and equally comforting, was piped in from somewhere. Patrons sat in small groups as if they were posing for a brochure. I went up to the main desk and asked for Anetka. The concierge led me to a private conference room down the main hallway.

I expected the room to be monitored. That didn't bother me. At this point, I still had nothing to hide. Anetka did, but this was her company's hotel. She could get the records, shut off the monitors, or have them destroyed. It would all be her choice.

To my surprise, she was waiting for me. She was wearing another dress, a blue diaphanous thing that looked so fragile I wondered how she managed to move from place to place. Her hair was up and pinned, with diamonds glinting from the soft folds. She also had diamonds glued to the ridge beneath her eyebrows, and trailing down her cheeks. The net effect was to accent her strength. Her broad shoulders held the gown as if it were air, and the folds parted to reveal the muscles on her arms and legs. She was like the diamonds she wore; pretty and glittering, but able to cut through all the objects in the room.

"Have you found anything?" she asked without preamble.

I shut the door and helped myself to the carafe of water on the bar against the nearest wall. There was a table in the center of the room—made, it seemed—of real wood, with matching chairs on the side. There was also a workstation, and a one-way mirror with a view of the lobby.

I leaned against the bar, holding my water glass. It was thick and heavy, sturdy like most things on the Moon. "Your father's will has been posted among the Legal Notices on all the nets for the last three years."

She nodded. "It's common for CEOs to do that to allay stockholder fears."

"It's common for CEOs to authorize the release after they've died. Not before."

Her smile was small, almost patronizing. "Smaller corporations, yes. But it's becoming a requirement for major shareholders in megacorps to do this even if they are not dead. Investigate farther, Mr. Flint, and you'll see that all of the Third Dynasty's major shareholders have posted their wills."

I had already checked the other shareholders' wills, and found that Anetka was right. I also looked for evidence that Carson Sobol was dead, and found none.

She took my silence to be disbelief. "It's the same with

the other megacorps. Personal dealings are no longer private in the galactic business world."

I had known that the changes were taking place. I had known, for example, that middle managers signed loyalty oaths to corporations, sometimes requiring them to forsake family if the corporation had called for it. This, one pundit had said, was the hidden cost of doing business with alien races. You had to be willing to abandon all you knew in the advent of a serious mistake. The upshot of the change was becoming obvious. People to whom family was important were staying away from positions of power in the megacorps.

I said, "You're not going to great lengths to hide this search from your father."

She placed a hand on the wooden chair. She was not wearing gloves, and mingled among the enhancements were more diamonds. "You seem obsessed with my father."

"Your mother disappeared because of him. I'm not going to find her only to have him kill her."

"He wouldn't."

"Says you."

"This is your hesitation?"

"Actually, no," I said. "My hesitation is that, according to all public records, you were born six months before your mother disappeared."

I didn't tell her that I knew all the databases had been tampered with, including the ones about her mother's disappearance. I couldn't tell if the information had been altered to show that the disappearance came later or that the child had been born earlier. The tampering was so old that the original material was lost forever.

"My father wanted me to look like a legitimate child."

"You are a clone. He knew cloning laws."

50

"But no one else had to know."

"Not even with his will posted?"

"I told you. It's only been posted for the last three years."

"Is that why you're not mentioned?"

She raised her chin. "I received my inheritance before—already," she said. I found the correction interesting. "The agreement between us about my sister is both confidential and binding."

" 'All of my worldly possessions shall go to my eldest child,' " I quoted. "That child isn't even listed by name."

"No," she said.

"And he isn't going to change the will for you?"

"The Disty won't do business with clones."

"I didn't know you had business with the Disty," I said.

She shrugged. "The Disty, the Emin, the Revs. You name them, we have business with them. And we have to be careful of some customs."

"Won't the stockholders be suspicious when you don't inherit?"

Her mouth formed a thin line. "That's why I'm hiring you," she said. "You need to find my sister."

I nodded. Then, for the first time in the meeting, I sat down. The chair was softer than I had expected it would be. I put my feet on the nearest chair. She glanced at them as if they were a lower lifeform.

"In order to search for people," I said, "I need to know who they're running from. If they're running from the Disty, for example, I'll avoid the Martian colonies, because they're overrun with Disty. No one would hide there. It would be impossible. If they were running from the Revs, I would start looking at plastic surgeons and doctors who specialize in genetic alteration because anyone who looks significantly different from the person the Revs have targeted is considered, by the Revs, to be a different being entirely."

She started to say something, but I held up my hand to silence her.

"Human spouses abuse each other," I said. "It seems to be part of the human experience. These days, the abused spouse moves out, and sometimes leaves the city, sometimes the planet, but more often than not stays in the same area. It's unusual to run, to go through a complete identity change, and to start a new life, especially in your parents' income bracket. So tell me, why did your mother really leave?"

Nothing changed in Anetka's expression. It remained so immobile that I knew she was struggling for control. The hardness that had been so prevalent the day before was gone, banished, it seemed, so that I wouldn't see anything amiss.

"My father has a lot of money," she said.

"So do other people. Their spouses don't disappear."

"He also controls a powerful megacorp with fingers all over the developing worlds. He has access to more information than anyone. He vowed to never let my mother out of his sight. My father believed that marriage vows were sacred, and no matter how much the parties wanted out, they were obligated by their promises to each other and to God to remain." Anetka's tone was flat too. "If she had just moved out, he would have forced her to move back in. If she had moved to the Moon, he would have come after her. If she had moved to some of the planets in the next solar system, he would have come for her. So she had no choice."

"According to your father."

"According to anyone who knew her." Anetka's voice

was soft. "You saw the vids."

I nodded.

"That was mild, I guess, for what he did to her."

I leaned back in the chair, lifting the front two legs off the ground. "So how come he didn't treat his other women that way?"

Something passed through her eyes so quickly that I wasn't able to see what the expression was. Suspicion? Fear? I couldn't tell.

"My father never allowed himself to get close to anyone else."

"Not even his Broadway actress?"

She frowned, then said, "Oh, Linda? No. Not even her. They were using each other to throw off the media. She had a more significant relationship with one of the major critics, and she didn't want that to get out."

"What about you?" I asked that last softly. "If he hurt your mother, why didn't he hurt you?"

She put her other hand on the chair as if she were steadying herself. "Who says he didn't?"

And in that flatness of tone, I heard all the complaints I'd ever heard from clones. She had legal protection, of course. She was fully human. But she didn't have familial protection. She wasn't part of any real group. She didn't have defenders, except those she hired herself.

But I didn't believe it, not entirely. She was still lying to me. She was still keeping me slightly off balance. Something was missing, but I couldn't find it. I'd done all the digging I could reasonably do. I had no direction to go except after the missing wife—if I chose to continue working on this case. This was the last point at which I could comfortably extricate myself from the entire mess.

"You're not telling me everything," I said.

Again, the movement with the eyes. So subtle. So quick. I wondered if she had learned to cover up her emotions from her father.

"My father won't harm her," she said. "If you want, I'll even sign a waver guaranteeing that."

It seemed the perfect solution to a superficial problem. I had a hunch there were other problems lurking below.

"I'll have one sent to you," I said.

"Are you still taking the case?"

"Are you still lying to me?"

She paused, the dress billowing around her in the static-charged air. "I need you to find my sister," she said.

And that much, we both knew to be true.

VI

My work is nine-tenths research and one-tenth excitement. Most of the research comes in the beginning, and it's dry to most people, although I still find the research fascinating. It's also idiosyncratic and part of the secret behind my reputation. I usually don't describe how I do the research—and I never explain it to clients. I usually summarize it, like this:

It took me four months to do the preliminary research on Sylvy Sobol. I started from the premise that she was pregnant with a single girl child. A pregnant woman did one of three things: she carried the baby to term, she miscarried, or she aborted. After dealing with hospital records for what seemed like weeks, I determined that she carried the baby to term. Or at least, she hadn't gotten rid of it before she disappeared.

A pregnant woman had fewer relocation options than a

non-pregnant one. She couldn't travel as far or on many forms of transport because it might harm the fetus. Several planets, hospitable to humans after they'd acclimatized, were not places someone in the middle of pregnancy was allowed to go. The pregnancy actually made my job easier, and I was glad for it.

Whoever had hidden her was good, but no disappearance service was perfect. They all had cracks in their systems, some revealing themselves in certain types of disappearance, others in all cases past a certain layer of complexity. I knew those flaws as well as I knew the scars and blemishes on my own hands. And I exploited them with ease.

At the end of four months, I had five leads on the former Mrs. Sobol. At the end of five months, I had eliminated two of those leads. At the end of six months, I had a pretty good idea which of the remaining three leads was the woman I was looking for.

I got in my ship, and headed for Mars.

VII

In the hundred years since the Disty first entered this solar system, they have taken over Mars. The human-run mineral operations and the ship bases are still there, but the colonies are all Disty run, and some are Disty built.

The Emmeline has clearance on most planets where humans make their homes. Mars is no difference. I docked at the Dunes, above the Arctic Circle, and wished I were going elsewhere. It was the Martian winter, and here, in the largest field of sand dunes in the solar system, that meant several months of unrelenting dark.

I had never understood how the locals put up with this. But I hadn't understood a lot of things. The domes here, mostly of human construction, had an artificial lighting system built in, but the Disty hated the approximation of a twenty-four-hour day. Since the Disty had taken over the northern most colonies, darkness outside and artificial lights inside were the hallmarks of winter.

The Disty made other alterations as well. The Disty were small creatures with large heads, large eyes, and narrow bodies. They hated the feeling of wide-open spaces, and so in many parts of the Sahara Dome, as Terrans called this place, false ceilings had been built in, and corridors had been compressed. Buildings were added into the wider spaces, getting rid of many passageways and making the entire place seem like a rat's warren. Most adult humans had to crouch to walk comfortably through the city streets and some, in disgust, had bought small carts so that they could ride. The result was a congestion that I found claustrophobic at the best of times. I hated crouching when I walked, and I hated the stink of so many beings in such a confined space.

Many Terran buildings rose higher than the ceiling level of the street, but to discourage that wide-open spaces feel, the Disty built more structures, many of them so close together that there was barely enough room for a human to stick his arm between them. Doors lined the crowded streets, and the only identifying marks on most places were carved into the frame along the door's side. The carvings were difficult to see in the weird lighting, even if there weren't the usual crowds struggling to get through the streets to God knew where.

My candidate lived in a building owned by the Disty. It

took me two passes to find the building's number, and another to realize that I had found the right place. A small sign, in English, advertised accommodations fit for humans, and my back and I hoped that the sign was right.

It was. The entire building had been designed with humans in mind. The Disty had proven themselves to be able interstellar traders, and quite willing to adapt to local customs when it suited them. It showed in the interior design of this place. Once I stepped through the door, I was able to stand upright, although the top of my head did brush the ceiling. To my left, a sign pointed toward the main office, another pointed to some cramped stairs, and a third pointed to the recreation area.

I glanced at the main office before I explored any farther. The office was up front, and had the same human-sized ceilings. In order to cope, the Disty running the place sat on its desk, its long feet pressed together in concentration. I passed it, and went to the recreation area. I would look for the woman here before I went door to door upstairs.

The recreation area was about half the size of an human-made room for the same purpose. Still, the Disty managed to cram a lot of stuff in here, and the closeness of everything—while comfortable for the Disty—made it uncomfortable for any human. All five humans in the room were huddled near the bar on the far end. It was the only place with a walking path large enough to allow a full-grown man through.

To get there, I had to go past the ping-pong table, and a small section set aside for Go players. Several Disty were playing Go—they felt it was the best thing they had discovered on the planet Earth, with ping-pong a close second—sitting on the tables so that their heads were as near the ceiling as they could get. Two more Disty were standing on the table, playing ping-pong. None of them paid me any attention at all.

I wound my way through the tight space between the Go players and the ping-pong table, ducking once to avoid being whapped in the head with an out-of-control ping-pong ball. I noted three other Disty watching the games with rapt interest. The humans, on the other hand, had their backs to the rest of the room. They were sitting on the tilting bar stools, drinking, and not looking too happy about anything.

A woman who could have been anywhere from thirty to seventy-five sat at one end of the bar. Her black hair fell to the middle of her back, and she wore make-up, an affectation that the Disty seemed to like. She was slender—anyone who wanted to live comfortably here had to be—and she wore a silver beaded dress that accented that slimness. Her legs were smooth, and did not bear any marks from mining or other harsh work.

"Susan Wilcox?" I asked as I put my hand on her shoulder and showed her my license.

I felt the tension run through her body, followed by several shivers, but her face gave no sign that anything was wrong.

"Want to go talk?"

She smiled at me, a smooth professional smile that made me feel a little more comfortable. "Sure."

She stood, took my hand as if we'd been friends a long time, and led me onto a little patio someone had cobbled together in a tiny space behind the recreation area. I didn't see the point of the thing until I looked up. This was one of the few places in Sahara where the dome was visible, and through its clear surface, you could see the sky. She pulled over a chair, and I grabbed one as well.

"How did you find me?" she asked.

"I'm not sure I did." I held out my hand. In it was one of my palmtop. "I want to do a DNA check."

She raised her chin slightly. "That's not legal."

"I could get a court order."

She looked at me. A court order would ruin any protection she had, no matter who—or what—she was running from.

"I'm not going to see who you are. I want to see if you're who I'm looking for. I have comparison DNA."

"You're lying," she said softly.

"Maybe," I said. "If I am, you're in trouble either way."

She knew I was right. She could either take her chances with me, or face the court order where she had no chance at all.

She extended her hand. I ran the edge of the computer along her palm, removing skin cells. The comparison program ran, and as I turned the palmtop face-up, I saw that there was no match. The only thing this woman shared in common with the former Mrs. Sobol was that they were both females of a similar age, and that they had both disappeared twenty-nine years ago while pregnant. Almost everything else was different.

I used my wrist-top for a double check, and then I sighed. She was watching me closely, her dark eyes reflecting the light from inside.

I smiled at her. "You're in the clear," I said. "But if it was this easy for me to find you, chances are that it'll be as easy for someone else. You might want to move on."

She shook her head once, as if the very idea were repugnant.

"Your child might appreciate it," I said.

She looked at me as if I had struck her. "She's not who—"

"No," I said. "She's safe. From me at least. And maybe from whoever's after you. But you've survived out here nearly thirty years. You know the value of caution."

She swallowed, hard. "You know a lot about me."

"Not really." I stood. "I only know what you have in common with the woman I'm looking for." I slipped the palmtop into my pocket and bowed slightly. "I appreciate your time."

Then I went back inside, slipped through the recreation area, walked past two more Disty in the foyer, and headed into the narrow passageway they called a street. There I shuddered. I hated the Disty. I'd worked so many cases in which people ran to avoid being caught by the Disty that I'd become averse to them myself.

At least, that was my explanation for my shudder. But I knew that it wasn't a real explanation. I had put a woman's life in jeopardy, and we both knew it. I hoped no one had been paying attention. But I was probably wrong. The only solace I had was that since she was hiding amongst the Disty, she probably wasn't being sought by one of them. If she had been pursued by a Disty, my actions probably would have signed her death warrant.

I spent a night in a cramped hotel room since the Disty didn't allow take-offs within thirty-six hours of landing. And then I got the hell away from Sahara Dome—and Mars.

VIII

My second possible was in New Orleans, which made my task a lot easier. I had former clients there who felt they owed me, some of whom were in related businesses. I had one of those clients break into the Disappeared's apartment, remove a strand of hair, and give it to another former client. A third brought me the strand in my room in the International Space Station. Because the strand proved not to be a match, and because I was so certain it would be, I repeated the procedure once more, this time getting another old friend to remove another hair strand from the suspect's person. Apparently, he passed her in a public place, and plucked. The strand matched the first one, but didn't belong to Sylvy Sobol.

I didn't warn this woman at all because I didn't feel as if I had put her in danger. If she were suspicious about the hair pulling incident, I felt it was her responsibility to leave town on her own.

The third candidate was on the Moon, in Hadley. I had no trouble finding her, which seemed odd, but she didn't check out either. I returned to Armstrong, both stumped and annoyed.

The logical conclusion was that my DNA sample was false—that it wasn't the sample for Sylvy Sobol. I had taken the sample from the Interstellar DNA database, and there was the possibility that the sample had been changed or tainted. I had heard of such a thing being done, but had always dismissed it as impossible. Those samples were the most heavily guarded in the universe. Even if someone managed to get into the system, they would encounter back-ups upon back-ups, and more encryption than I wanted to think about.

So I contacted Anetka and asked her to send me a DNA sample of her mother. She did, and I ran it against the sample I had. Mine had been accurate. The women I had seen were not Sylvy Sobol.

I had never, in my entire career, made an error of this magnitude. One of those women should have been the former Mrs. Sobol. Unless my information was wrong. Unless I was operating from incorrect assumptions. Still, the assumptions shouldn't have mattered in this search. A pregnant woman wasn't that difficult to hide, not when she was taking transport elsewhere. I'd even found the one who'd remained on Earth.

No. The incorrect assumption had to come after the pregnancy ended. The children. Transport registries always keep track of the sex of the fetus, partly as a response to a series of lawsuits where no one could prove that the woman who claimed she'd lost a fetus on board a transport had actually been pregnant. The transports do not do a DNA check—such things are considered violations of privacy in all but criminal matters—but they do require pregnant women to submit a doctor's report on the health of the mother and the fetus before the woman is allowed to board.

I'd searched out pregnant women, but only those carrying a single daughter. Not twins or multiples. And no males.

Anetka had mentioned failed clones. Clones failed for a variety of reasons, but they only failed in large numbers when someone was using a defective gene or was trying to make a significant change on the genetic level. If the changes didn't work at the genetic level, surgery was performed later to achieve the same result and the DNA remained the same.

I had Anetka's DNA. I'd taken it that first day without her knowing it. I ran client DNA only when I felt I had no other choice; sometimes to check identity, sometimes to check for past crimes. I hadn't run Anetka's—photographic, vid, and those enhancements made it obvious that she was who she said she was. I knew she wasn't concealing her identity, and there was no way she was fronting for a Disty or any other race. She had told me she was a clone. So I felt a DNA check was not only redundant, it was also unnecessary because it didn't give me the kind of information I was searching for.

But now things were different. I needed to check it to see if she was a repaired child, if there had been some flaw in the fetus that couldn't have been altered in the womb. I hadn't looked for repaired children when I'd done the hospital records scans. I hadn't looked for anything that complicated at all.

So I ran the DNA scan. It only took a second, and the results were not what I expected.

Anetka Sobol wasn't a repaired child, at least not in the sense that I had been looking for. Anetka Sobol was an altered child.

According to her DNA, Anetka Sobol had once been male.

IX

If the trail hadn't been so easy to follow once I realized I was looking for a woman pregnant with a boy, I wouldn't have traced it. I would have gone immediately to Anetka and called her on it. But the trail was easy to follow, and any one of my competitors would have done so—perhaps earlier because they had different methods than I did. I knew at least three of them that ran DNA scans on clients as a matter of course.

If Anetka went to any of them after I refused to complete

the work, they would find her mother. It would take them three days. It took me less, but that was because I was better.

X

Sylvy Sobol ran a small private university in the Gagarin Dome on the Moon. She went by the name Celia Walker, and she had transferred from a school out past the Disty homeworld where she had spent the first ten years of her exile. She had run the university for fifteen years.

Gagarin had been established fifty years after Armstrong, and was run by a governing board, the only colony that had such a government. The board placed covenants on any person who owned or rented property within the interior of the dome. The covenants covered everything from the important, such as oxygen regulators, to the unimportant, such as a maintenance schedule for each building, whether the place needed work or not. Gagarin did not tolerate any rules violations. If someone committed three such violations—whether they be failing to follow the maintenance schedule or murder—that person was banned from the dome for life.

The end result was that residents of Gagarin were quiet, law-abiding, and suspicious. They watched me as if I were a particularly distasteful bug when I got off the high-speed train from Armstrong. I learned later that I didn't meet the dome's strict dress code.

I had changed into something more appropriate after I got my hotel room, and then went to campus. The university was a technical school for undergraduates, most of them local, but a few came in from other parts of the Moon. The administrative offices were in low buildings with fake adobe facades. The classrooms were in some of Gagarin's only high rises, and were off limits to visitors.

I didn't care about that. I went straight to the Chancellor's office, and buzzed myself in, even though I didn't have an appointment. Apparently, the open campus policy that the on-line brochures proudly proclaimed extended to the administrative offices as well.

Sylvy Sobol sat behind a desk made of Moon clay. Ancient southwestern tapestries covered the walls, and matching rugs covered the floor. The permaplastic here had been covered with more fake adobe, and the net effect was to make this seem like the American Southwest hundreds of years before.

She looked no different than the age-enhancement programs on my computer led me to believe she'd look. Her dark hair was laced with silver, her eyes had laugh lines in the corners, and she was as slender as she had been when she disappeared. She wore a blouse made of the same weave as the tapestries, and a pair of tan cargo pants. Beneath the right sleeve of her blouse a stylish wrist-top glistened. When she saw me, she smiled. "May I help you?"

I closed the door, walked to her desk, and showed her my license. Her eyes widened ever so slightly, and then she covered the look.

"I came to warn you," I said.

"Warn me?" She straightened almost imperceptibly, but managed to look perplexed. Behind the tightness of her lips, I sensed fear.

"You and your son need to use a new service, and disappear again. It's not safe for you any more."

"I'm sorry, Mr.—Flint?—but I'm not following you."

"I can repeat what I said, or we can go somewhere where you'd feel more comfortable talking."

She shook her head once, then stood. "I'm not sure I know what we'd be talking about."

I reached out my hand. I had my palm scanner in it. Anyone who'd traveled a lot, anyone who had been on the run, would recognize it. "We can do this the old-fashioned way, Mrs. Sobol, or you can listen to me."

She sat down slowly. Her lower lip trembled. She didn't object to my use of her real name. "If you're what your identification says you are, you don't warn people. You take them in."

I let my hand drop. "I was hired by Anetka Sobol," I said. "She wanted me to find you. She claimed that she wanted to share her inheritance with her Original. She's a clone. The record supports this claim."

"So, you want to take us back." Her voice was calm, but her eyes weren't. I watched her hands. They remained on the desktop, flat, and she was without enhancement. So far, she hadn't signaled anyone for help.

"Normally, I would have taken you back. But when I discovered that Anetka's Original was male, I got confused."

Sylvy licked her lower lip, just like her cloned daughter did. An hereditary nervous trait.

I rested one leg on the corner of the desk. "Why would a man change the sex of a clone when the sex didn't matter? Especially if all he wanted was the child. A man with no violent tendencies, who stood accused of attacking his wife so savagely all she could do was leave him, all she could do was disappear. Why would he do that?"

She hadn't moved. She was watching me closely. Beads of perspiration had formed on her upper lip.

66

"So I went back through the records and found two curious things. You disappeared just after his business on Korsve failed. And once you moved to Gagarin, you and your son were often in other domed Moon colonies at the same time as your husband. Not a good way to hide from someone, now is it, Mrs. Sobol?"

She didn't respond.

I picked up a clay pot. It was small and very, very old. It was clearly an original, not a Moon-made copy. "And then there's the fact that your husband never bothered to change his will to favor the child he had raised. It wouldn't have mattered to most parents that the child was a clone, especially when the Original was long gone. He could have arranged a dispensation, and then made certain that the business remained in family hands." I set the pot down. "But he had already done that, hadn't he? He hoped that the Wygnin would forget."

She made a soft sound in the back of her throat, and backed away from me, clutching at her wrist. I reached across the desk and grabbed her left arm, keeping her hand away from her wrist-top. I wasn't ready for her to order someone to come in here. I still needed to talk to her alone.

"I'm not going to turn you in to the Wygnin," I said. "I'm not going to let anyone know where you are. But if you don't listen to me, someone else will find you, and soon."

She stared at me, the color high in her cheeks. Her arm was rigid beneath my hand.

"The will was your husband's only mistake," I said. "The Wygnin never forget. They targeted your firstborn, didn't they? The plants on Korsve didn't open and close without a fuss. Something else happened. The Wygnin only target firstborns for a crime that can't be undone."

She shook her arm free of me. She rubbed the spot

where my hand had touched her flesh, then she sighed. She seemed to know I wouldn't go away. When she spoke, her voice was soft. "No Wygnin were on the site planning committee. We bought the land, and built the plants according to our customs. At that point, the Wygnin didn't understand the concept of land purchase."

I noted the use of the word "we." She had been involved with the Third Dynasty, more involved than the records said.

"We built on a haven for nestlings. You understand nestlings?"

"I thought they were a food source."

She shook her head. "They're more than that. They're part of Wygnin society in a way we didn't understand. They become food only after they die. It's the shells that are eaten, not the nestlings themselves. The nestlings themselves are considered sentient."

I felt myself grow cold. "How many were killed?"

She shrugged. "The entire patch. No one knows for sure. We were told, when the Wygnin came to us, that they were letting us off easily by taking our firstborn—Carson's and mine. They could easily take all the children of anyone who was connected with the project, but they didn't."

They could have too. It was the Third Dynasty that acted without regard to local custom, which made it liable to local laws. Over the years, no interstellar court had overturned a ruling in instances like that.

"Carson agreed to it," she said. "He agreed so no one else would suffer. Then we got me out."

"And no one came looking for you until I did."

"That's right," she said.

"I don't think Anetka's going to stop," I said. "I suspect she wants her father to change the will—"

"What?" Sylvy clenched her collar with her right hand, revealing the wrist-top. It was one of the most sophisticated I'd seen.

"Anetka wants control of the Third Dynasty, and I was wondering why her father hadn't done a will favoring her. Now I know. She was probably hoping I couldn't find you so that her father would change the will in her favor."

"He can't," Sylvy said.

"I'm sure he might consider it, if your son's life is at stake," I said. "The Wygnin treat their captives like family—indeed, make them into family, but the techniques they use on adults of other species are—"

"No," she said. "It's too late for Carson to change his will."

She was frowning at me as if I didn't understand anything. And it took me a moment to realize how I'd been used.

Anetka Sobol had tricked me in more ways than I cared to think about. I wasn't half as good as I thought I was. I felt the beginnings of an anger I didn't need. I suppressed it. "He's dead, isn't he?"

Sylvy nodded. "He died three years ago. He installed a personal alarm that notified me the moment his heart stopped. My son has been voting his shares through a proxy program my husband set up during one of his trips here."

I glanced at the wrist-top. No wonder it was so sophisticated. Too sophisticated for a simple administrator. Carson Sobol had given it to her, and through it, had notified her of his death. Had it broken her heart? I couldn't tell, not from three years distance.

She caught me staring at it, and brought her arm down. I turned away, taking a deep breath as the reality of my situation hit me. Anetka Sobol had out-maneuvered me. She had put me in precisely the kind of case I never wanted.

I was working for the Tracker. I was leading a Disappeared to her death and probably the death of her son. "I don't get it," I said. "If something happens to your son, Anetka still won't inherit."

Sylvy's smile was small. "She inherits by default. My son will disappear, and stop voting the proxy program. She'll set up a new proxy program and continue to vote the shares. I'm sure the Board thinks she's the person behind the votes anyway. No one knows about our son."

"Except for you, and me, and the Wygnin." I closed my eyes. "Anetka had no idea you'd had a son."

"No one did," Sylvy said. "Until now."

I rubbed my nose with my thumb and forefinger. Anetka was good. She had discovered that I was the best and the quickest Retrieval Artist in the business. She had studied me and had known how to reach me. She had also known how to play at being an innocent, how to use my past history to her advantage. She hired me to find her Original, and once I did, she planned to get rid of him. It would have been easy for her too; no hitman, no attempt at killing. She wouldn't have had to do anything except somehow—surreptitiously—let the Wygnin know how to find the Original. They would have taken him in payment for the Third Dynasty's crimes, he would have stopped voting his shares, and she would have controlled the corporation.

Stopping Anetka wasn't going to be easy. Even if I refused to report, even if Sylvy and her son returned to hiding, Anetka would continue looking for them.

I had doomed them. If I left this case now, I ensured that one of my colleagues would take it. They would find Sylvy and her son. My colleagues weren't as good as I was, but they were good. And they were smart enough to follow the bits of my trail that I couldn't erase.

The only solution was to get rid of Anetka. I couldn't kill her. But I could think of one other way to stop her.

I opened my eyes. "If I could get Anetka out of the business, and allow you and your son to return home, would you do so?"

Sylvy shook her head. "This is my home," she said. She glanced at the fake adobe walls, the southwestern decor. Her fingers touched a blanket hanging on the wall beside her. "But I can't answer for my son."

"If he doesn't do anything, he'll be running for the rest of his life."

She nodded. "I still can't answer for him. He's an adult now. He makes his own choices."

As we all did.

"Think about it," I said, handing her a card with my chip on it. "I'll be here for two days."

XI

They hired me, of course. What thinking person wouldn't? I had to guarantee that I wouldn't kill Anetka when I got her out of the business—and I did that, by assuring Sylvy that I wasn't now nor would I ever be an assassin—and I had to guarantee that I would get the Wygnin off her son's trail.

I agreed to both conditions, and for the first time in years, I did something other than tracking a Disappeared.

Through channels, I let it drop that I was searching for the real heir to Carson Sobol's considerable fortune. Then I showed some of my actual research—into the daughter's history, the falsified birth date, the inaccurate records. I managed to dump information about Anetka's cloning and her sex change, and I tampered with the records to show that her clone mark had been faked just as her sex had. Alterations, done at birth, made her look like a clone when she really wasn't.

I made sure that my own work on-line looked like sloppy detecting, but I hid the changes I made in other files. I did all of this quickly and thoroughly, and by the time I was done, it appeared as though Carson Sobol had hidden his own heir—originally a son—by making him into a daughter and passing him off as a clone.

At that point, I could have sat back and let events move forward by themselves. But I didn't. This had become personal.

I had to see Anetka one last time.

I set an appointment to hand deliver my final bill.

XII

This time she was wearing emeralds, an entire sheath covered with them. I had heard that there would be a gala event honoring one of the galaxy's leaders, but I had forgotten that the event would be held in Armstrong, at one of the poshest restaurants on the Moon.

She was sweeping up her long hair, letting it fall just below the mark on the back of her head, when I entered. As she turned, she stabbed an emerald haircomb into the bun at the base of her neck.

"I don't have much time," she said.

"I know." I closed the door. "I wanted give you my final bill."

"You found my sister?" There was a barely concealed excitement in her voice.

"No." The room smelled of an illegal perfume. I was surprised no one had confiscated it when she got off the shuttle and then I realized she probably hadn't taken a shuttle. Even the personal items bag she wore that first day had been part of her act. "I'm resigning."

She shook her head slightly. "I might have known you would. You have enough money now, so you're going to quit."

"I have enough information now to know you're not the kind of person I relish working for."

She raised her eyebrows. The movement dislodged the tiny emerald attached to her left cheek. She caught it just before it fell to the floor. "I thought you were done investigating me."

"Your father's dead," I said. "He has been for three years, although the Third Dynasty has managed to keep that information secret, knowing the effect his death would have had on galactic confidence in the business."

She stared at me for a moment, clearly surprised. "Only five of us knew that."

"Six," I said.

"You found my mother." She stuck the emerald in its spot.

"You found the alarm. You knew she'd been notified of your father's death."

The emerald wasn't staying on her cheek. Anetka let out a puff of air, then set the entire kit down. "I really didn't appreciate the proxy program," she said. "It notified me of my insignificance an hour after my father breathed his last. It told me to go about my life with my own fortune and abandon my place in the Third Dynasty to my Original."

73

"Which you didn't do."

"Why should I? I knew more about the business than she ever would."

"Including the Wygnin."

She leaned against the dressing table. "You're much better than I thought."

"And you're a lot more devious than I gave you credit for."

She smiled and tapped her left cheek. "It's the face. Youth still fools."

Perhaps it did. I usually didn't fall for it, though. I couldn't believe I had this time. I had simply thought I was being as cautious as usual. What Anetka Sobol had taught me was that being as cautious as usual wasn't cautious enough.

"Pay me, and I'll get out of here," I said.

"You've found my mother. You may as well tell me where she is."

"So you can turn your Original over to the Wygnin?"

That flat look came back into her eyes. "I wouldn't do that."

"How would you prevent it? The Wygnin have a valid debt."

"It's twenty-seven years old."

"The Wygnin hold onto markers for generations." I paused, then added, "As you well know."

"You can't prove what I do and do not know."

I nodded. "True enough. Information is always tricky. It's so easy to tamper with."

Her eyes narrowed. She was smart, probably one of the smartest people I'd ever come up against. She knew I was referring to something besides our discussion.

"So I'm getting out." I handed her a paper copy of the

bill—rare, unnecessary, and expensive. She knew that as well as I did. Then, as soon as she took the paper from my hand, I pressed my wrist-top to send the electronic version. "You owe me money. I expect payment within the hour."

She crumpled the bill. "You'll get it."

"Good." I pulled open the door.

"You know," she said, just loud enough for me to hear, "if you can find my mother, anyone can."

"I've already thought of that," I said, and left.

XIII

The Wygnin came for her later that night, toward the end of the gala. Security tried to stop them until they showed a valid warrant for the heir of Carson Sobol. The entire transaction caused an interstellar incident, and the vidnets were filled with it for days. The Third Dynasty used its attorneys to try to prove that Anetka was the eighth clone, just as everyone thought she was, but the Wygnin didn't believe it.

The beautiful thing about a clone is that it is a human being. It's simply one whose heritage matches another person's exactly, and whose facts of birth are odder than most. These are facts, yes, but they are facts that can be explained in other ways. The Wygnin simply chose to believe my explanations, not Anetka's. It was the sex change that did it. The Wygnin believed that anyone who would change a child's sex to protect it would also brand it with a clone mark, even if the mark wasn't accurate.

Over time, the lawyers lost all of their appeals, and Anetka disappeared into the Wygnin culture, never to be heard from again.

Oh, of course, the Third Dynasty still believes it's being run by Anetka Sobol voting her shares, as she always has, through a proxy program. Her Original apparently decided not to return to claim his prize. He acts as he always planned to, secretly. Only Sylvy Sobol, her son, and I know the person voting those shares isn't Anetka.

After Anetka's future was sealed, I stopped paying attention to the business of the Third Dynasty. I still don't look. I don't want to know if I have traded one monster for another. Some cold-heartedness is trained—and I can make myself think that Carson Sobol never once treated young Anetka with love, affection, or anything bordering civility—but I am smart enough to know that most cold-heartedness is bred into the genes. Just because Anetka is gone, doesn't mean the Original won't act the same way in similar circumstances.

And what is my excuse for my cold-heartedness? I'd like to say I've never done anything like this before, but I have—always in the name of my client, or a Disappeared. This time, though, this time, I did it for me.

Anetka Sobol had out-thought me, had compromised me, and had made me do the kind of work I'd vowed I'd never do. I let a front use me to open a door that would allow other Trackers find a Disappeared.

People disappear because they want to. They disappear to escape a bad life, or a mistake they've made, or they disappear to save themselves from a horrible death. A person who has disappeared never wants to be found.

I always ignored that simple fact, thinking I knew better. But one man is never a good judge of another, even if he thinks he is.

I tell myself Anetka Sobol would have destroyed her Original if she had had the chance. I tell myself Anetka

Sobol was greedy and self-centered. I tell myself Anetka Sobol deserved her fate.

But I can't ignore the fact that when I learned that Anetka Sobol had used me, this case became personal, in a way I would never have expected. Maybe, just maybe, I might have found a different solution, if she hadn't angered me so.

And now she haunts me in the middle of the night. She wakes me out of many a sound sleep. She keeps me restless and questioning. Because I didn't go after her for who she was or what she was planning. I had worked with people far worse than she was. I had met others who had done horrible things, things that made me wonder if they were even human. Anetka Sobol wasn't in their league.

No. I had gone after her for what she had done to me. For what she had made me see about myself. And because I hadn't liked my reflection in the mirror she held up, I destroyed her.

I can't get her back. No one comes back intact from the Wygnin. She will spend the rest of her days there. And I will spend the rest of mine thinking about her.

Some would say that is justice. But I have come to realize, in a universe as complex as this one, justice no longer exists.

Dancers Like Children

1

I lie in this cool bed on Lina Base, my body coated with burn creams and wrapped in light bandages in the areas where the skin grafts have yet to take. I told my counselor that every time I wake up, I remember something else. I told her that I wanted to make notes, to organize my thoughts before the second round of questions begin. This morning she brought me the small, voice-activated computer that hangs on the side of my bed rail. I don't know if someone else can access what I write; I suspect anyone can. I don't care. I do need to get organized, for myself. I need to write down the entire story my way before too many questions taint it. I used to counsel my own patients to do that—fifteen years ago, when I was Justin Schafer, Ph.D., instead of Dr. Schafer, the man whose name is spoken in a cool, dismissive tone.

Fifteen years ago. When I had friends, respect, and a future, when people believed in me, even more than I believed in myself.

11

They brought me in after the fifth murder.

The shuttle dropped me on the landing site at the salt cliffs, overlooking the golden waters of the Singing Sea. Apparently, something in the shuttle fuel harmed the vegetation near the small colony, so they developed a landing strip on the barren cliff tops at the beginning of the desert. Winds and salt had destroyed the plastic shelter, so I wore the required body scarf and some specially developed reflective cream. Before he left, the shuttle pilot pointed out the domed city in the distance. He said he had radioed them to send someone for me. I clutched my water bottle tightly, refusing to drink until I was parched.

A hot, dry breeze rustled the scarf around my face. The breeze smelled of daffodils, or so it seemed. It had been so long since I had been to Earth, I was no longer sure what daffodils smelled like.

The desert spanned between me and the domed city. I wasn't sure if the reflections I saw were dome lights or a mirage. To my left, salt continually eroded down the cliff face, little crystals rolling and tumbling to the white beach below. The Singing Sea devoured the crystals, leaving a salt scum that reflected the harsh light of the sun. I wondered if this was where, decades ago, the miners had begun their slaughter of the Dancers. The Dancers were a protected species now, perhaps one one-hundredth of their original numbers.

This place had a number of protected species, but most lived far away from the colony. The only known Dancer habitat was at the edge of the domed city. All the materials sent to me on Minar Base pointed to the Dancers as the cause of the murders. The colonists wanted me to make a recommendation that would be used in a preliminary injunction, a recommendation on whether the Dancers had acted with malicious intent. That idea left me queasy and brought the dreams back.

I glanced back at the barren brown land leading to the dome. The colonists called this Bountiful. Colonists who escaped the planet called it the Gateway to Hell. I could understand why, with the endless heat, the oxygen-poor air, and the salt-polluted water. Just before I left the base, I spoke with an old man who had spent his childhood on this planet. The old man's skin was shriveled and dried from too many hours in an unkind sun. He ate no salt, and he filled his quarters with fresh, cool water. He said he was so relieved to become an adult, because then he could legally escape the planet. He had warned me to stay away. And if I had had a choice, I would never have come.

"Justin Schafer?"

I turned. A woman stood at the edge of the trail leading back to the dome. Her body-length white sand scarf fluttered with the breeze.

"I'm Netta Goldin. I'm to take you to the colony."

"We're walking?"

She smiled. "The ecology here is fragile. We have learned to accept a number of inconveniences." The reflective white cream gathered in the lines on her face, making her appear creased. "I hear they brought you in from the base near Minar. Minar is supposed to be lovely."

"They closed the planet almost a decade ago." A shiver went through me. Minar was lovely, and I hated it. "Your name is familiar."

"I'm the head of the colony."

I remembered now. The scratchy female voice over the telecorder. "Then you're the one who had me brought in."

She adjusted my scarf hood. The heat seemed to increase, but the prickling on my scalp stopped. "You're the best person for the job."

"I deal in human aberration. You need a specialist."

"No." She threaded her arm through mine and walked down the trail. The salt crunched beneath our feet. "I need someone who knows human and xeno psychology. You seem to be the only one left on either nearby base."

"I thought you were convinced the natives are doing this."

"I think the deaths have happened because of interaction between our people and the Dancers. It's clear that the Dancers killed the children, but we don't know why. I want you to investigate those dynamics. I also want this done fast. I want to do something about the Dancers, protect my people better than I am now. But I understand that you need to investigate the natives in their own environment, so we have taken no action."

The wind played with my sand scarf. A runnel of sweat trickled down my back. "I'm not licensed to practice xenopsychology."

"That's a lie, Dr. Schafer. I researched you rather heavily before I went to the expense of bringing you here. The Ethics Committee suspended your license for one year as a formality. That was nine years ago. You're still licensed, and still interested in the field."

I pulled my arm from hers. I had sat by the sea that first morning on Minar, too. I had been thirty years old and so sure I could understand everyone, human or alien. And I did understand, finally, too late.

"I don't want to do this job," I said.

"You're the only one who can do it." She had clasped her hands behind her back. "All the other xeno-psychologists in the quadrant have specialized in one species or refuse to do forensic work. Besides, no one is better at this than you."

"They charged me with inciting genocide on Minar."

"And acquitted you. Your actions were logical, given the evidence."

Logical. I should have seen how the land encroached, poisoned, ate away human skin. We learned later that Minaran skin oils were also acidic, but didn't cause the same kind of damage. The original colonists had died first because of land poisoning, not because the Minarans were acting on an old vendetta. All the work the natives had done, they had done to save the colonists. I had ascribed a human motive—the wrong human motive—and had decimated a sentient race. "I don't want to make the same mistake again."

"Good," she said. The wind blew her scarf across her face. She brushed the cloth away with a cream-covered hand. "Because then you won't."

III

The cool air in the meeting room smelled of metallic processing.

I shifted in my chair. Despite the reflective cream and clothing, my skin had turned a blotchy red. My scalp itched. Little raised bumps had formed underneath my hair. I was afraid to touch them, afraid they might burst.

I glanced at the others. Davis, a thin, wiry man from Lina Base, headed the laboratory team. Sanders, head of the medical unit, had hands half the size of mine. I found myself staring at her, wondering how someone so petite could spend her time sifting through the clues left in a dead body. And of course, Netta. Her hair was dark, her skin bronzed by the planet's sun. Netta had brought them all in to brief me. The only person missing was the head of the city's security.

The artificial lighting seemed pale after the brightness of the sun. The building was made of old white terraplastic— the kind colonists brought with them to form temporary structures until they could build from the planet's natural materials. Wood and stone were not scarce commodities here, yet it was almost as if the original colonists had been afraid to use anything native.

Finally a small man, his hair greased back and his face darkened by the sun, entered. He dumped papers and holotubes on the desk in front of Netta. "Thank you," she said. She pushed her chair back and caught the small man by the arm. "Justin, this is D. Marvin Tanner. He heads the security forces for this area. If you have any questions about the investigative work prior to this time, you should direct those questions to him."

Tanner's gaze darted around the room, touching everyone but settling on no one. I wondered what made Tanner so nervous. He had worked with the others. I was the only new person in the room.

"Most of what I will tell you is in your packet, for your own personal review later," Netta said. "But let me give you a general briefing now before we show the holos." She let go of Tanner's arm. He sat down next to me. He smelled of sweat and cologne. "They found the first victim three Earth months ago. Linette Bisson was eleven years old. She had been propped against the front door of her home like a rag doll. Someone had removed her hands, heart, and lungs.

"The next victim, David Tomlinson, appeared three weeks later. Same M.O. Three more children—Katie Dengler, Andrew Liser, and Henry Illn—were found two weeks apart. Again, same M.O. These children all played together. They were the same age. And, according to their parents, none of the last three seemed too terribly frightened by the deaths of their friends."

She paused, glanced at me. Children often had no concept of death, and the things they feared were not the things adults feared. That the children were not frightened had less significance for me than it seemed to have for Netta.

"The Dancers mature differently than we do," Sanders said. Her voice was soft and as delicate as she was. "They do grow, a little, but their heart, lungs, and hands work like our teeth. The old ones must be removed before the new ones can grow into place. They have developed an elaborate rite of passage that ends with the ceremonial removal of the adolescent's organs."

I turned to Netta. "You said the Dancers interacted with the colonists."

She nodded. "For decades we've had an informal relationship. They develop the herbs we use in our exports. We haven't had any trouble, until now."

"And the Dancers were allowed inside the dome?"

"We restricted them when the killings started, and now they're not allowed at all."

"We also set up dome guards," Tanner said. "The dome doors have no locks and can be operated from the inside or the outside. We had done that as a precaution so no colonist would die trapped outside the dome."

Colonists, colony. Fascinating the way that language had not evolved here. The "colony" had been settled for nearly a century. Gradually, it should have eased into "settlement" or "city." The domed area had no name, and even people like Tanner, who had lived on the planet their entire lives, felt no sense of permanence.

"We have some holos we'd like to show you," Tanner said. He had set up the equipment at the edge of the table. He moved chairs and a garbage can away from the wall, leaving a wide, blank space. He flicked on the switch, and a holo leaped into being before us.

Laughter filled the room, children's laughter. Twelve children huddled on the floor, playing a game I did not recognize. The children all appeared the same age, except for one, who sat off to one side and watched. He appeared to be about eight. The older children would pound their fists on the ground three times, then touch hands. One child would moan or roll away. The others would laugh.

Tanner froze the image. "These are the children," he said. He moved near the images, stopping by a slim, blonde girl whose face was bright with laughter. "Linette Bisson," he said. Then he moved to a solid boy with rugged features who was leaning forward, his hand in a small fist. "David Tomlinson."

Tanner moved to the next child, his body visible through the holos in front of him. I shivered. Seeing the living Tanner move through the projected bodies of dead children raised hackles on the back of my neck. Superstition. Racial memory. My ancestors believed in ghosts.

He looked at a dark-haired girl who frowned at the little boy who sat alone. "Katie Dengler. Beside her, Andrew Liser and Henry Illn." The boys were rolling on the ground, holding their stomachs. Their mirth would have been catching if I hadn't known the circumstances of their deaths. Tanner went back to the holojecter.

"Who are the other children?" I asked. At least eight were not accounted for.

"You'll meet them," Netta said. "They still run together."

I nodded and watched. Tanner switched images, and the projection moved again. The children's clothing changed. They wore scarves and reflective cream. A middle-aged woman with sun-black skin stood beside them. "Do as I say," she said. "Nothing more." They turned their backs on me and walked past trees and houses until the dome appeared. The woman flicked a switch, and the dome rose. The children waved, and the dome closed behind them. The younger boy ran into the picture, but an adult suddenly appeared and stopped him.

Tanner froze the image. I stared at the boy, seeing the dejection in his shoulders. I had stood like that so many times since Minar, watching my colleagues move to other projects, while I had to stay behind.

"We think this is the first time the Dancers met with the children," Tanner said.

"Who is that boy?" I asked.

"Katie Dengler's brother. Michael."

"And the woman?"

"Latona Etanl. She's a member of the Extra-Species Alliance." Netta answered that question. Her voice dripped with bitterness. "She believed that having the children learn about the Dancers would ease relations between us."

I glanced at her. "There have been problems?"

"No. The Alliance believes that we are abusing the Dancers because we do not understand their culture." Netta leaned back in her chair, but her body remained tense. "I thought we had a strong cooperative relationship until she tried to change things."

I frowned. The Alliance was a small, independent group with bases on all settled planets. Theoretically, the Alliance was supposed to promote understanding between the colonists and the natives. In some areas, Alliance members spent so much time with the natives that they absorbed and practiced native beliefs. On those lands the Alliance became a champion for the downtrodden native. In other lands the group assisted the colonists in systematically destroying native culture. And sometimes the group actually fulfilled its mission. The Alliance representatives I had met were as varied as the planets they worked on.

"How long ago was this holo taken?" I asked.

"Almost a year," Tanner said. "But the children weren't as taken with the Dancers as Latona thought they would be. I believe that was the only visit."

"What has changed since then? What has provoked the Dancers?"

Netta glanced at Tanner. She sighed. "We want to take control of the xaredon, leredon, and ededon plants."

The basis of Salt Juice, the colonists' chief export. Salt Juice was one of the most exhilarating intoxicants the galaxy had ever known. It mixed quickly with the bloodstream, left the user euphoric, and had no known side effects: no hangovers, no hallucinations, no addictions, and no dangerous physical responses. That export alone brought in a small fortune. "I didn't know the Dancers controlled the herbs," I said.

"They grow the herbs and give us the adult plants. We've been trying to get them to teach us to grow the plants, but they refuse." Netta shook her head. "I don't know why, either. We don't pay them. We don't give them anything for their help."

"And the negotiations broke off?"

"About a week before the first death." The deep voice surprised me. It belonged to Davis. I had forgotten he was there.

Another fact that I would have to investigate. I was developing quite a mental checklist.

"Let me show you the final image," Tanner said. "It's of the first death. You can see the others if you want in the viewing library. This one begins the pattern carried through on the rest."

He clicked the image. The scene in front of me was grim. Linette, her hair longer and sun-blonde, her skin darker than it had been in the first projection, leaned against one of the terraformed doors. Her feet stretched out in front of her; her arms rested at her sides. Her chest was open, dark, and matted with blood. Tanner froze the projection, and this time I got up, examining the halo from all sides. The stumps at the ends of her arms were blood-covered. Her clothing was also bloodstained, but that could have been caused by her bleeding arms. Blood did coat the chest cavity, though. Whoever had killed her had acted quickly. The girl's eyes were wide and had an inquisitive expression. Her mouth was drawn in a slight O of surprise or pain.

"The wounds match the wounds made by Dancer ceremonial tools," Davis said. "I can show you more down in the lab later if you want."

I nodded, feeling sick. "Please shut that off," I said. Tanner flicked a switch, and the image disappeared. Five children, dead and mutilated. I had to get out of the room. I had received too much information, and seen too much. My stomach threatened to betray me. The others stared at me.

"This packet and the information you've given so far should be enough for me to get started," I said. I stood up and clutched the chair for support. "I'm sure that I will return with questions." I let myself out of the room and took a deep breath. The image of the child remained at the edge of my brain, mingling with that of other dead colonists on a world ten years away.

I heard rustling inside the conference room, and knew I had to be gone before they emerged. I hurried through the dimly lit corridor. Sunlight glared through the cracks around the outside door. I stopped and examined the almost inch-wide space between the door and its frame, forcing myself to think about things other than holographic images. Clearly, the people who lived inside the dome had no fear of the elements or of each other. Anyone, or anything, could open that door by wedging something inside the crack.

I felt better outside the room. The people inside made me feel uncomfortable. They had discovered what they could through instruments and measures and other "scientific" things. I had to crawl inside alien minds and see what had caused such murders. If the colonists had suspected a human killer, they would have brought any one of half a dozen other specialists to the planet. Instead they had brought me.

I had to see the Dancers clearly, without dead Minarans clouding my vision. If the Dancers killed with malicious intent, the colony had to be protected or moved. I would simply approach things differently this time. Instead of going to the leaders of the colony, I would go to Galactic Security. That might prevent slaughter. The Dancers, with their small population, were easier prey than the Minarans.

I stepped outside and blinked at the blue-tinted light. The dome filtered the sunlight, deflecting the dangerous ultraviolet rays and allowing only a modicum of heat inside.

Roses grew beside the door, and young maples lined the walks. Patches of grass peeked through, hidden by bushes and other flowering plants. The care that the colonists had not placed in their homes, they had placed in making the interior of the dome look like Earth. It felt odd to stand here, among familiar trees and lush vegetation, and to know that just outside the dome, a different alien world waited.

I crouched beside the roses and put my hand in the soil. Perhaps it was less alkaline than the salt cliffs had led me to believe. Or perhaps the colonists had imported the soil, as they had imported everything else. I saw no reason to live in a new place if I were going to try so hard to make it look like the place I had left. That attitude was a difference between me and the colonists. I would collect thousands of differences before I was through. The problem was whether thousands were enough or if they meant anything at all. The differences I had to concentrate on were the differences between human and Dancer thought. Something that should have taken a lifetime to study, I would have to discover in a matter of weeks.

IV

That night I dreamed of the Minarans. Their sleek sealbodies dripped with water. They hovered around me, oversized eyes reproachful, as if they were trying to warn me of something I would never understand. They reached out to touch me, and I slapped their fingered fins away. Shudders ran through my body. They had caused the murders. But I knew if I told the colonists, they would slaughter the Minarans—the fat mothers, the tiny males, and the white pups that, not that much earlier, the children had watched as if they were pets. Minaran blood was colorless but thick. It still coated my hands, leaving them sticky and useless.

I blinked myself awake. A fan whirred in the darkness. The blanket covering me was scratchy and too hot. I coughed, and tasted metallic air in the back of my throat. The apartment Netta had given me seemed small and close.

I had done nothing right since the Minaran trial. I should have resigned from psychology, let my licenses lapse, and bought back my contract. I had had the money then. I hadn't had to serve out my time on Minar Base, the planet hovering in my viewscreen like an ugly reminder. Instead I stayed, wrote abstracts and papers, conducted studies, and worked with an intensity that I hadn't known I had. My colleagues ignored me, and I tried to ignore myself. Just before she left me, Carol accused me of idolizing the Minarans. She said that I had buried my emotions in the search for the cause of my own flaws. Perhaps I did idolize the Minarans, and I knew that I had stored my emotions far away from myself. But I thought I knew the cause of my own flaws. I didn't hide in my work. I liked to think that I was atoning.

I rolled over. The sheets were cool on the far side of the bed. Maybe my sense of guilt allowed me to let my contract safeguards lapse so that someone like Netta could buy my services for the next Earth year. The darkness seemed to close around me, press on me. When I closed my eyes, I saw the Minarans.

I could, I supposed, cancel the contract and head to Lina Base for reeducation, never to practice psychology again. But the work was all I had. Perhaps I was atoning. Or perhaps I hadn't learned.

V

I rose early and drank my coffee outside, watching the colony wake up. I sat on the stoop of the apartment building, looking over some sort of evergreen bush at the street beyond. The apartments were clearly for guests of the colony. I had heard no one in the building during the night, and no one passed me on the way to work.

The streets were full, however. Adults carrying satchels and briefcases walked by, chatting. Others wore grubby clothes and carried nothing. A few wore sand scarves and helped each other apply reflective cream. Work seemed to start at the same time. I would have wagered that the workday ended at the same time, too.

In my wanderings I had noticed no taverns and no restaurants, no place for the colonists to gather and socialize after the workday had ended. I wondered what the colonists did for recreation besides garden.

I got up, went inside, and put my mug into the washer. Then I went back outside. The last of the stragglers had gone up the street, and in the near silence, I heard a squeal of laughter, followed by a child's voice. I followed the sound. It didn't seem too far away. The laughter came again, and again, guiding me to it. I walked the opposite direction of the workers, past terraplastic homes with no windows, large gardens that passed for lawns, and fences dividing property. The laughter grew closer. I turned and saw a small corner park, marked off by three weeping willows. Flowers grew like a fence along the walkway, and inside, on the grass, about ten children sat in a circle, playing the game I had seen them play on the hologram.

One child stood back, leaning on the gate. He was tall for his age, but the longing expression on his face made him seem even younger than he was. I wondered if my face used to look like that on nights after the Minar trial, when I used to pass my colleagues in the middle of heated round-table discussions. I suppressed a sigh and stood beside the boy. It took a moment for me to recall his name. Michael Dengler.

"What are they playing?"

He glanced over at me, seemingly surprised that someone would talk to him. "Race."

The children pounded their fists on the ground three times, then made different hand gestures. They laughed. I watched the muscles bulge in their arms, wondering what kind of exercise program they were on. One girl rolled away, stood up, arched her back, and growled. "Limabog!" "Arachni!" "Cat!" "Illnea!" the children called. At each name the girl shook her head. Finally someone yelled, "Bear!" She nodded, joined the circle again, and the fist pounding started all over.

"How do you play?" I asked.

His frown grew until his entire face turned blood-red. "I don't," he said.

The hair on the back of my neck prickled, and for a moment I heard the hushed whispers of former friends gossiping about my failures. I swallowed, determined to distance myself from the boy. "Don't you play with friends your own age?"

Michael stopped leaning on the fence. "You're one of the strangers here for the Salt Juice, aren't you?"

I gave a half-nod, not bothering to correct his misconception.

"You got kids?"

"No," I said.

He shrugged. "Then it stays the same. I'm the only kid my age. My mom and dad didn't follow the rules."

The children burst into laughter, and another child rolled away, this time approaching the group on all fours. Apparently, this colony still followed the practice of having children in certain age groups, then spacing the next group at least four years away. It was a survival tactic for many new colonies.

"So you want to play with the older kids," I said.

"Yeah." I could feel the wistfulness in his voice. He watched from the outside; I had written papers about other people's work. Michael glanced over at the children, his hands clenching. "But they won't let me play until I grow and learn to think like a big kid. Mom says they should take me for who I am." He looked at me, his mouth set in a thin line. "What do you think?"

Such an easy question, asked to the wrong person. I had always thought for myself, and it had gained me respect and a following—until Minar. After that, I stood at the edge of the roundtable discussions instead of leading them, waiting for someone to pull back a chair and let me in. If I had said I was sorry, opened myself up for dissection, perhaps I wouldn't be standing friendless on an unfamiliar planet.

"In the ideal world, your mom is right," I said. "But sometimes you have to do what the group wants if you're going to be accepted."

Michael crossed his arms in front of his chest, his fists still clenched. His body language made his thoughts clear: he didn't want to believe what I said. I wouldn't have, either, in his position, but I hoped he would take my advice. Standing outside the group, watching, was much more painful than playing inside.

"Could you explain the game to me?" I asked softly.

"No!" He spun, started down the pathway. "Maybe they will. They talk to grown-ups."

95

He half-ran away from me. I almost started after him, then let him go. The boy reached me because I saw a similarity between us. He didn't have a lot to do with my investigation.

The children laughed behind me as if they hadn't noticed his outburst. I took Michael's place at the fence and watched, to see if I could learn the game from observation before I tried talking with the children.

VI

By midday the dome filter changed, giving the colony a sepia tone. The children had refused to talk to me, running when I approached. I decided that I would get Netta to arrange a time for me to talk with them. Then I walked to the office of the Extra-Species Alliance, hoping to talk to Latona Etanl.

The office was clearly marked, one of the few buildings with any identification at all. Tulips and lilies of the valley blossomed across the yard, and two maple trees shaded the pathway. The office building itself was made of terraplastic, but it seemed larger, perhaps because of the windows beside the door.

I mounted the stoop and saw, through the window, a woman get up from her desk. The door swung open in front of me, and I found myself staring at the woman from the holos. I recognized her sun-blackened face. It took me a moment to realize she wasn't wearing a sand scarf. Her long black hair went down to her knees and wrapped around her like a second skin.

"Ms. Etanl," I said, "I'm—"

"You're Dr. Schafer. I've been waiting for you." She stood away from the door, and I stepped inside.

The room had the rich, potent aroma of lilies of the valley. A bunch of flowers was gathered in a vase by the window. Other vases rested on end tables beside the wide couch and easy chairs that filled the rest of the space. A hallway opened beyond the desk, leading to other, smaller rooms. The sepia-colored light shining through the windows made the outdoors muddy and the interior even brighter than it should have been.

"Your offices are lovely," I said to cover my surprise at her greeting.

"We like to have pleasant surroundings," she said, and I thought I heard a kind of condemnation in her voice. "Care for a seat?"

She moved over to one of the easy chairs and waited for me to follow. I sat on the couch, sinking into the soft cushions. She sat down at the edge of her seat, looking as if she were going to spring up at a moment's notice.

"Ms. Etanl—"

"Latona."

"Latona. I'm surprised you knew who I was."

"The colony's small. And Netta told us you would come." She adjusted her hair over her legs as if it were a skirt. "She blames me for taking the children out of the colony. She thinks I started the Dancers on this."

Latona hadn't looked at me. "What do you think?" I asked.

She shook her head. "I don't think the Dancers are capable of such killings."

"From my understanding," I said slowly, "Dancers don't kill their young. They perform the mutilations to help adolescents reach maturity. Could something have happened in

97

that one meeting that would have made the Dancers try to help human children?"

She finally looked at me. Her eyes were wide and black, the color of her hair. "You haven't seen the Dancers yet, have you?"

I shook my head.

"You need to. And then you can ask me questions." She took a deep breath, as if hesitating about what she was about to say. "I'll take you if you like."

"Now?"

She nodded. "We have protective gear in the back."

My heart thudded against my chest. I hadn't expected to see the Dancers yet, but I was ready. A little thrill ran down my spine.

We got up, and she led me down the hall to one of the black offices. As she walked past an open office door, she peeked inside. A man sat behind a desk, his bald head bowed over a small computer screen. "Daniel, I'm taking Dr. Schafer to see the Dancers."

He glanced up, and I realized he was younger than I first thought—thirty or less. "Would you like a second?"

She shook her head. "Unless he thinks we need one."

She was asking me a question without directing it at me. I shook my head. "If she thinks the two of us will be fine, I'm not going to second-guess."

Daniel smiled, showing a row of very white teeth. "Latona is our best. She's studied the Dancers her entire life."

Latona had already started down the hall. I nodded at Daniel, then followed her. The room she entered was the size of a small closet. She flicked on a light and pulled two sand scarves from pegs. She took out a jar of reflective cream and handed it to me. I applied it. The goo was cold against my face, and smelled faintly sweet. Then I wrapped the sand scarf around me and waited as Latona did the same. She tied a small pack to her waist. Finally she pulled two pairs of sunglasses out of a drawer and handed me one.

"Put these on after we leave the dome," she said.

We left through a door on the back side. The sepia tone of the dome seemed to have grown darker. Latona led me across the yard along an empty pathway until we reached the dome. Two men stood beside the structure, looking bored. Latona nodded at them.

"I'm taking Dr. Schafer to see the Dancers."

"Netta permit this?" one of the men asked.

Latona sighed. "She doesn't have to. Dr. Schafer is off-world."

The man looked as if he were about to say more, but his partner grabbed his arm. He pushed a button, and the dome door slid open. Dry heat seeped in, making the air inside the dome feel as plastic as the buildings. I followed Latona outside and heard the doors squeak closed behind us.

Sunlight reflected off the white cream on my face, momentarily blinding me. The wind rustled my sand scarf. I already felt overdressed. The air smelled of salt, daffodils, and promises.

Latona tugged her hood over her face and headed into the wind. I bent and followed, wishing that I could see more of the desert. But the wind was strong and blew the sand at a dangerous rate. I put on the glasses, thankful for the way they eased the glare.

"Netta hates it when I visit the Dancers," Latona said, "but she can't stop me. I'm not officially a colony member. Neither are you."

"Why did you bring the children out here?" The sand

was deep and thick, and I was having trouble walking.

Latona seemed to follow no trail. "There are a lot of creatures on this planet that the colonists ignore. Little sand devils that burrow tunnels below the surface, birds with helicopter-like wings, and insects. Daniel is studying the birds to see if they're intelligent. Micah, one of my other colleagues, has determined that the sand devils are not. But the Dancers are intelligent, in their own way."

The sand became thin and packed, almost a mud-like surface. I glanced back. The dome was a small bubble in the distance.

"The early miners hated the Dancers and killed them. The killing stopped, though, when the colonists discovered Salt Juice."

"This is history," I said. My voice sounded breathless. "I want to know about now."

"I'm getting to now. The Dancers grow the herbs for Salt Juice, and although the colonists have tried, they can't. So they need the Dancers as another intelligent species. The colonists take the plants without recompense, and the Dancers just grow more. I know some of the colonists think the children's deaths are retaliation."

"And you don't think so."

Latona shook her head. "That's a human reaction. The Dancers are a different species. They have very alien thought processes."

The wind had eased, but my skin felt battered. I brought a hand up to my cheek and felt sand on the cream. Sweat ran down my back, and my throat was dry. "You have water in the pack?" I asked.

Latona stopped, opened the pack, and handed me a small plastic bottle. I saw others lined in rows of six. I put the bottle to my lips and drank. The water was flat and warm, but the wetness felt good. I handed the bottle back to Latona, and she finished the water, putting the empty bottle into her pack.

"We're almost there," she said. "I want you to do what I tell you and nothing else. The Dancers will come when I call them, and will touch you. They're only trying to see what you are. Their fingers are more sensitive than their eyes."

We stepped into a shadowy darkness, and it took me a moment to realize that we had reached trees. They had dark, spindly trunks, wind-whipped and twisted. Sand caught in the ridges, making the trees look scarred. The tops of the trees unfolded like umbrellas, the ropelike leaves entangled and braided to form a canopy. Latona took her hood down, removed her glasses, and whistled.

Dark shapes approached from ahead of us. I let my hood down and pocketed my sunglasses. The creatures weren't walking, although they were upright. They almost glided along the hard-packed sand, their feet barely touching. The creatures had long, twig-thin bodies with shiny black skin, two legs, two arms, and a wide, oblong head with large silver eyes. It was easy to see why the colonists had called them dancers; they moved with a fluid grace, as if they made every step in time to a music that I couldn't hear.

My heart pounded against my chest. The Dancers surrounded us and touched us lightly. I clutched my hands into fists, fighting the feeling of being trapped. Latona held her head back, eyes closed, and I did the same. Fingers with skin like soft rubber touched my mouth, my nose, my eyelids. I didn't move. The Dancers smelled of cinnamon and something tangy, something I couldn't identify. The bumps on my scalp burned as the Dancers touched them. I wanted to move my head away, but I didn't. I heard whistling and low hums. The sounds seemed to follow a pattern, and felt, after a moment, as familiar as a bird's call. I opened my eyes. Latona had stepped away from the Dancers a little. She was gesturing and churring. One of the Dancers touched her face and then whistled three times, in short bursts.

"He said they would be pleased to have you visit their homes."

I pulled away from the Dancers near me. Even though they were no longer touching me, I could still feel their rubbery fingers against my skin. I glanced at Latona and then at the Dancers again. They had no visible, recognizable sexual characteristics. I wondered how she knew the speaker's gender. "Thank him."

She did. We walked with the single Dancer through the canopied trees. My heartbeat slowed. I could feel myself growing calmer. If the Dancers were going to hurt us, they would have done so when we met them at the edge of the forest. Perhaps. I was assigning human logic. I shook my head and tried to clear my mind.

The vegetation grew thicker and the air cooler as we hit areas without sunlight. My eyes adjusted to the darkness, and I saw clothlike material stretched around four trees like handmade tents. The Dancer continued talking, touching things as if he were giving us a tour. Latona did not translate.

We followed him inside one of the tents. There the tangy cinnamon scent was stronger. I touched the tent material, and it felt like waterproof canvas. Rugs made from leaves covered the ground, and in the corners sat glass jars that cast a phosphorescent glow around the room.

"He says he would like to welcome us to his home."

"Tell him we're honored."

She responded. I examined the glass jars. They were crude. The glass had bubbles, ripples, and waves. The light inside moved as if it were caused by something living.

Our host whistled and churred. Latona watched me. "What is he saying?" I asked.

She glanced at the Dancer as if she hadn't heard him. Then she smiled. "Right now he's saying that if he were a good host, he would give you a jar, but the jars are valuable, too valuable to give to a guest who will disappear before the day ends."

"Tell him that I plan to return—"

She shook her head. "It doesn't matter." She slipped out of the tent. "You need to see the rest of the homes."

I followed her into the shaded darkness of outside. "Shouldn't you thank him?"

"No." She led me toward more of the tent-like structures. Dancers emerged, hands reaching for our faces. Latona ducked this time. I did, too. I was a bit more at ease, but I didn't want them to touch me again.

From appearances, the Dancers seemed to be a hunter-gatherer culture. The entire area lacked permanence. The ground seemed untended and wild. I saw no signs of cultivation. But then, I didn't know what I was looking for. For all I knew, the canopied trees were an edible, renewable resource.

"This is it," Latona said.

I stared at the tents, the scattered possessions, the Dancers huddled around me like shadows in the late-afternoon sunlight. "Which ones are the children?"

"The children live elsewhere. Let me ask permission to see them." Latona turned to a Dancer beside her and spoke. The Dancer whistled and churred in response, gesturing at me. Latona nodded once, and then the Dancer walked forward. "Come on," Latona said.

I followed. The hard-packed mud curved inward, as if feet had worn a smooth path through the trees. There were no tents here, and the vegetation had grown lush. I realized then that the land behind us had been tended, that the Dancers did the opposite of the colonists. The Dancers removed vegetation except for the thin, spindly trees.

Sunlight began to break through the overhead canopy. We reached a sun-mottled area where the undergrowth had again been thinned. Here the canvas material had been tied to the trees sideways to form a gate. We approached the gate and stared over the edge. Inside, small, dark creatures scrabbled in the dirt, tussling and fighting. Some sat off to the sides, leaning on the gate—sleeping, perhaps. Toward the back, larger children lay on the ground, their skin gray in the filtered sunlight. Their fingers seemed claw-like, and their eyes were dark, empty, and hollow.

I nodded toward the children. "Are they ill?"

"No," Latona said. "They've hit puberty."

"Do these children ever interact with the adults?"

"Not really. The adults treat them like animals. Education into the life of a Dancer begins after puberty."

I shivered a little, wondering at life that began in a cage under a harsh sun. The gray-skinned children did not move, but lay in the sunlight as if they were dead.

The Dancer churred and hovered over us. I glanced at it. Latona spoke briefly, then said to me, "We have to leave."

The Dancer corralled us, as if pushing us away from the children. Latona took my arm and led me in a different direction. The Dancer watched from behind.

"This is a quicker way back to the dome," Latona said. Some of the cream had melted off her face, making her appear lopsided and slightly alien.

The gray-skinned, sickly-looking creatures with the clawed hands haunted me. "You never told me why you brought the children here."

"I wanted them to learn respect for the Dancers." Latona kept her head down. We moved out of the trees.

"Why? The arrangement seems to be working."

"They're living beings," Latona snapped. "Humans have a history of mistreating beings they don't understand."

"And you think the colonists are mistreating the Dancers."

"Yes." Latona pushed a ropy branch aside and stepped into a patch of sunlight. Her sand scarf glowed white. "But I don't know what the Dancers think."

"That's why the Alliance is here, to find out what the Dancers think?"

"And to negotiate an agreement over the Salt Juice herbs."

I frowned. I stepped into the sun, and the heat prickled along my back. "But there is no agreement."

"You can't negotiate with the Dancers," she said. "They have an instinctual memory, and a memory for patterns that allows them to learn language and establish routines. Past events have no meaning for them, only future events that they hold in their minds. It poses an interesting problem: if we negotiate a treaty with them, the treaty will not exist, because they will have forgotten it. If we plan to negotiate a treaty in the future, as their language and customs allow, the treaty will not exist because the negotiations haven't started yet."

"Their language has no past tense?"

"Not even a subtle past. They speak only in present and future tenses. They also have a very active subjunctive. Their lives are very fluid and very emotional."

"And when one of them dies?"

"He ceases to be." She glanced at me, her lips set in a thin line. "And then they skin the body, eat the flesh, throw the bones to the children, and cure the skin. They stretch it and mount it until it becomes firm. And then they use it to form their tents."

I knew then what was glowing at me through the jars in the tents. Silver eyes. Wide silver eyes that had absorbed the light from the planet's powerful sun. "Where did the jars come from?"

"The miners made them. The Dancers used to live closer to the salt cliffs."

My mind felt cold and information-heavy. Heat rose in waves from the sand. "What did the children think of the Dancer children?"

Latona shrugged. She took out the cream and reapplied it. "They seemed fascinated. Who knows what would have happened? Netta banned any child contact with the Dancers."

"Before the murders?"

"Yes." Latona handed me the cream. "I am not supposed to bring them back."

I nodded, done asking questions. I drank the water Latona gave me, then looked across the desert. The dome looked small and far away. I wrapped my scarf around my face and followed Latona, too tired to do anything other than walk.

VII

Latona promised to show me a time-lapse holo of the Dancers' puberty rite. I eased my way out of the apartment the next morning, unable to comb my hair because some of the bumps had burst, leaking pus on my scalp. My skin, which had been a light red the night before, had eased into an even lighter tan. It would take many hours wearing reflective cream under the sun before my skin color even approached that of Netta or Latona.

I had barely missed the morning work rush. I walked along the pathway, staring at yards and the windowless plastic homes. These people made the most euphoric drug in the galaxy, and they were humorless stay-at-homes who created beautiful yards, but refused to look at their handiwork from inside the house.

The yards had different flowering plants from different climates and different seasons. Roses seemed to be predominant, but some blocks preferred rhododendrons, while others had hyacinths. All of the flowers bloomed, too, the tulips with the pansies, the daisies with the sunflowers. It seemed odd to me that a colony with such botanical expertise could not learn to grow native herbs from seeds.

Children's laughter caught me again, near the same block it had before. I glanced down. The children were playing in their park, sitting in a circle, pounding their fists against the ground. I walked over slowly, hoping that this time they would talk to me. Michael Dengler sat in the middle of the group, smiling as if he had found his own personal heaven. I relaxed a little. Maybe my advice had helped him. Maybe my wasted ten years had helped someone.

One of the boys pointed at me. The children got up and backed away, as if I were an enemy; then, as a group, they turned and ran.

I stopped and watched them go. Only one child glanced

back as he ran. Michael Dengler. I waved at him. He didn't wave back.

I continued to the offices of the Extra-Species Alliance. A woman sat at the desk. She was petite, with close-cropped hair and wide eyes. "Latona couldn't be here," she said, "but she told me to show you the holo, and she said she'd answer any of your questions this afternoon."

I nodded, and followed the woman into another closet-sized room with a holojecter set up. She flicked on the 'jecter, flicked off the lights, and left me.

Dancers filled the room, less frightening without their tangy cinnamon scent. They circled around a gray-skinned child, huddled on the desert floor. The circling seemed to last forever, then a Dancer grabbed a ceremonial knife and slit open the breastbone, reached and removed something small, blackened, and round. A heart, I assumed. The Dancer handed the black object to another Dancer, who set it in a jar. Then the Dancer slit again, removing two thin, shriveled bits of flesh from the child's interior. The child didn't move. Another Dancer put the flesh into a jar beside the heart. Finally the first Dancer lifted the child's hands by a single finger and sliced once along the wrists. The hands fell off, and the child's arms fell to its side. The Dancers carried the child to a tree and leaned the child against the tree. They wrapped the child's chest with rope leaves, and as they placed the arms on the child's lap, I could see small fingers peeking out of the hollow wrists like human hands hidden in the sleeves of a jacket one size too big.

The Dancer child did not bleed. Latona's comparison to a human child losing its baby teeth was an apt one.

Then the time-lapse became clear. The child's hands grew; its skin grew dark like that of other Dancers. Gradually, it moved on its own, and the adult Dancers helped it crawl into a nearby tent. Then the holo ended.

I replayed it three times, memorizing each action, and confirming that there was no blood.

Things weren't adding up: things Latona said, things I had seen. I shut off the 'jecter and left the room, thankful that the woman was not at the front desk. I needed to read my briefing packet, to see if the information in there differed from the information Latona had given me about the Dancers.

I hurried back to my apartment and sat in the front room reading. Latona was right. The Dancers showed no ability to remember things from visit to visit or even within visits. During the murders by the miners, the Dancers returned to the sites of the deaths and continued to interact with the miners as if nothing had happened. They never tried retaliation, and they never mutilated any of the miners.

Dancer preadolescents were gray and motionless, looking more dead than alive. The human children Latona had taken to the Dancers were fluid and energetic, as lively as the little creatures I had seen scrabbling in the dirt.

I set aside the packet, not liking what I was thinking. The Dancers were a protected species, so they could not be killed or relocated without interference from Lina Base. The colonists were great botanists and had been trying for years to learn the way to grow the Salt Juice herbs. The Dancers were impossible to negotiate with, and they guarded the seeds jealously. What if a colonist had figured out how to grow an herb from seed? The Dancers were no longer necessary; were, in fact, a hindrance. The murders allowed Lina Base to send in one expert instead of a gaggle of people—and also put the expert on a strict timetable. Netta had requested an expert with a flawed background, known for his rash judgments. My impetuous decision-making had led one colony to spray an alkaline solution in an acidic ocean filled with intelligent life. Perhaps this colony wanted me to make another bad decision, and use that as an excuse to murder the rest of the Dancers.

I leaned my head on the back of the chair. I had no evidence supporting my theory, had only suspicions as I had had with the Minarans. I stood up. I had to go to Communications Central and wire for more help. I could not make my decision alone.

VIII

A knock on the door startled me out of a sound sleep. I was lying on the packet on the couch in the apartment's front room. The knock echoed again. It sounded loud in the nearly empty room. Before I could respond, the door eased open and spread a wide patch of yellow light across the floor.

"Dr. Schafer?"

I squinted, and sat up, reaching for a light. As the lights came on, I closed my eyes, wincing even more. "Yes?"

"We have another one."

I blinked. My eyes finally adjusted to the brightness. D. Marvin Tanner, the head of the dome's security, stood before me. He seemed calm. "Another one?"

"Yes," he said. "Netta sent me to get you. We have another dead child."

The flat tone he used to deliver those words sent a shiver down my back. The security officer on Minar had come to me in the middle of the night, his hands shaking, his mouth set in a rigid line. His voice would crack as he spoke of the dead and his own feelings of helplessness. Tanner didn't seem to care. Perhaps that was because this was no longer his investigation. Or perhaps he was one of those borderline psychopaths himself, the kind that went into law enforcement because it provided them with a legal way of abusing others.

I wondered how he was able to get into the apartment so easily. Netta had assured me that I had the only key to the lock.

"What happened?" I rubbed my face, adjusted my clothes.

"You'll be able to see," he said. "No one is allowed to work the scene until the entire team has been assembled."

I got up and followed Tanner outside. The dome filter had changed again, this time to one that left everything looking gray and grainy, probably the colony's equivalent of dawn. Shadows seemed darker, and the dome filter leached the color from the plants. Only the white plastic seemed unchanged, but startling for the contrast against the physical environment.

People had stepped to the edges of their gardens and were watching us pass. The street seemed unusually quiet. I waited for someone to say something or to follow us. No one did. They stared as if we were a two-man funeral procession and they were distant relatives there only for the reading of the will.

We turned the corner and arrived at the murder scene. A dozen people stood in a half-circle on the cultivated lawn. Netta and Saunders crouched near the door. I pushed through the people and walked up the sidewalk.

"Netta?"

She turned, saw me, and moved out of the way. This body was headless. I stared for a moment at the gap where the head should have been, noting as calmly as I could that no blood stained the white plastic door. This child was smaller than the others. Its chest had been opened, and its hands were missing.

"You need to see this, too, Justin." She walked down the steps and rounded the building. I followed. There, in between two spindly rose bushes, the head rested. I stared at it, feeling hollow, noting other details while my stomach turned. Michael Dengler's empty eyes stared back at me. His mouth was caught in a cry of pain. His hands were crossed in front of his chin, but I couldn't see his heart or his lungs.

The last time I had seen him, he was smiling, running with the other children. I crouched down beside him, wanting to touch his face, to soothe him, to offer to take his place. My life was empty. His had just been starting.

"Michael Dengler," Netta said, startling me. I took a deep breath. "His sister, Katie, was one of the earlier victims. His mother is over there."

A woman stood at the very edge of the semicircle, her hands clutched to her chest. The silence was unnerving me. I could hear myself breathe. The rose scent was cloying. I turned back to Michael and thought, for a moment, that I was staring at myself.

"This is the first time we have ever found the missing body parts. We have to confirm, of course, that the hands are his, but they look small enough," Netta said.

I made myself concentrate on Netta's words. Michael Dengler was dead. I was part of the investigative team. I had to remain calm.

"I need a light," I said. Someone came up behind me and handed me a handlight. I cupped my hand around the metal surface and flicked the switch, running the light around the head. The boy was pale, the pale of a human body that had never, ever tanned. "How old was he?"

"Eight."

Eight. Too young for puberty, even on the outside edges of human physiology. If he had been female, maybe. But even that was doubtful. This was a little boy, a child, with no traces of adulthood—and no possibilities for it. *Mom says they should take me for who I am,* he had said. *What do you think?*

Professional, I reminded myself. I had to be professional. I took a deep breath, stood up, and dusted my knees.

"Someone needs to talk with the mother," Netta said. "I think you're the best choice."

My heart froze. I didn't want to deal with someone else's emotions. I wanted to go back to my apartment, close the door, and cry for the little boy who had lost everything, as I had. I didn't want to talk with his mother, even if I was the best choice because I had been trained in a helping profession. Helping. I made a small, quiet sound. I had never been able to help myself. How could I help a woman who had lost two children by murder in a few months?

"Go on," Netta said. Her words had the effect of a strong push. My movements were jerky as I walked over to Michael's mother.

She was half my height, in her early thirties, her eyes dark and haunted. "Ma'am," I said. "I'm Dr. Schafer."

"He's beyond doctors now." Her voice sounded rusty, as if she hadn't used it for a long time.

"Yes, he is, but you're not. Let me talk with you for a moment."

"Talk?" The word seemed to snap something inside her. "We talked the last time, and talked and talked. I have two more babies, and I want to leave the planet. I wanted to leave before, with those crazy aliens out there, killing and killing. You want my whole family to die!"

Her words echoed in the silence. I didn't want anyone to die, especially her son. She pushed away from me and walked to the edge of the steps, staring at what remained of Michael. I watched her for a moment, and could think of nothing to say to comfort her. I wasn't even sure she needed comforting. There was something reassuringly human about her pain.

I was the one who needed to remain calm. My hands were shaking, and the back of my throat was dry. I had missed something in the shock of Michael's death. Something was not making sense. I went to Davis, who was examining the ground near the rosebushes. "Leave the weapon this time?" I asked. The killer had, each time in the past, removed the body parts and left the weapon, a thin flensing knife chipped from native rock. Davis pointed. The knife sat on the other side of the bush, away from Michael's head.

"It's smaller than I thought," I said.

"But powerful." Davis leaned over toward me. "See the edge? It's firm. Anyone could use this knife. If the victim is unconscious, the killer doesn't need much strength."

"Not even to cut through bone?" I shuddered, thinking of Michael screaming as the knife sliced his skin.

Davis shook his head. "It's a Dancer knife. They do this stuff all the time and have had centuries to perfect it. We've had people cut themselves in the lab, nearly losing fingers, just handling the things."

The feeling still bothered me. I glanced around me. The houses were close together, the lawns well tended. How could a Dancer sneak in here, steal a child, and return it in such a grisly condition without anyone seeing? And how could a Dancer get past the dome guards?

I stood up and took a deep breath. I had to get away from the roses. Their rich scent was making me dizzy. And I hated the silence. I pushed past the semicircle out to the street and glanced once more at the scene in front of me.

Poor little Michael Dengler. He had wanted so much to grow up, to be part of the group. I shook my head. At least he had been able to play with them that one last time. At least he had gotten part of his wish.

IX

I leaned against the desk at the office of the Extra-Species Alliance. The cool plastic bit into my palms. Latona stood in front of me, her arms crossed in front of her chest. She had contacted me as soon as she heard about Michael Dengler's death.

"Dancers do not behead their children," she said. "I can show you document after document, holo after holo. It's not part of the ritual. A beheading would kill the child. Someone is killing them. Someone human."

A chill ran down my back. She had come to the same conclusion I had. "But the other children died. Perhaps the Dancers thought that the beheadings might work?"

Latona shook her head. "They don't learn as we do. They think instinctually, perform rituals. Beings with rituals and no memory would not experiment. That's not within their capability."

"But couldn't they modify—"

"No." Latona leaned toward me. "Dr. Schafer, they remove the lungs and heart to make way for larger organs.

They remove the hands to make way for sexually mature genitals. They mate with their hands. The head remains— their heads are like ours, the center of their being. They can't live without the head, and the Dancers do not kill each other. They never have, not even mercy killings. They had no concept of it."

And when they die, they cease to be. I shivered. "Why would someone kill children like this?"

Latona shook her head. "I don't know. I wish I did. Maybe the children know. Maybe they've seen something strange."

I nodded. The children, of course. If anyone had seen something, the children would have. They were the only ones free during the day. I ducked out of the office. I had to talk to Netta.

X

Netta's office was a small room in the back of Command Central. I had already been to the building once during the past two days—to wire for extra help before Michael Dengler's death. Lina Base had promised me assistance within the week; they had to pull people off of other assignments and shuttle them to us. During that visit, though, I hadn't seen Netta's office. I wasn't prepared for it.

The room smelled of roses. Plants hung from the ceiling and crowded under grow lamps attached to shelves on the far wall. Salt Juice ad posters from various nations, bases, and colony planets covered the white wall space.

Netta sat on a large brown chair behind a desk covered

with computer equipment and more plants. "You have something to report?"

"No." I had to stand. She had no other chair in her office. "I would like to make a request, though."

She nodded, encouraging me to continue. She looked tired and worn, as if Michael Dengler's death affected her as much as it had affected his mother.

"I would like to interview the older children."

"Why?" Netta sat up, suddenly alert.

"I think they might know something, something the rest of us don't."

She templed her fingers and tapped them against her lips. "You've seen the reports, and the holos, and Latona has taken you to see the Dancers. I'm sure you have enough to make a preliminary recommendation without bothering the children."

"No, actually, I don't." I looked around for a chair or available wall space, anything to lean on to ease my discomfort. "Some things aren't adding up."

"Everything doesn't have to add up for a preliminary ruling," Netta said. "I want quick action on this, Justin. Another child died yesterday. I need to protect my people from these Dancers."

"And what happens if I get an injunction against the Dancers? By intergalactic law, that removes their protected status. Michael Dengler died inside the dome. His killer might not have been native to this planet."

Netta's lips turned white. "I brought you here to make a ruling on the Dancers' motivation, not to solve a crime that has already been solved. Those children died by Dancer methods. I need to know what methods I can use to protect my people from those creatures."

"I want to talk to the children," I said. The office was

117

unusually hot, probably for the plants. "I want office space by tomorrow, and the children brought to me one by one. I'm doing this investigation by the book, Netta."

Her eyes widened a little, and for a moment I felt my suspicions confirmed. Then she reached over and tapped a few lines into the computer. "You'll have a room and a place, and someone will bring the children to you," she said.

"Thank you," I said. Then I took a deep breath. "You aren't paying the Dancers for the Salt Juice herbs, are you?"

Netta leaned away from the computer, her fingers still touching the screen. "Why?"

"I'm wondering what they'll lose now that you've discovered how to grow your own herbs." My hands were shaking, revealing my nervousness at my guess. I clasped them behind my back.

Netta studied me for a moment, as if she were tempted to find out where I had gotten the information. Her eyes flicked to the left, then down. It seemed as if hundreds of thoughts crossed her mind before she spoke. "We think the seeds have a religious significance for the Dancers. We don't know for sure. We don't know anything about them for certain, despite what the Alliance says."

A curious elation filled me. I had guessed right. The colonists had learned the secret to making Salt Juice. The Dancers were dispensable.

"The Dancers are dangerous, Justin," Netta said. "I don't think you need any more proof of that. I want some action in the next three days on this. I need quick movement."

I nodded, thinking of the team shuttling in. They would arrive soon. Netta would get her movement, although it might not be the kind she wanted.

XI

The room she gave me to interview the children was the same one in which we had held our initial briefing. It was almost too big and very cold. A table sat in the middle of the room, my chair on one side, a child-sized chair with booster on the other—a setup almost guaranteed to make the child uncomfortable. I made sure the computer took meticulous notes, but the first half a dozen interviews ran together in my mind.

"What is the game you play?" I asked.

"Race." The boy was tall with dark hair.

"How do you play it?"

"You pound your fist on the ground three times." This time the speaker was a girl, a redhead with sun-dark skin. "After that you either make a fist, lay your hand flat, or put up two fingers. If you do something different from most of the group, you have to imitate something, and we have to guess. If we can't guess it, you're out."

"Did the Dancers teach you the game?"

"No." Another little girl, this one with black curly hair.

"What did the Dancers teach you?"

"We only saw them once."

"Why didn't you want Michael Dengler to play?"

The fat boy scrunched up his face. "He was too little."

"But he played with you the last time I saw him."

The blonde girl shrugged. "He followed us around."

I didn't get much information from them, and what information I got was the same, except repeated in different words. By midday I was tired and discouraged. I planned to see only a few more children and then quit, ready to let the team take over when they arrived.

The next child who entered was named Beth. She was

tiny for an eleven-year-old, with long black hair, dark eyes, and brownish black skin.

She sat stiffly on the chair, ignoring the anatomically correct dolls I had placed beside her, after pausing momentarily to examine the doll that had been altered to represent a Dancer.

I poised a hand over the computer screen, to highlight anything of importance. Such a standard gesture usually made people more comfortable. But nothing seemed to ease these children. And I knew their answers by heart.

"Let's talk a little bit about what's going on," I said.

"I don't know anything," Beth said. Over her soft voice, I heard six other voices murmuring the same thing.

"You'd be surprised what you know."

The others had shrugged. Beth's lower lip trembled. I watched it, trying not to take too much hope from such a small sign.

"I understand you've met the Dancers." She nodded.

"Latona took us."

"What did you think of them?"

"They're kinda spooky, but neat. They grow up fast."

A new response. I tried not to be too eager. "What makes you say that?" She shrugged. I waited in silence for her to say something. When she did not volunteer any more information, I asked, "How often have you seen the Dancers?"

"Just the once." Back into the rote response. Her eyes were slightly glazed, as if she were concentrating on something else.

"Did you know Michael Dengler?"

She looked at me then. Her eyes were stricken, haunted. I had to work to meet her gaze because pain was so deep. "I always played with him when the others weren't around," she said. I nodded once to let her know I was listening and interested. "John and Katie say we aren't supposed to be nice to him because that means he'll keep following us. I told John that Mikey was too little, and John said that little didn't matter. He said he knew a way to make him grow faster. But he's not going to grow at all, is he, Dr. Schafer?"

"No," I said. Her use of the present tense bothered me.

"The Dancers do," she said. "They grow into adults."

My hands had become cold. "Do you want to be an adult, Beth?"

"Not anymore," she whispered.

XII

My entire body was shaking as I returned to my apartment, a 'jecter under my arm. I no longer trusted myself after the mistakes with the Minarans. I had to double-check every suspicion, every thought. The remaining children that I interviewed said nothing about the Dancers, nothing about growing up. But Beth's soft voice kept echoing in my head.

John said that little didn't matter. He said he knew a way to make him grow faster. But he's not going to grow at all, is he, Dr. Schafer?

None of them grew, Beth. The experiment failed.

I pulled out the holos and the file. I stared at the 2-D photos, examining the color closely. Then I watched the holos. Katie Dengler's face was as pale as her brother's on the day she left to see the Dancers for the first time. When she died, her skin was as dark as Latona's. All the other children had pale skin in the earlier holo, and dark skin at the time of their death. They had gotten the dark, dark tan from the harsh sun. They had been outside the dome—a lot. My skin, despite its off-planet weakness, had turned only a light brown. The children's skin was almost black.

The dome guards were new since the death before Michael Dengler's. The dome doors were easy to use and didn't latch. The children were unsupervised except for occasional school days, when workers could be spared to teach. No one watched the children, so the children went off to watch the Dancers.

Do you want to be an adult, Beth?

Not anymore, she whispered.

The Dancers wouldn't remember from time to time, and would show the ritual to the children over and over again. The children could take the knives without the Dancers realizing it. The Dancers' lack of a past probably meant that they lost a lot of things over the years and thought nothing of it.

John said that little didn't matter. He said he knew a way to make him grow faster. But he's not going to grow at all, is he, Dr. Schafer?

"None of them are," I whispered. The old man I had seen before I left, the old man who had lived here as a child, had said he could hardly wait to become an adult because then he could legally leave the planet. Shuttle pilots rarely checked IDs. They figured if a person was large enough to work on any of the nearby bases, they would ferry that person off-planet, away from a colony, away from home.

Away from a sterile place with no windows, lots of rules, and no real place to play.

I shut off the 'jecter and hugged my knees to my chest. Then I sat in the darkness and rocked, as the pieces came together in my mind.

XIII

Sometime toward morning I decided to go to Command Central. The building was only a few buildings away from mine. As I walked, I listened to the silence of the community. The dome filter was a thin gray, as it had been the morning of Michael Dengler's death. The colony itself was quiet, with no indication of people waking.

My back muscles were tight, and an ache throbbed in my skull. I lacked the skill, the expertise, and the authority for this case. I had to contact Lina Base, push to get the help here as soon as possible. If my suspicions were right and the children were mutilating each other in an attempt to grow up, then something had to be done, quickly. Some of the children, like Beth, were beginning to realize that the experiment didn't work. The others, though, the ones who answered me by rote, still believed in what they were doing.

The children must have visited the Dancers daily since Latona took them the first time. Young minds were particularly susceptible to new cultures—and these children must have absorbed the Dancers' beliefs, modified them, and interpreted them a new way. If Dancer children became adults by losing their hands, hearts, and lungs, then human children would, too. Maybe, they must have thought when they carved Michael, human children grew taller if their heads were removed.

John said that little didn't matter. He said he knew a way to make him grow faster. But he's not going to grow at all, is he, Dr. Schafer?

The children experimented, the adults took the bodies away, and the children never knew if the experiments worked. I remembered seeing the children's muscles bulge in play. Perhaps they had participated in Dancer rituals before trying the same ritual on Linette Bisson.

I walked into Central, spoke briefly to the man who monitored the equipment, and then took a private console. Each console was housed in a booth of white plastic, walls so thin that I could shake them apart. I jacked in my private number, sent a signal to Lina Base, and requested that help arrive immediately.

"Good work, Justin."

I turned. Netta stood behind me, her arms crossed, a half-smile on her face. "The tech let me know that you were here."

"I'm sending a private communication," I said. My hands were shaking. Her attitude disturbed me.

"And it's perfect. When they arrive, I'll tell them that you ran into an emergency, you slapped an injunction against the Dancers, and they rose in a frenzy of slaughter. No one will question the fact that you're gone."

I gripped the console. "You've been killing the children?" It didn't make sense; why would she behead Michael Dengler?

Netta shook her head. Her smile grew. "The children gave me a problem when they started killing each other. I solved it—and another one, with your help. There won't be any more killing. And there won't be any more Dancers."

My throat was dry. I stood slowly, bowing my head slightly, playing the docile prisoner. "Where are you going to take me?"

"I'm not going to take you anywhere," she said. "I think right here will be—"

I pushed past her and leaped out into the main room. Two guards stood behind her, startled at my sudden movement. I ran down the slick plastic floors, past the tech who had betrayed me, and through the open door.

The dome filter was losing its gray. Some of the sunlight peeked through, illuminating the pathway. My heart caught in my throat. I was out of shape, not used to running.

Damn her. Damn her for using me. For using all of us. The children killed each other in a misguided attempt to imitate the Dancers, and she let the deaths occur. Then she discovered me, with my flaws and my history, and the loophole in galactic law that allowed one person to make a decision for an entire species. She manipulated us all, and in that manipulating, she caused the deaths of more children, including Michael Dengler.

Michael Dengler. His wistful face rose in my mind. Netta would act before the shuttle came. I had to stop her.

I ran through the twisting streets until I reached the offices of the Extra-Species Alliance. I pounded on the door. Daniel opened it. He seemed sleep-weary. I pushed past him. The computer screen on the main desk was blinking. "I'm looking for Latona," I said.

She stood at one of the side doors, her long hair flowing around her. "A message about you just came across the net. Netta says you have decided that the children are killing each other in an imitation Dancer ritual, and you believe all of the children under the dome should die."

So Netta knew how close I had been to the truth. She must have been monitoring me. "Netta's trying to figure out a way to stop me. I radioed Lina Base for help."

"I'm not going to help you kill children," Latona said.

"I'm not trying to hurt the children. I'm trying to save your Dancers."

"The Dancers?"

"Listen," I said, "I don't have time. I need someone who can talk with the Dancers. We need to get them out of here."

"Why would Netta want to hurt the Dancers?"

"Salt Juice," I said. "She doesn't need them anymore. You got me on this track when we talked about Michael Dengler. There is a human killer, which means someone is trying to pin this whole thing on the Dancers." I decided the entire truth was too complicated to explain at the moment.

"But Netta—"

"I don't think Netta is working alone."

"She's not." The voice came from behind me. Daniel still stood in the doorway. He stepped into the front rooms. His hands were empty. "Some of the dome leaders have been trying to cancel our contracts here. The negotiations have grown too cumbersome. They want to harvest their own Salt Juice plants, but the Dancers won't let them near the plant site. And even though the colonists know how to grow from seed, they still need the atmospheric conditions and the special soil of the Dancer lands."

Latona whirled. "You never said anything about canceled contracts."

Daniel shrugged. "I was working with it. So was Lina Base. It would have worried you and interfered with your work."

"Shit." Latona grabbed her sand scarf and a small handheld heat weapon. "Will you stay here, Daniel, stall them?"

He nodded. "I'll also contact Lina Base and tell them we need emergency personnel now."

"They know," I said. "Netta plans to use that as an excuse to make up some story, something about an emergency that required the colonists to kill the Dancers—with my permission."

"O.K.," Daniel said. "I'll make my message explicit. Colonists trying to illegally kill Dancers. Need emergency assistance. Good enough?"

"If the assistance arrives in time," Latona said. "Come on, Dr. Schafer."

I followed her outside. "They flashed that message. I won't be able to get out," I said.

"There're other ways out of the dome." Latona hurried to the dome edge and touched a seam. A small panel slid back, and bright sunshine eased in. If the children had wanted to avoid the doors, they could have used these panels. "You don't have a sand scarf," she said.

"We don't have time to get one. Let's go."

We slid through the dome opening and into the light. The heat was searing. I felt it burn into my skin. Latona threw me her cream, and I rubbed it on as we ran. I wondered if this was the way the children went when they went to study the Dancers. I would ask Latona sometime.

It seemed to take forever to cross the hot sand. Finally we reached the canopied trees. When we did, Latona let out a long, shrill whistle. My skin was crackling and dry. I already saw heat blisters forming beneath the surface.

The Dancers appeared, hurrying through the trees. Latona stepped back as they tried to touch her. She spoke rapidly. One of the Dancers spoke back, gesturing with its hands. She shook her head and tried again. The Dancer repeated the gesture.

"What?" I asked.

"I've told them to leave," she said. "They think it's a ploy to get the plants." I peered through the canopied trees. I thought I saw air cars shimmering in the distance. Perhaps it was my own overactive imagination. I thought they didn't have air cars here. We had to do something. We had to get the Dancers out of the area, if only for a short time. The shuttles would arrive within a few days. The Dancers needed that much of an advantage. "Give me your weapon," I said.

"Why?"

"Have them show us the plants."

"But—"

"Now! I think we've been followed out of the dome."

She spoke to the Dancer. The Dancer churred in response, then grabbed Latona and pulled her through the trees. We walked the path we had walked before, the one that led to the children's pen.

"The plants are all around us," Latona said.

"Give me your weapon," I repeated.

"What do you want to do with it?"

"I want to start these plants on fire, to show the Dancers how unimportant they are."

"But the children—"

"There'll be time to get the children out of the gates."

She bit her lower lip.

"If you're worried, tell him what we're going to do. Have him send people to the children."

She spoke to the Dancer. The Dancer made a whirring sound. Latona reached down and touched a plant with the weapon, searing the leaves. The Dancer whistled shrilly, and others ran down the path.

"Tell him that we're not bluffing. Tell him that we have to destroy the plants, and that they have to leave. I don't care what reasons you give them. Just get them out of here."

Latona spoke quickly. The Dancer listened, then repeated Latona's sounds loudly. My ears felt as if they were being pierced. I grabbed the weapon from Latona, studied it for a moment, saw the finger control on the side and the open mouth along another side. I pointed the mouth at the plants and pushed the control. Heat whooshed out of the mouth, catching the leaves and sending fire along the plants. The Dancer beside us screamed and ran down the path. Other Dancers were running, too, like the shadows of animals running before a forest fire. In the distance I saw the Dancers lifting the children from the gate and tucking them under one arm as they continued to run.

The heat was getting under my skin, making my body ache. The smoke felt faintly sweet. I giggled, feeling giddy: The canopy was keeping the smoke in the forest. We would pass out if we didn't get out. I grabbed Latona's arm and pulled her with me.

When we reached the desert, I saw no air cars. Hallucination, then, maybe. But I did see a small band of people in sand scarves, walking determinedly across the sand. I remembered watching other colonists walk like that, carrying laser weapons to beaches that lined their island home, and blasting small, seal-like creatures until clear blood coated the sand, while helicopters circled overhead dropping alkaline solution into the acidic ocean. I sank down against a tree. My whole body itched. I didn't want to watch again.

Latona slipped away from my side. The smoke smell had grown cloying, and the giddiness had grown with it. I wondered where I could stay until the ship arrived. I glanced down at my skin. It was black. Large lumps had risen on the surface, with pus bubbles on top. They would be painful when they burst.

"They're gone," Latona said.

I looked at her, then at the colonists. They weren't gone. They were getting closer.

"The Dancers," she said. "They're gone."

I felt the relief run through me like a cool draft of air. I took a deep breath to speak, and toppled face forward into the sunbaked sand.

XIV

Now I lie here in this cool bed on Lina Base, my body coated with burn creams and wrapped in light bandages in the areas where the skin grafts have yet to take.

The rooms here have yellow walls. Green plants hang in the corners, and windows look out onto a wide and vast galaxy. Latona has visited me. She tells me the Dancers have moved to a similar canopied forest, near the Salt Cliffs, the place historians believe was their earlier home. Lina Base is dismantling the colony on Bountiful. Netta and the dome leaders are going to stand trial. I will have to testify at that. Latona also says that some chemists here on Lina Base are trying to duplicate the chemical properties of Salt Juice. I hope, if only for the Dancers' sake, that they have some success.

So I lie here in the coolness, my burns itching and rubbing me raw, and think, Dancer-like, about what is ahead. I have regained my stature, atoned for my culpability in the minds of others, I guess. The Minarans no longer visit me in dreams, but the children do, particularly Michael Dengler.

When I am well, I am to work with the children to determine their mental state. The psychologists here share my fear: that the children have learned Dancer behavior, that it is normal to them. That presents a sticky point of law. We have to determine if the children are insane or are capable of standing trial. And if they are capable of standing trial, what standards do we use, ours or the Dancers? The irony hasn't missed me, since I had gone to determine if the Dancers were mentally capable of standing trial in our system.

I spent all those years after Minar, trying to regain the

respect of my colleagues, trying to regain my own self-respect. And now I think of writing papers about the children, about my experience, as if that ten-year period never happened. My colleagues have become friendly again. They call me "Justin"; they send me cards; they wish me well. I seem to have vindicated myself, to have won acceptance with the group.

But sometimes I wake up in the middle of the night and see Michael's face, his mouth forming a startled O. Michael's group accepted him, and took in payment his head, his heart, his lungs, his hands, and his life.

I smile at my colleagues when they visit. I thank them for their attentiveness and their interest.

And I wait for the flash of a knife, for the bite of an extra-sharp blade against my wrist.

Alien Influences

I

The corridor smelled stale. John huddled against the display panel, replacing microchips with the latest models—more memory, more function. The near-robotic feel of the work was all that mattered: pull, grab, replace; pull, grab, replace. They should have had a 'droid doing this, but they had given the work to John, sure sign that his contract was nearly up.

He didn't mind. He had been on the trader ship for nearly a month, and it was making him nervous. Too many people, too close. They watched him as if they expected him to go suddenly berserk and murder them all in their sleep. He wouldn't have minded if their wariness had been based on his work as a bounty hunter. But it wasn't. It was based on the events on Bountiful, things he had done—and paid for—when he was little more than a child.

Footsteps along the plastic floor. He didn't move, figuring whoever it was would have nothing to say to him. A faint whiff of cologne and expensive illegal tobacco. The captain.

"John, someone to see you."

133

John looked up. The captain stood on the other side of the corridor, the lights from the display giving his skin a greenish cast. Once, John had fancied this man his friend, but John hadn't had any real friends. Not since he was fifteen years old. The day Harper betrayed him. The day they took Beth away.

"I will not see anyone," John said. Sometimes he played the role, the Dancer child everyone thought he was. The one who never spoke in past tense, only present and future, using the subjunctive whenever possible. The one who couched his thoughts in emotion because he had nothing else, no memory, no ethics, no soul.

The captain didn't even blink. "She flew in special from Rotan Base."

John stood and closed the display. A client, then. The time on the trader ship would end sooner than he had expected.

He followed the captain through the winding corridors. The ventilation system was out. The entire ship smelled of wet socks and too many people. Down one of the corridors, the techs were discussing whether they wanted to fix the system or whether they wanted to wait until next planetfall. John would have argued for fixing it.

The captain stopped at his personal suite and keyed in the access code. John had never seen this room; it was off-limits to all but the captain himself. John stepped in, but the captain remained outside. The door snicked shut.

Computer-generated music—technically proficient and lifeless—played in the background. The room itself was decorated in whites, but the lighting gave everything a reddish cast. The couch was thick and plush. Through open doors, he could see the bed, suspended in the air, cushions piled on top of it. A room built for comfort, and for seduction.

A woman stood at the back of the room, gazing out the portals at the stars. Her long black hair trailed down her back, her body wrapped in expensive silks. She looked the part of the seductee, although she was the one who wanted to hire him.

John never hired out for anything but bounty work. He would tell her that if he had to.

"I would like you to work for me, John." She didn't even turn around to acknowledge him. He felt his hackles rise. She was establishing herself as the adult, him the child in this relationship. He hated being treated like a child. The claustrophobia inched back on him, tighter than it had been in months.

He leaned against the door, fcigning a casualness he didn't fecl. He wanted her to turn around, to look at him. "Why should I work for you?"

"Forgive me." This time she moved, smoothing her hair as she did. Her face was stunning: full lips, long nose, wide eyes. And familiar. "I'm Anita Miles. I run an art gallery on Rotan Base. We specialize in unusual objects d'art. . . ."

He stopped listening, not needing the explanation. He recognized her face from a hundred vids. She was perhaps one of the most powerful people in this sector—controlling trade and commodities. Her gallery sold anything that could be considered art. Once, she sold a baby Minaran, claiming that since the species was nearly extinct, the Minarans could be appreciated only in an aesthetic way. He couldn't remember if she had won or lost the ensuing law-suit.

Baby trader. The entire galaxy as an art object. If she had been in business when he was a boy, what would she have done with the Dancers?

"Why should I work for you?" he repeated.

She closed her mouth and gave him a once-over. He recognized the look. *How much does he understand? I thought I was explaining in clear terms. This is going to be more difficult than I thought.* "You're the best," she said, apparently deciding on simplicity. "And I need the best."

He often wondered how these people thought he could bounty hunt with no memory. He shook off the thought. He needed the money. "What will you pay me?"

"Expenses, of course, a ship at your command because you may have to travel a bit, and three times your daily rate—which is, I believe, the equivalent of four hundred Rotan zepeatas."

"Eight hundred."

Her expression froze for just a moment, and then she had the grace to flush. John crossed his arms. Too many clients tried to cheat him. He took them on anyway. If he tried to avoid those who treated him like a Dancer, he would have no business.

"I'm not a Dancer." He kept his tone soft, but made sure the sarcasm was there. "I wasn't even raised by them. Just influenced. The trial is over, and I've served my time. When they released me, they declared me sane, and sane for a human being means an understanding of time and an ability to remember. After that little stunt, I won't work with you for anything less than five times my rate, one month payable in advance."

The flush grew, making those spectacular eyes shine brighter. Not embarrassment after all. Anger. "You tricked me."

"Not at all." John didn't move. He felt more comfortable now with this little hint of emotion. He could ride on emotion, play it. That he had learned from the Dancers. "You had expectations. You shouldn't believe everything you hear."

For a moment, she drew herself up, as if she were going to renounce him and leave. But she didn't. She reached into her pocket and removed a credit flask. She must have needed him badly.

She handed him two chips, which he immediately put into his account. One-hundred-and-twenty-thousand zepeatas. Perfect. He smiled for the first time. "What do you want from me?" he asked.

She glanced at the portals, as if the stars would give her strength. The story was an embarrassment, then. An illegality perhaps or some mistake she had made. "Several weeks ago," she said, "I acquired a Bodean wind sculpture."

Awe rippled through him. He had seen Bodean wind sculptures once, on their home planet. The deserts were full of them, swirling beautifully across the sands. No one knew how to tame them; they remained an isolated art form on a lone planet. Someone must have figured out a way to capture them, wind currents and all.

"That's not the best part," she said. Her tone had changed. She still wasn't treating him like an equal, but she was closer. "The best part is the mystery inside the sculpture. My equipment indicates a life-form trapped in there."

No, no. Not allowed to leave the room, the wing—If we grow up, we'll be able to leave, never see Bountiful again. If we grow up. . . .

He shook the memory voices away, made himself concentrate on her words. Something inside the sculpture. A bodeangenie? But they were the stuff of legends. Traders to Bodean claimed that the sculptures originated to capture little magical beings to prevent them from causing harm to the desert. When the Extra-Species Alliance went to study the sculptures, however, they found no evidence of life in or around them.

His hands were shaking. She trapped things and called them art. "You don't need me," he said. "You need a specialist."

"I need you." She turned, her hair spiraling out around her. Beautiful, dramatic. "The wind sculpture's been stolen."

II

Sleep. Narrow trader bunk, not built for his long frame. Dream voices, half-remembered:

   . . . *we'll be able to leave* . . .

   . . . *the Dancers do it* . . .

   . . . *It'll hurt, but that won't matter. You'll grow up* . . .

   . . . *Stop, please* . . .

   . . . *Just another minute* . . .

   . . . *Stop!!!* . . .

   . . . *the other hand* . . .

   . . . *ssstttooooppp* . . .

He forced himself awake, heart pounding, mouth dry. The trapped feeling still filled him. He rolled off the bunk, stood, listened to the even breathing of the other sleepers. He hadn't had the dream since when? The penal colony? The last trading ship? He couldn't remember. He had tried to put it out of his mind. Obviously that hadn't worked.

Trapped. He had started the spiral when she said the word *trapped*. He leaned against the door, felt the cool plastic against his forehead. The memory voices still rang in his head. If someone had listened, then maybe. . . .

But no. The past was past. He would work for her, but he would follow his own reasons.

III

Her gallery was less than he had expected. Shoved into a small corner of the merchant's wing of Rotan Base, the gallery had a storefront of only a few meters. Inside hung the standard work by standard artists: an Ashley rendition of the galaxy, done in blacks and pinks; a D.B. portrait of the sphynix, a red-haired catlike creature from Yster; a Dugas statue of a young girl dancing. Nothing new, nothing unique, not even in the manner of display. All the pieces were self-illuminated against dark walls and stands, a small red light beside each indicating the place for credit purchases.

The gallery was even more of a surprise after she had told him her tale of woe: she claimed to have the best guards on Rotan, an elaborate security system, and special checking. He saw no evidence of them. Her storefront was the same as the others, complete with mesh framing that cascaded at closing each evening.

The gallery smelled dry, dustless. He wanted to sneeze, just to see particles in the air. The air's cleanliness, at least, was unusual. He would have to check the filtration system. The sculpture probably hadn't disappeared at all. Some overeager viewer probably opened the container, the wind escaped, and the sculpture returned to the grains of sand it was. No great mystery, certainly not worth 120,000 zepeatas. But he wouldn't tell her that.

Anita threaded her way through the displays to the back. He felt himself relax. There he would find the artwork he sought—the priceless, the illegal, the works that had made her famous. But when the door slid open, his mood vanished.

Crates, cartons, holoshippers, transmission machines,

more credit slots. The faint odor of food. A desk covered with hard-copy invoices and credit records. A small cache of wine behind the overstuffed chair, and a microprocessor for late-night meals. A work space, nothing more.

She let the door close behind them, her gaze measuring him. He was missing something. He would lose the entire commission if he didn't find it.

He closed his eyes and saw in his imagination what his actual vision had missed. The dimensions of the rooms were off. The front was twice the size of the back. Base regulations required square sales—each purchased compartment had to form a box equal on all sides. She had divided her box into three sections—showroom, back workroom, and special gallery. But where?

Where something didn't fit. The wine. She sold wine as art—nectar of the gods, never drinking it, always collecting it. Wine didn't belong with the boxes and invoices.

He opened his eyes, crouched down, scanned the wine rack. Most bottles came from Earth. They were made with the heavy, too-thick glass that suggested work centuries old. Only one didn't belong: a thin bottle of the base-made synth stuff. He pulled it, felt something small fall into his hand. He clenched his hand to hold it as the wall slid back.

Inside was the gallery he had been expecting.

Holos of previous artifacts danced across the back wall. In those holos the baby Minaran swam. He wondered where it was now; if it could feel happiness, exploitation. He made himself look away.

A tiny helldog from Frizos clawed at a glass cage. A mobile ice sculpture from Ngela rotated under cool lights. Four canisters in a bowl indicated a Colleician scent painting. He had seen only one before; all he had to do was touch it, and he would be bathed in alien memories.

More valuables drifted off in the distance. Some hung on walls, some rested on pedestals, and some floated around him. None had the standard red credit slot beside them. They were all set up for negotiation, bargaining, and extortion.

"Impressed?" She sounded sarcastic, as if a man with his background could not help but be impressed.

He was, but not for the reasons she thought. He knew how much skill it took to capture each item, to bring it onto a base with strict limitations for importing. "You have your own hunters. Why hire me?"

She tapped on the helldog's cage. John winced. The dog didn't move. "I would have had to hire a hunter no matter what," she said. "If I removed one of my own people from a normal routine, I would have to hire a replacement. I choose not to do that. My people have their own lives, their own beats, and their own predilections. This incident calls for someone a bit more adaptable, a free-lancer. A person like you."

He nodded, deciding that was the best answer he would get from her. Perhaps she had chosen him, and not one of his colleagues, on a whim. Or perhaps she thought she could control him, with his Dancer mind. It didn't matter. She was paying him. And he had a being to free.

IV

Working late into the night so that the dreams would stay away, he did the standard checks: exploring the gallery for bits of the sculpture, contacting the base engineers to see if sand had lodged in the filters, examining particulate material for foreign readings. Nothing. The sculpture appeared to have vanished.

Except for the small item he had found near the wine cache. He set it in the light, examined it, and froze. A sticker. Lina Base used them as temporary IDs. Stickers weren't the proper term. Actually, they were little light tabs that allowed the bearer to enter secured areas for brief periods of time, and were called stickers because most spacers stuck them to the tops of their boots.

He hadn't touched one since he had left Lina Base nearly two decades before. The memories tickled around his head: Beth, her eyes wide, hands grasping, as Harper's people carried her away; sitting on his own bed, arms wrapped around his head, eyes burning but tearless, staring at his own sticker-covered boots—signifying temporary, even though he had been there for nearly two years.

Dancer mind. He snorted. If only he could forget. He was cursed with too much remembrance.

He set the sticker down, made himself move. He had to check arrival records, see who had come from Lina Base, who frequented it. Then he would know who had taken the sculpture.

V

The next morning he walked into the gallery. The showroom was filled with Elegian tourists, fondling the merchandise. The security system had to be elaborate to allow such touching without any obvious watchful presence. The room smelled of animal sweat and damp fur. No wonder her filtration system was good. He pushed his way through and let himself into the back.

Anita was cataloging chip-sized gems that had arrived

the day before. She wore a jeweler's eye and didn't look up when he entered.

"I need that ship," he said.

"You found something?"

He nodded. "A lead. Some traders."

This time she did look up. The jeweler's eye gave her face a foreign feel. "Who?"

A small ship out of Lina Base named *Runner*. Owned by a man named Minx. He worked with four others on odd jobs no one else wanted—domestic cats from Earth to a colony of miners on Cadmium; a cargo of worthless Moon rocks to scientists on Mina Base. No records older than twenty years. No recording of illegal trading of any kind. But he didn't tell her that. He still wasn't sure if he was going to tell her anything.

"No one you'd know," he said. "If it turns out to be them, I'll introduce you."

She removed the jeweler's eye. Her own looked less threatening. "You're working for me, which gives me the right to know what you've found."

"You *contracted* with me," he corrected. "And I have the right to walk away anytime I choose—keeping the retainer. Now, do I get that ship?"

She stared at him for a minute, then put the eye back in. "I'll call down," she said.

VI

The ship was nearly a decade old, and designed to carry fewer than five people in comfort. He had computer access, games and holos, as much food and drink as he wanted.

Only rules were not to disturb the pilot—for any reason. He guessed she had found out about his past, and wanted nothing to do with him.

He slept most of the time. His way of escape on ships. When he was awake, they reminded him of the penal ship, of the hands grabbing, voices prodding, violence, stink, and finally isolation, ostensibly for his own good. When he was asleep, they were the only places that allowed him rest without dreams.

His alarm went off an hour before landing, and he paced. He hadn't been to Lina Base for twenty years. He had left as a boy, alone, without Beth, without even Harper, the man who had once been his savior and became his betrayer. Harper, who had healed his mind, and broken his heart.

When the ship landed, John didn't move. He was crazy to go back, crazy to look at the past he had been avoiding. No job was worth that, especially a job he only half-believed in.

You have to face your past, face yourself. And once you see clearly what happened and why, you must forgive yourself. Only then will you be whole.

Harper's voice. John shook himself, as if he could force the voice from his head. He had promised himself, when he left Lina Base on the penal ship, that he would never listen to Harper again.

He had a job. His stay on Lina Base would be short.

He drew himself to his full height and let himself out of his room. The pilot was at the door. She stopped moving when she saw him, her gaze wary. He nodded. She nodded back. Then he went out of the ship before her.

The docking bay had shiny new walls and state-of-the-art flooring. But it smelled the same: dusty, tangy, harsh with chemical cleaners. He gripped the railing, cool against his hand.

. . . *cringing in the back of the ship, safe behind the uphol-stered chairs. Voices urging him to get off, and he knowing they were going to kill him. They believed he had done something wrong, and he was going to get a punishment worse than any his parents could dish out. . . .*

"You O.K.?" the pilot asked.

He snapped back to the present. He was not twelve, not landing on Lina Base for the first time. He was an adult, a man who could handle himself.

Down the stairs and into the base. No crowds this time, no holoteams, no reporters. No Harper, no savior, no friends beside him. Only ships and shuttles of various sizes. Lina Base had grown since the last time he had been there. Now it had three docking facilities instead of one. It was one of the main trading bases in the galaxy, and had grown instead of declined when the officials had closed Bountiful to any and all aliens. He stopped, remembered: If he went to one of the portals, he would be able to see Bountiful, its deserts and mountains etched across the surface like a painting, the Singing Sea adding a touch of blue to the art.

Odd that he missed the place when, as a boy, all he had wanted to do was leave it.

"You seriously O.K.?"

"Yes." He whirled, expecting his anger to deflate her concern. Then understood that she was speaking from obligation. He was her charge until he left the docking bay, and she didn't want the responsibility of handling him.

"Then get to deck three for inspection and hosing. They need to clean this bay for other arrivals."

He nodded, felt a bit numb at her lack of concern. Procedures. After an outbreak of Malanian flu almost three decades before, Lina Base had become fanatic for keeping unwanted elements off the station. During his first visit here, he had been quarantined for three Earth months.

He turned his back on the pilot, sought the elevator, and took it to a tiny corridor on deck three. There a blinking light indicated the room he was to use. He went inside.

The room was better than the one they had given him as a child. This one had a couch, and a servo tray filled with beverages. He stripped, let the robot arms whisk away his clothes, and then stepped under the pale blue light in the corner of the room.

Streams of light invaded his orifices, tickling with the warmth of their touch. He closed his eyes, holding himself still, knowing that, on some bases, they still used hand searches, and wondering how he could ever stand that when he found this procedure so invasive. When the light had finished, he stepped into the autodoc and let it search him for viruses, traces of alien matter, alien materials, and—probably—alien thought.

Alien influences. . . .

A shiver ran through him. He had been twelve years old. Twelve years old and not realizing that what they had done was abnormal. Not human. Yet he was still human enough to feel terror at separation from all that he knew. Knowing, deep down, that the horror was only beginning.

The autodoc was beeping, and, for a long moment, he was afraid it had found something. Then he realized that it wanted him to leave its little chamber. He stepped back into the main room and retrieved his clothes—now cleaned and purified—dressed, and pressed the map to find out where he was and where he wanted to be.

VII

John huddled in the shuttle records bay. Dark, cramped, smelling of sweat and skin oils, it was as familiar as any other place on the base. Only, this was a different kind of familiarity. Every base had a records bay. And every base had an operator like Donnie.

He was small, wiry, scrawny enough to be comfortable in such a small place. His own stink didn't bother him—he was used to being alone. He monitored the traffic to and from the base, maintained licenses, and refused admittance if necessary.

"Left just as you were docking," he said. His lips barely parted, but his teeth were visible—half fake white, half rotted. "In a hurry, too. Gave 'em the day's last slot."

The day's last slot. No other craft could be cleared for leaving, then, until the next day. John clenched his fists. So close.

"Where did they go?"

Donnie checked the hard copy, then punched a button. The display on the screen was almost unreadable. He punched another button, lower lip out, grimy fingers shaking.

"Got a valid pass," he mumbled.

The shiver again, something a bit off. "Where?" John asked.

"Bountiful."

The word shimmered through him. Heat, thin and dry; deep, flowery perfume; the rubbery feel of Dancer fingers.

"You done?" Donnie asked.

John took a deep breath, calmed himself. "You need to get me to Bountiful."

"Nope." Donnie leaned back in the chair. "I know who

you are. Even if Bountiful were open, I couldn't let you go there."

Trapped. This time outside Bountiful. John's fingernails dug into his palms. The pain kept him awake, sane. He made his voice sound calmer than he felt. "Where do I get the dispensation?"

Donnie gazed at him, scared of nothing, so secure in his small world of records, passes. "Level five. But they won't help—"

"They will," John said.

VIII

He put in a call to Anita, told her to hurry, or she would never get her sculpture back. She would pull the strings and dole out the cash. He would spend his time digging out information about the traders.

Lina Base's paranoia about its traders led to a wealth of information. He spent half an Earth day alone with a small computer linked up to the base's mainframe.

And found the information he had already known, plus some. Lina Base was their main base of operation. They were well known, not popular. Two men worked with Minx: Dunnigan, trained as a linguist; and Carter, no formal training at all. The women, Parena and Nox, provided muscle and contacts. They had gotten the jobs on Cadmium and Mina Base. And they had all hooked up twenty years ago.

After Bountiful had been closed to aliens.

When Minx had to expand his operation.

When Salt Juice had become illegal.

148

Salt Juice. That little piece of information sent ripples of fear through John. Food. He had to get food. Take care of himself. He stood, unable to stop his mind.

Salt Juice had started it all.

The very smell of it gave him tremors, made him revert, close all the doors on himself, close out the memories and the emotions and the pain. He would focus on the future for protection, Dancer-like, and no one—except Harper, base kiddie therapist—had been able to get in. The only way to keep himself intact, human, was to take care of his body so that the damaged part of his mind could recover.

He went to the cafeteria.

Wide, spacious, with long windows open to space, and hanging plants from all sides, the cafeteria gave him a feeling of safety. He ordered off the servo, picked his table, and ran the credit voucher through. His food appeared on the table almost before the voucher stopped running. He walked over, sat down, and sniffed.

Roast chicken, steamed broccoli, mashed potatoes. Not a normal spacer's meal. Heaven. He made himself eat, feeling the food warm the cold places inside him. As he nourished himself, he allowed his mind to roam.

Salt Juice had been one of the most potent intoxicants in the galaxy. It was manufactured on Bountiful, using herbs grown by the Dancers. The main reason for the dispute with the Dancers was those herbs—and when the colony finally learned how to grow them without Dancer assistance, they tried to wipe out the Dancers.

With the help of children. Poor misguided children. Lonely little children who wanted only to leave the hell they were trapped in.

Once Lina Base discovered the scheme, Bountiful was closed. The best herbalists and chemists tried to manufacture Salt Juice away from the colony, but it proved impossible. A good thing. Later they learned that the drug everyone thought addiction-free had some nasty side effects.

Minx traded in Salt Juice. Then Moon rocks, cats. Worthless cargo. But Cadmium's northern water supply had a drug as pure as crystal meth. And the Minaran skin was poison that, taken in small amounts, induced a dangerous kind of high.

The five were drug runners. Good, competent, skilled drug runners.

So the bodeangenie had more than artistic value to them. It also had some kind of stimulant value. He leaned back. What kind, he was sure he would find out.

IX

But things happened too quickly. The call came from Anita. She had bought him a window—three Earth days—and she let him know that it had cost her a fortune. He smiled. He was glad to put her money to good use.

He located the pilot, and together they flew to the place from which he had been banned for life.

X

Once again he sat in his room on the ship, far from the uncommunicative pilot. He was glad for the solitude, even on such a short trip. He hadn't been to Bountiful since he was twelve. Then he had hated the planet, wanted nothing more

150

than to be free of it. But the freedom he obtained wasn't the freedom he had expected.

. . . *The plastic frame dug into his forehead. Through the portal, he could see Bountiful, swirling away from him. They had isolated him, considering him the ringleader—and perhaps he was. He hadn't understood the depths of their anger. He was experimenting, as they had; only, he was trying to save the others . . .*

He sighed and walked to the portal. Bountiful loomed, dark and empty. Only five humans on the planet. Five humans and hundreds of Dancers, thousands of other species. After the announcement of the murders, the authorities had declared the planet unsafe and had closed it to all colonization. Even researchers needed special dispensation to go. The Dancers were too powerful, their thought too destructive. He shook his head. But the Dancers hadn't been the real problem. Salt Juice had.

Without Salt Juice, the Dancers would never have become an endangered species. Without Salt Juice, the colony wouldn't have made money, and wouldn't have tried to protect that base by allowing ill-conceived killings to go on. The colonists had tried to blame the Dancers for the murders to exterminate the entire species; the intergalactic shock had been great when investigators discovered that the murderers were children.

Salt Juice. He still remembered the fumes, the glazed looks in his parents' eyes. Colonists weren't supposed to indulge—and none did—but they all suffered from Salt Juice intoxication because of their exposure during manufacturing. Perhaps if he had had a better lawyer, if the effects of Salt Juice had been better understood at the time, he would have gotten off, been put in rehabilitation instead of incarceration.

A slight ponging warned him that the shuttle would land soon. He dug in his duffel and removed the sand scarf and some ointment. The woven material felt familiar, warm, a touch of the past. As children, they had stopped wearing sand scarves, and he had gotten so crisped by Bountiful's sun that he still had tan lines. He was older now, and wiser. He would wear the offered protection.

His throat had gone dry. Three days alone on Bountiful. The pilot wouldn't stay—probably due to fear of him. John strapped himself in, knowing it was too late to turn back.

The shuttle bumped and scuttled its way to a stop. Already the temperature inside had changed from cool to the kind of almost-cool developed when the outside air was extremely hot. John unstrapped himself, put on the sand scarf, and rubbed oil over his exposed skin. Then he slung the duffel over his back and got up and went into the flight deck.

The pilot made an exasperated, fearful noise. John ignored her. Through the windows, he could see the salt cliffs and the Singing Sea. The shuttle landed where they had always landed, on the edge of the desert, half a day's walk from the colony itself. He realized with a shudder that no one lived on the planet but the natives. The five traders and the sand sculpture were the aliens here.

He had no plan. He had been too lost in his memories.

"Familiar?" the pilot asked. Her expression was wary. She knew his history. Perhaps she thought that once he set foot on the planet, he would pull out a Dancer ritual knife and slice off her hands and feet.

He didn't answer her. "You're coming back in three days?"

She nodded. Her hands were shaking on the controls. What kind of lies had the authorities made up about Bountiful to keep the curious away? That one touch of the desert sand would lead to madness? That one view of the Dancers would lead to murder?

"Wait for me. Even if I'm not here right away, I'll be coming." The words sounded hollow to his own ears. She nodded again, but he knew at that moment that she wouldn't wait. He would have to be here precisely on time or be stranded on Bountiful forever. Trapped.

The child inside him shivered.

He tugged on the duffel strap, adjusting it, and let himself out. A hot, dry breeze caressed his face. The air smelled like flowers, decaying flowers too long in the sun. Twelve years of memories, familiarity, and fear rose within him—and suddenly he didn't want to be here anymore. He turned to the shuttle, but the bay door had already closed. He reached up to flag her down—and turned the gesture into a wave. He was not twelve anymore. The adults were gone. The colony was gone. He was the adult now, and he wouldn't let himself down.

XI

The traders had made a brilliant decision to come to Bountiful with the wind sculpture. Here they had a ready-made empty colony, a desert filled with sand, and winds aplenty. They could experiment until they were able to duplicate whatever effect they needed, or they could use the planet as a base from which to travel back to Bodean. No one would have caught on if Anita hadn't started the search for her sculpture.

The colony's dome shone like glass in the sunlight. The

walk wasn't as long as John remembered. Still, he would have loved an air car. Air cars had always been forbidden here; they destroyed the desert's delicate ecological balance.

He stopped in front of the dome, stunned to see it covered with little sand particles. In another generation the dome would be a mound of sand, with no indication that anything had ever existed beneath it. The desert reclaimed its own.

He brushed the sand aside, feeling the grains cling to the oil on his skin. The dome was hot, hotter than he cared to touch, but still he felt for the fingerholds that he knew would be there.

And found them. Smaller than he remembered, and filled with sand, but there. He tugged, and, with a groan, the section moved. He slipped inside, bumping his head on the surface. He was a man now, not a boy, and crawling through small spaces wasn't as easy as it used to be.

Once inside, he closed the hatch and took a deep breath. The air wasn't stale as he had expected it to be. It tasted metallic, dusty, like air from a machine that had been turned off for a long time. Decades, probably.

The traders had been in here. Of course they would know that the dome could be breached from the outside. Bountiful's colonists had had a terror of being trapped in the desert.

All he had to do was go to the municipal building, and track them from there. So easy. They would have to wait three lousy Earth days together for the shuttle pilot to return.

He turned onto a street and started walking. He had made it halfway down the block, before the things he saw registered and his emotions stopped him.

The houses hadn't collapsed. They were old-time regulation colony homes, built for short term, but used on Bountiful for nearly a century. The lawns were dead. Brown hulks of plants remained, crumbling now that the air had come back on.

The lawns, the gardens, had been the colonists' joy. They were so pleased that they had been able to tame this little space of land, turn it into their ideal of Earth. Plastic homes with no windows, and Earth flowers everywhere. The dome used to change color with the quality of the light: sometimes gray, sometimes blue, sometimes an odd sepia to protect the colonists from the UV rays.

All of that gone now. No voices, no hum of the Salt Juice factory, no movement. Just John on a long, empty street, facing long, empty ghosts.

There, on the house to the left, he and the other children had placed Michael Dengler's body. He had been the last one, the true failure. It had seemed so logical that if they removed his head along with his hands, his heart, and his lungs, he would grow taller and stronger than the adults. But like the others, he didn't grow at all.

John sunk to the ground, wrapped his arms around his head as if he could shield himself from his own memories. He and the others weren't covered under the Alien Influences Act. They weren't crazy. They were, according to the prosecuting attorney, evil children with an evil plan.

All they had wanted to do was escape. And they thought the Dancers held the secret to that escape.

He remembered huddling behind the canopied trees, watching the Dancer puberty ritual, thinking it made so much sense: remove the hands, the heart, and the lungs so that the new ones would grow in. He was on a different planet now, the third generation born in a new place. Of

155

course, he wasn't growing up. He wasn't following the traditions of the new world.

The attorneys asked him, over and over: if he believed that, why hadn't he gone first? He had wanted to go last, thinking that to be the ultimate sacrifice. Dancer children didn't move for days. He didn't understand the adult reaction—the children weren't dead; they were growing new limbs. Or at least, that was what he had thought. Until Michael Dengler. Then John understood what he had done.

He stayed on his knees for a long time. Then he made himself rise slowly. He did bounty now. He traveled all over the galaxy. He had served his sentence. This was done, gone. He had a wind sculpture to recover, and the people were within his grasp.

He made himself walk, and concentrate on the future.

XII

He found where they had gotten in. Another section had been dislodged, letting too-bright sunlight into the dome. Footprints marred the dirt, and several brown plant stalks were newly broken. Being this close usually excited him— one of the few excitements that he had—but this time he felt empty inside.

His breathing rasped in his throat. He had a dual feeling; that of being watched and that of being totally alone. The hairs prickled on the back of his neck. Something was wrong here.

He followed the footprints to the municipal building. The door was open—an invitation almost. He couldn't go around to the windows, since there were none, and most buildings didn't have another doorway. He braced himself, and slipped in.

The silence was heavier in here. The buildings always had a bit of white noise—the rustle of a fan, the whisper of air filtering through the ceiling. Here nothing. Perhaps they had found the controls only for the dome itself. Perhaps they wanted it quiet so that they could hear him.

The walls and floors were spotless, so clean that they looked as if they had been washed days before. Only the dirt-covered tracks of the traders marred the whiteness, a trail leading him forward, like an Earth dog on the trail of a scent.

He followed it, willing to play out his little role in this drama. Some action would take his mind off the remains of the colony, of the hollow vestiges of his past.

He rounded the corner—and found the first body.

It leaned against the wall, skin toughened, mummified into a near skeleton. For a minute, he thought it had been there since the colony closed, and the air shut down, then he noticed the weapon in its left hand. A small hand-held laser, keyed to a person's print. Last year's model.

He made himself swallow and lean in. One of the traders. For a minute, he couldn't determine which one. He ripped at the clothes, discovered gender—male—then studied the wrinkled, freeze-dried face.

Not the old trader, Minx, who had run Salt Juice. One of the younger males. Tension crept up his back. He held himself still. He had seen this kind of death before, but where?

The answer required that he let down some internal shields, reach into his own memory. He did so slowly, feeling the hot spots, the oppression the colony imposed on him. Then it came:

A Cadmium miner on one of the many cargo ships he

had worked for. The miner had slipped into the hold, trying to get safe passage somewhere, not realizing that to get out of those mines, he needed a series of shots, shots that protected him from the ways that the mining had destroyed his body, processes that wouldn't start until the mining ended.

The captain of the cargo ship had leaned over to John, expressing the view for the entire ship. "God," he had said. "I hope I don't die like that."

John touched the corpse again, figuring that if he was contaminated, there wasn't much he could do about it. Amazing that he hadn't died when he left Cadmium. They had been away from that planet for years. Amazing that the death would come now, here, in this faraway place, with a weapon in his hand.

He took the laser from the body, ran the diagnostic. It worked. He pocketed the laser. Better to use that weapon than his own. Cover his tracks, if he had to.

The footprint path continued down the hall. He brushed off his hands and followed it. All the doors were closed, locks blinking, as if they hadn't been touched since the colony had been evacuated.

He followed the trail around another corner, and found another body: this one a woman. She was sprawled across the floor, clothing shredded, blood everywhere, eyes wide with terror. No desiccation, no mummification. This time the reek of death and the lingering scent of fear.

She appeared to have been brutalized and beaten to death, but as he got closer, he realized that she didn't have a scratch on her. John's throat had gone dry, and his hands were shaking. He had never before encountered anything as odd as this. How did people die on a dead planet? Nothing here would do this, not in this fashion, and not so quickly. He knew about death on Bountiful, and it didn't work like this.

He pulled the laser out of his pocket and kept going. The dirt path didn't look like footprints anymore, just a swirl of dirt along a once-clean floor. He half-expected a crazed trader to leap out from behind one of the doors, but he knew that wouldn't happen. The deaths were too bizarre, too different to be the work of a maniac. They had been planned. And a little scared voice inside told him they had been planned for him.

XIII

John reached the main control room, surprised to find it empty and silent. Lights blinked and flashed on a grid panel nearly two centuries old. He checked the patterns, using guesswork, experience with odd grids, and a half-worn-down diagram near the top of the room to figure out how it should run. His instincts warned him to absorb the knowledge in this room—and absorbing it he was, as quickly as he could.

A door slammed somewhere in the building.

His skin prickled. He whirled. No one visible. No sounds. Nothing except the slight breeze caused by his own actions. He moved slowly, with a deliberation he didn't feel. He checked the corridor, both directions, noting that it was empty. Then he left the main control room. There was nothing more he could do inside. He walked toward the direction of the slammed door. Someone else was alive in here, and he would find that person. He didn't know what he would do then.

His heart was pounding against his chest. Death had never frightened him before. He had never felt it as a threat, only as a partner, an accident. He never saw the murders as deaths, just failed experiments. No one he loved had ever died. They had just disappeared.

Another body littered the corridor. He didn't examine it. A quick glance told him the cause of death. Parts were scattered all over, hanging in the ritual position of Fetin killings, something he had seen too much of in his own exile.

The fourth body was crucified against a wall, upside down, blood still dripping onto the pristine floor. Perhaps he was wrong. One madman with a lot of determination, and perhaps some kind of toxic brain poisoning from a drug he wasn't used to. One man, Minx, the old trader, under the influence of the Bodean wind sculpture.

He hated to think Minx had done this in a rational frame of mind.

John had circled nearly the entire building. From his position, he could see the door, still standing open. Minx had to be outside, waiting for him. He tensed, holding the laser, setting his own systems on alert.

The dirt spread all over the floor, and a bit on the walls. Odd, without anyone tracking it. Was Minx's entire body grimy? John crept along as quietly as he could, trying to disturb nothing. Seemed eerie, as if Minx had been planning for this. It felt as if he had been watching, waiting, as if John were part of a plan. Even eerier that Minx had managed to kill so many people in such diverse ways—and in such a short period of time.

It made no sense.

John reached the front door—and went rigid, except for a trembling at the very base of his spine. Minx was there, all right; waiting, all right—but not in the way John had expected.

Minx was dead.

The blood still trickled from the stumps where his hands used to be. His chest was flayed open, heart and lungs missing. Head tilted back, neck half-cut, as if whoever had done this couldn't decide whether or not to slice it through.

He hadn't been there when John had gone into the building. Minx couldn't have died here—it took too long to chop up a human being like that. John knew. He had done it half a dozen times—with willing victims. Minx didn't look willing.

The blood was everywhere, spraying everything. Minx had to have died while John was inside.

To kill an adult the size of Minx would have taken a lot of strength, or a lot of time.

The shivering ran up John's spine, into his hands. *I didn't mean to kill him!* the little boy inside him cried. *We just wanted to grow up, like Dancers. Please. I didn't mean . . .*

He quashed the voice. He had to think. All five were dead. Something—

"John?"

He looked up. Beth stood before him, clutching a Dancer ritual blade. It was blood-covered, and so was she. Streaks had splattered across her face, her hands. He hadn't seen her since she was fifteen, since the afternoon the authorities caught them comforting each other, him inside her, her legs wrapped around him like a hug.

The first and last time John had been intimate with anyone.

She had hated the killings, had never wanted to do them. Always sat quietly when Harper made the group talk about them. Three years of sessions, one afternoon of love. Then prison ship and separation, and him bounty hunting, alone, forever.

"Beth?" He knew it wasn't her, couldn't be her. She

161

would never do anything like this, not alone, and not now, so many years in the future. He walked toward her anyway, wanting to wipe the blood off her precious face. He reached for her, hand shaking, to touch that still-rosy cheek, to see if it was as soft as he remembered, when his hand went through her.

She was as solid as wind.

Wind.

She laughed and grew bigger, Minx now, even though he remained dead at John's feet. "Took you long enough," the bodeangenie said. "And you call yourself the best."

John glanced at the body, the ritual knife, found the laser in his own hand. A laser could not cut through wind.

"No," the bodeangenie said. "It can't."

John stopped breathing. He took a step back as the realization hit. The bodeangenie was telepathic. It had been inside John's head, inside his mind. He shuddered, wiped himself off, as if, in brushing away the sand, he brushed away the touch, the intimacy that he had never wanted. Had the others died of things they feared? That would explain the lack of external marks, the suddenness. That would explain all except Minx. Minx, who had died of something John feared.

Then the images assaulted him: the trader ship, full of sweat, laughter, and drink, hurtling toward the planet; the traders themselves, dipping into the bodeangenie like forbidden fruit, using him to enhance their own powers, tap each other's mind, playing; the Dancers, stalking out of the woods, into the desert; John, sitting in the cafeteria, his memories displayed before him; Anita, counting credits, peering into the bottle; the trap closing tight, holding him fast, a bit of wind, a bit of sand, a bit of plastic. . . .

John was the bodeangenie's freedom if Bountiful didn't

work. He could pilot the traders' ship back to Bodean, back to the 'genie's home. Fear pounded inside his skull. He didn't want to die like that. He had never wanted to die like that . . .

He slid to his knees, hands around his head as if to protect it. Harper's voice: *if you want protection, build a wall. Not a firm wall, a permeable one, to help you survive the alone times. The wall must come down when you need it to, so that things don't remain hidden. But sometimes, to protect yourself, build a wall.*

The sheets came up, slowly, but more easily than he had hoped because they were already half there. The bodeangenie chuckled, Beth again, laughter infectious. She went to the dome, touched it, and John saw Dancers, hundreds of them, their fingers rubbing against the plastic, their movements graceful and soft, the thing that had given them their name.

"Three choices," the bodeangenie said. "Me, or death, or them."

A little light went on behind his wall. The bodeangenie thought the Dancers frightened him. The 'genie could tap only what was on the surface, not what was buried deep, no matter what its threats.

Wind, and sand, and plastic.

John hurled himself at the dome, pushing out and sliding through. The Dancers vanished as if they had never been. He rolled in the sand, using all his strength to close the dome doors. The bodeangenie pushed against him with the power of wind. His muscles shook; his arms ached. The bodeangenie changed form, started to slip out, when John slammed the portal shut.

Trapping the 'genie inside.

The bodeangenie howled and raged against the plastic

wall. The side of the dome shook, but the 'genie was trapped. A little boy appeared in his mind, alone in a foreign place, hands pounding on a door. *Let me out,* the little boy said with John's voice. *Please, I didn't mean to*—His words, his past. Trapped. The 'genie was trapped. It had to be, or it would kill him. Trapped.

John started to run, as if that would drown out the voice. Across the sands toward the forest, toward something familiar. The sun beat down on him, and he realized he had forgotten his scarf, his ointment, his protection. The little boy kept pounding, sobbing. Torture. He wouldn't be able to survive it. Two more days until the shuttle arrived.

He could take the traders' ship, if he could find it.

The forest still looked charred, decades after the fire that had happened just before John had left the planet. But the canopied trees had grown back, and John could smell the familiar scent of tangy cinnamon. Dancers.

No!!! the little boy screamed in his head.

They came toward him, two-legged, two-armed, gliding like ballerinas on one of the bases. They chirruped in greeting, and he chirruped back, the language as fresh as if he had used it the day before.

His mind drifted into the future, into emotion, into their world.

I would like to stay, John said, placing his memories behind him. *I would like to be home.*

XIV

Sometimes he would wake in the middle of the night, stare through the canopies at the stars, and think: *Someday I will touch them.* Then he would return to sleep, incident forgotten.

Sometimes he would be touching a Dancer's hand, performing a ritual ceremony, and a child's scream would filter through his mind. He would drop the knife, plead apology, and wonder at it, since none of the others seemed to mind.

He loved the trees and the grass, but the hot, dry wind against his face would make him shiver. Sometimes he would think he was crazy, but usually he thought nothing at all.

XV

Perhaps days, perhaps months later, John found himself in the desert, searching for small plants. Food, he was thinking; he would like food—when fists, a little-boy voice, pounded their way into his mind. *Let me out; please let me out.* Puzzlement, a touch of fear, and something against a block—

The memories came flooding back, the shuttle, the bodeangenie. He sat down, examined his fried skin. Human. No matter how much he wanted to be Dancer, he would always be human, with memories, guilt, and regrets.

The bodeangenie was still trapped. The shuttle was long gone, and John was trapped here, presumed dead, doomed to die if he didn't get out of the harsh sun and eat human foods instead of Dancer foods.

He looked back into the forest. He had no memories of the past few days (months?). Dancer thought. Dancers had no memories. He had achieved it, ever so briefly. And it would kill him, just as it had nearly killed him when he had been a boy. They were his drug, as potent as Salt Juice, and as deadly.

Please.

He stood, wiped himself off. The trader shuttle was hidden near the Singing Sea. The bodeangenie was trapped, the planet closed. He was thought dead, and Anita had lost her money.

Beth rose in his mind, pleading against the dome.

Beth. Her screams, his cries. Nights clutching a pillow pretending it was her, wanting the warmth she provided, the understanding of shared experience, shared terror.

Trapped.

The adults had punished him because he had felt trapped, abandoned, because he had killed to set himself free.

Like the bodeangenie.

John was the adult now.

He sank to the sand, examined his sunbaked skin. Much longer, and he would have died of exposure. He was already weak. His need to run, his longing for the Dancers, had trapped him as neatly as he had trapped the bodeangenie. He had been imprisoned so long that even when he had freedom, he imprisoned himself.

Beth and a handful of children huddled near the edges of the dome, waiting for him. Children he had killed, others he had destroyed. The genie was using their memories to reach him, to remind him how it felt to be trapped.

He needed no reminding. He had never been free.

He got up, wiped the sand off his skin. His clothing was tattered, his feet callused. He had been hiding for a long time. The 'genie wasn't able to touch the Dancer part of his mind.

John started to walk, feet leading him away from the

Dancers. He glanced back once, to the canopied forest, the life without thought, without memory. Alien influence. The reaction was not human.

And he was all too human.

Please! I didn't mean . . .

Yes, he had. Just as the 'genie had. It was the only way they knew how to survive.

The sand burned under his bare feet. He wasn't too far from the dome. Perhaps that was how the 'genie's thoughts had penetrated. Saving him. Saving them both.

John nodded, a plan forming. He would take the 'genie back home on the trader ship, using Anita's credits for fuel. She would know that he was alive then, and she would be angry.

Then he would deal with her, and all the creatures she had trapped. He would find the Minaran, free it; free the little helldog. He would destroy her before she destroyed too much else.

Sand blew across the dome's surface. Almost buried, almost gone. He got closer, felt the presence inside.

Please. . . .

In his mind's eye, half a dozen children pushed their faces against the plastic, waiting for him. Beth, a woman now, held them in place. No 'genie. Just his past. *Face it,* Harper had said.

He had been running from it too long.

He reached the dome, brushed the sand away, searching for a portal.

The 'genie needed him. It wouldn't kill him. Wind couldn't pilot a spaceship alone.

"I'm coming," John said.

And inside the dome, the children rejoiced.

Flowers and the Last Hurrah

It's amazing how life can change in the space of a day, an hour, a minute. That's a fact of my business. *Gossip Hourly* specializes in change—sometimes even initiates it.

But I didn't expect the changes that came after Detective Frank Forino's last official visit to my office. When he barged in, I thought the entire interaction was going to be routine.

He came through the doors unannounced—somehow he scared my receptionist—carrying a palmtop as thin as a piece of paper, and before I could decide whether I wanted to greet him or throw him out, he thrust the tiny screen at me.

"Looks like one of yours," he said.

Now that statement could have meant anything. My entire office was screens, except for the computers on and in my desk, the desk itself, and my chair. Plants dripped off every other surface, although I rarely paid them any attention. Some old guy with tattoos and piercing scars changed them every week.

But I knew Frank wasn't talking about the screen. He was talking about the pix on it. He usually brought me a pix, combined with some accusation or another. I usually lied, ignored him, or sent him to my lawyer.

I dropped Frank's palmtop on my desk, kicked my chair back and put my feet up, nearly slamming the screen with my right heel. Frank winced at me. He was a big guy, with florid features, and they could make a wince twice as effective. I ignored him too. I laced my hands behind my head and leaned back.

"You gonna answer me, Colin?" To his credit, Frank hadn't tried to get me to move my feet or to take the pix back. Half the cops in the city would have. But Frank and I had an understanding.

"Why should I?" I asked.

"Because, idiot," he said. "This ain't no trademark tampering case. Not this time."

I glanced back at him. His face was red and the collar of his blue shirt was damp with sweat. His brown eyes had something unusual in them, so unusual I couldn't read them.

"Is it more serious?" I asked.

"You bet your ass," he said.

"Then I'm not answering any questions, officer. Not without my lawyer."

"Colin, you and me, we go back a long way," Frank said.

"I know," I said, "and that line has never gotten me anywhere with you, not even when I was reporting. Why should it get you something?"

"Because," he said. "This might be a you-scratch-mine, I'll-scratch-yours-kinda deal."

"Off the record?" I asked.

"No can do," he said. "Strictly by the book."

"I don't do strictly by the book," I said.

"You might want to this time," he said. "Take a look at that shot."

This was how it started. First Frank would get me to

170

look at the pix. Then he'd get me to comment on it. Then he'd get me to admit that one or more of the parties involved were not who we purported them to be.

At least, that's what he tried to do. It hadn't worked yet.

I sighed and brought my feet off the desk. "I'm not going to confirm or deny anything," I said, as I reached for the 'top. Then my hand stopped inches above it.

It wasn't, as I expected, a download off our website. *Gossip Hourly* never published a pix like this, no matter what the case. We did murders, sure, and grisly ones. But we made it a point to avoid the more explicit shots, especially after the New York State Legislature made it a crime to publish visuals that might hamper murder investigations.

"Well?" Frank asked.

He was speaking to fill the silence. I knew that. Frank always did. He wasn't long on patience, but for all his bad grammar, he was long on smarts.

I had to play it just right.

I slid the 'top closer. The pix was a standard morgue shot, grim, yes, but also of little interest to our subscribers, who expect a bit more creativity from our 2-D stills. The woman involved was laid out on the metal medical table, arms at her side, the Y autopsy incision scarring what had once been a very beautiful torso. The pix was taken by someone who had been crouching by her feet. They showed recent signs of hard use: five burst blisters and an ingrown nail on the left big toe.

"We don't take pix this dull, Frank," I said.

"It ain't the pix, nimrod," he said. "The pix clearly ain't yours. It's the body. The body's yours."

I was about to protest that the body wasn't mine, and then comment that it was a good thing too because otherwise Frank and I wouldn't be having this scintillating conversation when I realized what he really meant.

The woman had a small number embedded in the arch of her right foot.

Frank was on to something; she could have been one of ours after all.

"Okay," I said, wondering if even saying this much was a bad idea without my lawyer. My stomach churned, and I envisioned a new ulcer. I'd just paid off the bill for capping last year's. "I see the mark. She's a flower, Frank. It's not my fault she's dead."

"We'll talk the ethics of flowers later," he said. "She didn't die of no Accelerated Age Syndrome. She was murdered."

"Why would anyone murder a flower?" I asked. "She'd be dead in a few weeks anyway."

"Now you're thinking," Frank said. "She one of yours?"

I almost snapped that I couldn't tell, not from the angle of that shot, and then I caught myself. To admit that would be to admit we financed the making of flowers, and admitting that would make us the victims of potentially damaging trademark infringement suits not to mention criminal charges if someone could link our operation with flower-making.

"We have nothing to do with flowers, Frank," I said in my prissiest voice.

"Yeah, right," he said. "And I got nothing to do with the criminal element in the Big Apple."

"Your sarcasm needs work," I said.

"So does your honesty," Frank snapped. "I'm coming to you for help on this one."

I shoved the 'top back at him. "You never said that."

"I said scratch-your-back—"

"But not help. Not the let's-do-this-entirely-off-the-record kind. You wanted by the book."

"You know something then?"

I didn't. But I could. It was only a matter of a few calls. "No."

"Ah, jeez, Colin. I already been to every pimp in Manhattan. You and them, you're the only one what uses this kinda flower."

I threaded my fingers together and rested my chin on them. "You don't read your nets, do you, Frank? Flowers are used in all sorts of industries, from medicine to fashion. I resent the fact that you try to lump us with the shady underbelly of New York Society—"

"When you'd rather be lumped with the doctors and models," he said.

Caught me. I smiled. "I was talking about two different issues here, Frank. The first was on flowers. The second was the other part of your sentence. The one where you said that only pimps and tabloids use flowers."

"I didn't say that," he said, taking the pix as if I didn't deserve to look at it any more.

"What did you say, then?" I asked.

"I said 'that kinda flower.' You both used that kinda flower."

"What kind is that?"

"That kind," he said, pointing at the screen so hard I thought his finger would poke a hole in it. "The kind that looks like somebody else."

"All clones look like someone else, Frank. That's why they're clones."

"But not somebody that famous," he said. "Medical researchers don't need 'em famous, and the fashion industry, well, they don't like getting sued."

Neither did we, but it was part of the business. I

snatched the 'top from him again.

"She doesn't look like anyone to me," I said.

"Naw," he said. "Only Shardeen."

Shardeen, the biggest Christian superstar of the twenties. She was drop-dead gorgeous with chocolate skin, upswept blue eyes, and a figure on her six-foot frame that made every man believe there is a God. She sang on pay-for-play downloads, had her own vids, and starred in wholesome VR programs designed by her Christian backer. She and her husband, Davis Drew, the head of Mogul Media Productions (and a former alcoholic who claimed he knocked off the bad habits when he heard a voice from heaven) had a picture perfect marriage that, rumor had it, was as deep as the picture and not quite as wide. We'd been trying to nail that relationship for years, and hadn't had a chance. Shardeen and Davis were more media savvy than the media, if that was possible.

I looked at the pix again. The hair didn't matter: Shardeen changed hers weekly, but the eyes were the right shade of blue and the skin was Shardeen's creamy brown.

"I don't see any resemblance," I said, and tossed the 'top back at him.

"Don't play me for dumb, Colin," he said. "It'll blow up on you."

"I'm not playing you for anything, Frank," I said. "We have nothing to do with this, although you could give us an exclusive for the 2:20 Celebrity site update."

"By the book?" he asked.

By the book in this instance meant that we could report the death, by murder, of a female Jane Doe, mixed ancestry, unknown type. New York had dozens of those every day. They weren't worth the pixels.

"What'd she die of?" I asked.

"You gonna run the story?"

"When it becomes one, which it isn't right now. I'm asking for me, Frank. I'm curious."

"Curious about a Jane Doe?" He smiled. "She was poisoned, Colin."

Now he really had my interest and he knew it. That smile was smug. He watched as I sat up, as I punched the button which made my desk computer rise from the glass top.

"Can I get a copy of the autopsy report?" I asked.

"Thought you'd never ask," he said. "Access 267, use the usual voice code. That should get you in. It's the 18th Jane Doe for June 20th."

"Thanks," I said.

"Don't mention it." He headed for the door. Then he stopped. "I mean it. Don't mention it."

"I won't," I said and waited until he left before adding, "at least, not yet."

The death of a flower wasn't news. Flowers died all the time. It was their nature. Flowers were illegal, but useful, as they had been since the teens. Cloning was easy, cheap, and fast—one cell could generate a dozen copies. The cloners grew the copies to the right age—taking care of the high maintenance early years.

Medical researchers discovered the flower technique the way most things get discovered—while they were looking for something else. As they made clones, an illegal practice anyway, they tampered with genes. Tamper with one area on one clone to see how it affected the body; tamper on another area with a different clone from the same cell to monitor another effect. Eventually, the researchers discovered how to accelerate the aging process, which accelerated the

175

experiment process, and of course, some enterprising researchers saw the possibility for side money, using the rapidly aging clones. No one would miss them, the researchers thought, and they could generate a lot of quick cash—which they did. An entire black market industry in flowers grew up almost as fast as the flowers themselves.

Some of the lesser tabloids still doctored pictures, but that was riskier than flower work. Every time a new technique made doctored photos "perfect," someone discovered a way to find the flaws. Over the last twenty years, the law stopped protecting our rights to publish what we wanted. Now we had to prove that the story was "true to the best of our knowledge." Flowers enabled us to do that because no one could tell flowers from the real person—at least, not without removing their shoes.

For our purposes at *Gossip Hourly*, the best flowers stayed fresh for about three weeks. That actually meant a seven-week life span, with two weeks growth, three weeks of use, and two weeks of deterioration expense, which we usually got some of the less reputable medical labs to cover.

Flowers died all the time.

No one cared. Few humans considered lives of such a short duration important. Sure there were the Save the Flowers freaks, and the sincere ethical folks who were constantly testifying before Congress trying to get laws passed to legalize and regulate flower-making, but they weren't having any success.

Flowers never lived long enough to vote.

Besides, flowers were human, despite their life spans and origins. Once made, they were covered under the same laws as the rest of us. If a flower was murdered, and they were more often than you'd think, the perps rarely got prosecuted—rarely got caught. It was only the most flagrant

cases that made headlines, and the most disgusting operations that got shut down. When the kiddie porn folks got
into flowers, the cops swooped in. When the fringe VR pro-
ducers based their product on flower snuff, the cops
swooped again. But the rest of us got harassed sometimes,
got sniffed sometimes, but otherwise we didn't get bothered.

We gave flowers work, kept them off the streets, and
paid for their upkeep during their brief sojourn on this
earth. It really wasn't that expensive. We rarely had the
same flower on the payroll for more than a month.

So flowers died. At the hands of inept researchers or in
random shootings or in crimes of passion, usually committed by an overzealous john.

But flowers weren't poisoned. Poison suggested a deliberate killing. A premeditated death. A *reason* for taking an
already shortened life.

So that was the essence of the you-scratch-my-back-I'll-
scratch-yours case. Frank knew I wouldn't be able to let
this one alone. The puzzle was too great.

If I could get official word on this, we'd be on-line with
it in a matter of hours, and the story would hang for days.

Maybe weeks.

I didn't download immediately after Frank left, although
he expected me to. I had other business first.

I left my office and wandered into Celebrity Headquar-
ters. CHQ leader Jacques DuFriesne was running audio on
the latest lead while he was fact-checking another story on
screen. I noted as I approached his desk that he had a split
screen working, one with his notes, and one which instantly
reported the notes of his favorite source.

I put a hand on his narrow shoulder.

"Sorry to interrupt, Jacques," I said. "It's important."

"It better be," he said. "I'm supposed to upload in fifteen."

Each section of *Gossip Hourly* had its specific upload time. Celebrity uploaded at twenty after, City uploaded at twenty-one after, and so on, with our display changing every minute of every hour of every day. The tabloid really should have been named *Gossip Minutely*, but that didn't have the right ring to it. So we settled for *Hourly*. A person could instant download every hour, and have a new tab in front of him. Publishing like this took diligence, it took coordination, and it took minds like DuFriesne, who could do three things at once, and still consider himself slacking off.

"Prepare someone else to do the upload," I said. "I'm not sure how long this'll take."

"I'm working on a delicate piece," he said.

"It'll have to wait an hour, then."

"We'll get scooped by the *Globe*."

I shrugged.

"It's your neck," he said and beckoned his assistant, one Gerda Hockstader, to his desk. Gerda was slender and blonde and had more implants than a Major League ball player. He showed her what he was doing, and pushed away from his desk.

"Okay, what?" Jacques asked as he stood. I beckoned him out of Celebrity and into the hallway between. I wrapped a casual arm around his shoulder as if I were chastising him for something. It was an old habit of mine, and it guaranteed that the curious would leave us alone.

"You do a flower for that piece on Shardeen?"

"Yeah," he said, "but the first deployment was a complete failure. I was planning a second, but never got around to it."

"Why not?" I didn't like hearing that he had wasted company funds on a failed story.

I felt his shoulders stiffen beneath my hand. "I lost the flower."

"You lost it?"

He shrugged and looked away.

Flowers did get lost sometimes. They were left to themselves a lot, and even though they had neural implants, the implants were not a great substitute for real learning and experience. It was rather like having a three-year-old child with the body of an adult, the intelligence of a dog, and more useless knowledge than the *Encyclopedia Britannica*. Anything could go wrong—and often did.

"Who was babysitting it?"

"Gerda," he said. "But she got called out on assignment."

Gerda. The one he'd left in charge. The one he said I'd regret.

"Get her," I said.

"Someone's got to do the update," he said. "These things can be delicate. We don't dare miss a detail."

Sometimes he forgot that I worked my way up through the ranks. "What's the story?"

"The President's Lesbian Love Affair."

"I thought the *Star* did that this morning."

"They did," he said, "but not with footage."

"Is ours real or is it flower-footage?"

He looked hurt. "Does it matter?"

Of course it did. It mattered, and I needed to know. I just stared at him.

He sighed. "We don't have a flower for the president."

"I know," I said. We had an evergreen, developed rapidly enough for use at the end of the election, but with a life span of a good dozen years. Evergreens were used only for people with staying power; presidents, Elvis, and the occasional superstar.

"Why would any president allow someone to film her having sex?"

"Stevens did in '08."

"You sure?" he asked.

"It was pre rapid-growth cloning techniques," I said.

"And no one has allowed it since. They all remember the scandal."

So our video was flower-footage. Once, just once, I would have liked our stories to have more than verisimilitude. I would have liked them to be real. But in this flower-heavy world, I no longer knew how to make real interesting.

"Sir?" he asked, in a tone that suggested he had said the word before. "You want me to get Gerda?"

"Yeah. Send her to my office." I let go of his shoulder, and let him return to Celebrity. The place would be complete chaos in there for the next ten minutes. They did have an update to finish. The moments before a deadline were always hectic.

It was a good thing they had fifty minutes in between. They could use the time cleaning up the stories they did manage to get.

I went back to my office, my mind spinning. A dead flower, a failed story, and a lot of money out of my company's pocket.

I didn't like how this was shaping up.

Flower creation was a lot more delicate than it initially sounded. A man, a company, couldn't just order up any old flower. He needed a cell, some DNA, something that would regenerate. And then he had to find someone who would make the flower, no questions asked.

Since flowers were illegal anyway, the questions weren't asked. But no one wanted to get caught. And the folks most likely to get caught were the ones in charge of famous faces. Under my tenure, *Gossip Hourly* had suffered weekly investigations, and nearly 35 trademark infringement lawsuits, all of which we had won. None of the celebrities who claimed we had misused their trademarked image—pix, vids, holograms and VR representations of their famous faces, bodies and voices—could prove we were responsible for the flower. They couldn't even prove that we had known the difference between the flower and the celebrity.

We had a good team of lawyers but they weren't the only ones responsible for our excellent luck in defending our publication. We kept our activities as separate from the flower makers' as we could. So far, Frank and his minions had proven inept at database robbing or easy encryption decoding. They also lacked the manpower, and I hoped it would stay that way, because we had to keep track of expenses and inventory.

Everybody did.

And that could create problems in the wrong hands.

When Gerda Hockstader had arrived in my office, she had already been prepared. She wafted in on a wave of *Charlie* so thick, it made me think of my great-grandmother. Gerda's implants made her cheeks a bit too red, her eyes a bit too large, and her body so out of proportion that I wondered if she'd topple forward onto my desk.

"I didn't lose her intentional," she said, smacking on a piece of gum, and sitting, uninvited, in the cracked leather chair beside my desk.

"I would hope not," I said, trying to remember if I had

approved this woman's hire or if the approval had come directly from personnel. I wondered who had interviewed her, and if it had bothered that person that this Gerda Hockstader preferred to speak in ungrammatical English.

A tabloid had to have some standards.

"Why don't you tell me what happened?" I asked.

"I ain't gonna lose my job, am I?" She peered at me sideways with those buggy eyes. I assumed that she assumed that the look was seductive.

It wasn't. It was creepy.

And I wasn't going to answer her question. "Ms. Hockstader, I called you into my office to ask about the flower you lost, not to discuss your employment."

Although we would discuss her employment if I decided that she lost the flower through her own complete ineptitude.

"Well, it wasn't my fault," she said, and I suppressed a sigh. With her type, it never was. "They didn't have no apartment for her, you know? Sports was supposed to give up Apartment A, but they still had some soccer guy in there. Good news for the real one, they said, because in person years, he'da been about 130 years old. They were trying to farm the soccer flower off to some Aging Research Institute, but they claimed they already had too many flowers of this guy, and they didn't need no more."

I remembered the problem. The soccer player's clone had tied up the apartment for an extra two weeks. We had sixteen apartments that usually went from flower to flower. Sometimes an apartment or two stood empty, but rarely did we have none empty at all. And never before had we had one tied up by a flower who seemed to be morphing into an evergreen.

"Go on," I said, when it became clear we were getting to

the heart of the story, and she didn't want to incriminate herself.

"So she's supposed to stay with me," Gerda said. And there it was. The center. "I gave her the code, even implanted it in that neural thing, and gave her instructions on how to find the place, and told her when to meet me."

"What went wrong?" I asked.

"If I knew, we wouldn't be missing one flower, now would we?" she snapped.

"She didn't show?" I asked.

"How'm I supposed ta know?"

"You were supposed to meet her," I said, none too gently.

She shrugged. "Deadlines."

"I'm sure you've shepherded flowers around deadlines," I said, beginning to really dislike this woman. I would call up her personnel file the moment she left.

"I have," she said. "But this was an *evolving* deadline."

The staff hated evolving deadlines, and for some reason, they blamed me for them. I suppose they had a point, since I was the one who mandated that only two people cover any one story. But usually stories popped and fizzled within six hours. Every now and then we had stories that lasted for days, and the two in charge of it had to learn to work in shifts of twelve hours each. The first day of this marathon usually caused an all-nighter, and that, in turn, created animosity towards me.

My staff hated to go without sleep.

They should have had my job.

And my annual ulcer.

"So that was Day One of your evolving deadline. And you couldn't contact her? Warn her?"

"A flower?" Gerda asked. "Like I'm supposed to have

her e-mail address? This babe wouldn't have known an e-mail message from a voice from God."

"She was dumb?"

"She didn't know ta wait for me, now did she?"

"I don't think that's prima facie evidence, Ms. Hockstader."

She blinked at me. I had used the phrase on purpose. All of my staffers should know a few specialized terms and "prima facie" in connection with "evidence" was one of them.

"I don't see how that's the issue," she said archly, obviously not clear at all on what I had just said.

"Oh?" I asked. "The issue is what, then?"

"Why this company don't have no policy for lost flowers."

"We're not even supposed to have flowers, Ms. Hockstader. How could we have a policy dealing with them? I thought this was explained to you when you were placed on Jacques's team."

"I signed a few papers."

"Did you read them?"

She shrugged. "That was six months ago. 4300 hours ago, you know?"

"Actually," I said, "it was 4380 hours ago, if we're going to be exact."

"You like lording stuff over people, don't ya?"

I guess I did. It was one of the reasons I'd been promoted. "It's my job to know how many hours there are in a day, a week, a month, or a year, Ms. Hockstader. We say that's how many issues we put out, even though that's not technically true. Technically, we put out a new issue every minute, which would mean that you signed those papers two hundred sixty two thousand eight hundred issues ago. By my lights."

"As if you read all those issues."

"I read every story we put in *Gossip Hourly*, Ms. Hockstader," I said. I wasn't quite sure why she was irritating me. Probably because she was subtly complaining about her workload, when all she had to do was concentrate on one story, sometimes for days. I had to concentrate on as many as 1440 stories per day plus the business of employee management, the *Hourly*'s financing, and making certain we had site space. I also had to handle cops and flowers and other nefarious aspects of running this business.

She complained about an occasional all-nighter; I was lucky to get sleep. And people wondered why folks in my profession burn out after a few years. There's nothing left.

"So what is the policy?" she asked and I nearly groaned aloud. If she didn't know, then other employees didn't know either, and we were in deep trouble. Before I fired her, I'd better make certain she signed the confidentiality agreement, and that she understood that she had signed it, and that everything she owned was forfeit if she failed to live up to it.

"It doesn't matter," I lied. "When did you start looking for the flower?"

"I didn't," she said. "I forgot until Jacques reminded me."

"And when was that?"

She had the grace to flush. For a few moments there I thought she had no conscience at all. "When he told me you wanted to see me."

I bit my tongue to keep from firing her then and there. Confidentiality. Frank. Flowers, and whatever else she might know. Those were all reasons to keep her on staff until I could shut her up.

Now I knew why all those Mafiosos from the past century killed people who knew too much.

It was easier.

I made myself smile. "Thank you, Ms. Hockstader."

"That's all?" she asked.

"That's all," I said.

"Really?"

"Did you expect something else?"

She stood slowly. "I kinda thought you might, you know, be a bit upset at me or something."

I shrugged, half amazed that she was buying this entire routine of mine. But then, Frank bought it damn near every week.

"Why should I be upset at you, Ms. Hockstader? After all, she was just a flower."

Just a flower.

Special ordered through one of our holding companies, bought and paid for through another, and lost by an inept Celebrity writer who hadn't even had the decency to mention it the following day.

If Frank got his hands on this one, there'd be no bargaining.

Someone had murdered the flower because we had been careless. I tried to console myself with the idea that she would have died anyway, but it didn't wash.

Something about the poison.

It meant that someone had had time to consider killing her.

And that someone knew how to find her.

I contacted personnel and had them look up all the paperwork in Hockstader's file. Then I used the access number Frank had given me and called up the code. Then I asked for the 18th Jane Doe file for the 20th day of the month.

The autopsy appeared on my screen. The file number was in the high six figures. They had realized she was a flower, and gave her case the lowest priority possible.

Made me wonder why Frank was even investigating it, even in a I'll-scratch-your-back, you-scratch-mine, by-the-book fashion.

Something nagged at me about that.

I skipped the part about the poison. I would come back to that later. What I wanted to find out was where the flower died.

I scrolled through a mountain of information in the space of a minute. My reporter's skills hadn't left me. In the old days, I could pull the good pieces out of an autopsy in 35 seconds flat, and be accurate.

They found the flower in Trump's Last Hurrah.

Actually, the name of the building was the Gold Building, and it was a crown jewel in Trump New York. It was in the middle of some behind the scenes power jockeying, had been since the Donald died, at the very ripe old age of 85. The Gold Building had just been under construction then, but the Donald had said, in one of his last announcements, that it would be the building everyone would remember him by, and the name Trump's Last Hurrah had stuck ever since.

A mere flower couldn't afford the Hurrah. Hell, the editor and business manager of a tabloid couldn't afford it either. Was her assignation at the Hurrah? That wouldn't make sense. If we needed a Hurrah-like setting, we usually used the Set, a series of interiors that looked like New York hotels. Our pix people were good at avoiding things like the missing wall or the lack of a ceiling.

But the Hurrah was an interesting case in point because

Now, sometimes I did use flowers to destroy perfectly innocent lives, and those are the stories that still haunt me. Like the case of the soccer player and the latest operatic diva—you know who I mean. The rumors were hot, they were heavy, and they were wrong. The marriage was happy—had been, that is, until the pix of our floral soccer player clone with that no-name flower in one of our VR sets became the greatest scandal of all time.

I'd had no idea that the diva would swallow so many pills, or that the primitive stomach pumping techniques still in use in the greater New York area hospitals could ruin a larynx.

I had no idea at all.

Not that ignorance is an excuse.

Heads rolled after that one, and I was a lot more careful about which targets we went after on flower-like stories.

Like Shardeen.

Shardeen was a prime target. She paraded herself as a great Christian lady with a heart of gold, but she was no Christian and she had no heart.

We just couldn't prove it. For every story we heard, we couldn't get anyone to talk on the record. Her husband controlled too many jobs, in a wide variety of businesses. And he seemed to believe all that crap he and Shardeen prattled about their fairy tale relationship.

Even though I knew she had her eye on other men. She'd even had her eye on me for a nanosecond. But I didn't go for Christian hypocrites. When I approved the Shardeen flower, I had done it with her husband in mind. No man needed to be made a fool of in quite that way.

All of this is a roundabout way of explaining why I left the rag in the capable hands of Debora, my assistant who lusted, equally capably, after my job, and ventured into the wilds of Brooklyn, a place where no one of my status and reputation went any more.

I went because, for the first time in nearly a decade of covering illicit affairs and trying to scandalize an occasional head of state, Frank had surprised me. Intrigued me. Made me feel like a cub again.

I hadn't felt like a cub in a very long time.

I had been a good reporter then. Back in my cubbing days, there were still opportunities for good reporters although folks who really cared about news and reporting it were being replaced with folks who were a lot more interested in being reported, or who wanted to make their names as scandal-mongers or commentators. I wasn't vapid enough to comment, and I really didn't care who was sleeping with whom.

I just wanted to have an effect on something.

I had a few minor successes. A few changed policies at some of the local precincts. A major story on the mayor. A few kids taken off the streets and given good homes.

But I was part of a dying breed, and I realized it long before the first flower came on the scene. I even covered the flower development story, and I remember worrying, even then, about the potential to exploit flowers. I never saw how the changes in my own industry would lead me to do it— not because it was cheaper up front, but because it was cheaper (and easier) in the long run.

In those early days, I thought of flowers as human.

I don't any longer.

Brooklyn hasn't changed a lot in the last hundred years. Parts of it have, of course—neighborhoods have gentrified, then shifted back to genteel poverty again, and many have regentrified. But a lot of the houses are still made of brownstone, and they have nice lots with yards, and they still have trees out front and the sound of children's voices in the early evening, the feel of a neighborhood—the kind where everyone knows everyone else.

It wasn't my set. My set lived in west side high rises and aspired to Park Avenue and Central Park. But sometimes I longed for this. I had just never managed to maintain a relationship, and these neighborhoods whispered family, something I was beginning to believe I would never have.

Frank's house was in the middle of the block, as brownstone as the others around it. Nothing to distinguish it, nothing to say a guy I'd known for nearly twenty years lived inside. The roots of an old tree pushed up the sidewalk, and the tree itself provided shade for three yards. The house had a front porch that looked like it'd been glassed in during the smog crisis of the early '00s, and the inside door, which was obviously from the same period, was made of steel. Otherwise the house hadn't been touched since it'd been built.

I wondered if Frank's family had lived there for generations.

Probably.

Housing in the Greater New York area was at such a premium that a cop, on a cop's salary, couldn't have afforded a dive apartment, let alone a place like this.

My weight on the porch stairs triggered the house security system. Bolts and steel cables slammed home behind all the windows, and a small red light blinked above the old-fashioned doorbell, the kind that went out of use when I was a kid.

"Hey, Frankie," I said in the direction of the light. "It's Colin. I decided my back needed scratching after all."

192

The light flicked off for a second which meant someone inside was checking my vitals, then all the bolts and locks and cables slid back. The porch door unlocked and slid open by itself. As I stepped inside, Frank pulled open the steel interior door.

"Didn'ja know you could get shot doing this?" he asked.

I shrugged. "I thought you lived in a safe neighborhood."

"You're lucky I do." He stood aside and let me into the dark interior. It smelled of old cabbage and fresh spaghetti sauce. The wood on the floors was warped and wavy. A staircase curved to my right. To my left was a large living room complete with two net chairs, a VR station, and a flat screen rolled up and hidden in one of those mural tubes near the ceiling. Pictures hung on every available wall, and some were as old as the house.

I was right; Frank had inherited the place.

He led me into the kitchen. A boy with Frank's features stirred two pots on the stove. A raw-boned woman with graying hair sat at the table, grading school assignments with a palm scan. She was Frank's mother. His wife, he explained, hadn't made it home yet. She worked luxury taxi in the City, and she was working extra hours because there was a big to-do at the Met and she wanted the cash.

I never gave other people's financial situations much thought, but I realized that even with the house, and the land, and the three-paycheck household, Frank's situation was tight.

Money was never something I worried about. Time was what I worried about.

Strange to see how things differed from person to person.

He led me to a small shop in the back. It had been built

in the middle of the previous century and it still smelled like oil. Only Frank had converted it to his office away from home. A tiny space heater gleamed on the ceiling, but in the summer months like these, only good old-fashioned windows provided any relief at all. He had computer equipment still stamped with the department's name on the side, and he had a lot of other gee-gaws, most for processing evidence. He obviously did a lot of work here, which didn't surprise me, given the cramped and uncomfortable conditions at his precinct.

He scooted a folding chair toward me, and pulled toward him a square-backed wooden chair that would have been an antique if it weren't for the layers of spray paint. The folding chair was like one my grandmother had; the metal was thick and old, and the chair squealed when I sat on it.

"So what's so urgent you had to risk life and limb to come down here?" he asked.

"Your case," I said.

"You got something?"

"Maybe," I said. "First I want to know why you're investigating this. Because she died in the Hurrah?"

A smile played at his lips. "You read the autopsy."

"Of course I did."

"Then you saw it was one of them designer poisons, working over several days."

I hadn't really noted that. I had just noted the name, and I hadn't recognized it. I had planned to look it up later.

The case got curiouser and curiouser.

"That," I said. "But I was wondering whose room she was in. It didn't say on the report. It just gave the room number."

"I thought you had some mole in reservations."

"I do," I said. "But I really didn't want to use him on something like this."

Frank's eyebrows went up. "It's a him?"

"It was last week." I grinned. "Might be different this week."

"Some day you're gonna tell me," he said.

"Some day you're going to put me out of business," I said.

He laughed. Then he sobered up. "If I tell you this, we're in that you-scratch-my-back-I'll-scratch-yours situation."

"Off the record," I said. "We're not reporting this story."

"You will once I tell you."

"Maybe not."

"Don't make promises you can't keep."

I sighed. "Look, either we do it by the book or we don't. But if we do, we go nowhere because you and I can't talk. Why don't we pretend that we're the partners this time?"

"And why is that?" he asked. "You know something?"

"Maybe," I said.

He shook his head. "All right. I don't say nothing about where I get information, and you don't report nothing until I say."

"And if you happen to learn something about another operation, say, or a piece of information that could possibly be harmful to, say, a company as a sideline in this investigation, you don't prosecute."

Frank held up his hands. "I don't make those kinda deals. You know that. The DA'd be all over me."

"You make those deals all the time," I said. "That's how you get information. It's a time-honored tradition among cops."

He sighed. "Yeah, but not with guys like you."

I stood. The folding chair groaned again. "I guess I came down here for nothing, then."

"Colin," he said, and I heard pleading in his voice.

I froze. "What do you need me for?"

"The flower." His voice was soft, regretful. "What I come to you for in the first place."

"Do we have a deal?" I asked.

"If upstairs finds out, it'll be my butt."

I shrugged, grabbed the handle on the hot metal door.

"All right," he said. "I ain't heard nothing, especially from you. You been as uncooperative as usual."

I nodded and returned to my chair.

He was staring at me. "My info says your guys ordered up the flower, and then lost her."

"Celebrity," I said, feeling the hair on the back of my neck prickle. I'd never admitted to anyone outside *Gossip Hourly* that we made flowers.

"Good," he said. Then more softly, he repeated, "Good."

"Why?" I asked.

He looked up, folded his hands as if he were imparting the most important information in the world, and said, "Because the room belonged to Davis Drew."

The implications were staggering. No wonder Frank was trying to cover his ass on this one.

Davis Drew, media mogul and Shardeen's husband, shared a room with the flower. She died of a slow-acting poison. Did he do it, thinking she was Shardeen? Thinking the designer poison was slight enough that no one would know that she'd been murdered?

Or did he knowingly kill the flower? And if so why? As a warning to *Gossip Hourly*, and other publications/programs/VR vids like us? Or to warn Shardeen that this would happen to her?

Or was there something else involved? Something I didn't see?

"Davis Drew wouldn't be that stupid," I said, trying to remain calm even though my brain was racing.

"That was my first thought," Frank said. "So I figured maybe the poison was for him. But why was he shacked up with the flower? Why not his wife?"

We were always good about reporting stories that could be true, especially when we used flowers. We were going to get pix of Shardeen with a lover in a New York hotel, because she was supposed to be at a New York hotel.

With Davis?

I'd have to check, but probably.

So was he shacking up with the flower, thinking she was Shardeen?

How could anyone mistake a flower for a real person?

Unless their relationship was based on something other than conversation.

That thought made me shudder.

"Don't add up, do it?" Frank said.

"No, it doesn't," I said. And Frank was right; the flower was the key. It gave him an edge knowing that Drew didn't order up the flower himself, or that someone else didn't send it in, as an exact duplicate, coached in the art of being Shardeen.

Our flowers just had to look good in the pix. They didn't have to talk right or pretend to have the same experiences. Our flower was as obvious a clone as they come.

"You talk to Drew yet?" I asked.

"No," Frank said. "His people keep tying us up with red tape."

"Cut through it," I said. "I'll work as your partner on this. You handle the official parts. I'll trace the flower."

He grabbed my arm. "I can trust you on this?"

"If you couldn't, you shouldn't have brought me into it."

"You know what could happen, don't you?"

I knew a million things could happen. I didn't know which one Frank was focusing on. "What?"

"This could bring down the whole *Gossip Hourly* flower business. You and your competitors, when this blows, could become villains."

I smiled at him. Frank was a good cop, but he didn't understand spin. "I doubt that, my friend," I said.

He shook his head. "Don't say I didn't warn you."

"All right," I said. "I won't."

There were too many players, I thought as I reached my office. I got off the elevator to find the normal chaos: a screaming fight in Sports because someone forgot to double-check information for the lead story in the hourly update; a process server, sitting beside the fern bed in the lobby, obviously waiting for someone he didn't recognize and of course the receptionist was giving him no help; a glitch in our daily subscription charge—we were charging viewers last year's day rate instead of this year's; and so on.

My life: One crisis after another.

I let the fight in Sports settle itself. I ignored the process server and he ignored me—so somehow I failed to meet the description he had. And I put a big notice on the front of this hour's magazine, claiming that the day rate was artificially lowered as an "unannounced special" for today only. By midnight, we would be back to the normal rate, and someone in subscriptions encoding would be unemployed.

All of this I managed before going to my inner sanctum.

There I closed the door, locked it, and booted up the other computer, the one Frank didn't know about. The one no one knew about except me, the installer (now employed at company offices in Sydney) and my boss who probably has forgotten the seven codes it takes simply to get the computer out of the secret drawer in the desk.

I sat in my leather chair, used the linen handkerchief that came with the suit to wipe the sweat off my face, and wished I had asked the secretary to order me a frappaccino. Old-fashioned, I know, but I had developed a taste for them as a boy on hot summer days, and when I was sweating this bad, nothing seemed to satisfy my thirst better.

Instead, I opened my mini-fridge, took out my last allotment of bottled water for the day, and downed it. The frappaccino would have to wait.

I called up the ordering service for flowers—not that ordering flowers was ordinarily my job, but I did double-check the invoices, particularly after we'd been double-billed for the presidential evergreen. The service was listed under a gardening company that did supply the office with all its green and blooming plants. Frank checked that one years ago, along with everything else in our data files, and found nothing suspicious. That was because the boss initially paid the service a hefty cash fee to duplicate their invoice system. Our flowers had numbers, all right, but they matched numbers on the growing plants that filled the offices. The only difference was a dash in the flower system that wasn't there in the gardening service system. The gardening service kept a copy of its invoice and so did we, only we assigned those numbers to flowers.

The billing went through another broker, and was infinitely more complicated than I want, or need, to explain here.

I pulled Frank's downloaded pix off my desk and peered at the number. Then I entered it in the item slot on my computer, and waited. The download was slow throughout this system because we decided not to use state-of-the-art. State-of the art encryption systems always had bugs, and we couldn't afford to have any. So in the nanosecond I was forced to wait, my stomach churned.

I hoped the flower wasn't ours.

I worried that it was.

I wondered what I would do if it wasn't, since I'd already confessed to Frank about our flower service. Halfway through the download, I worried that Frank had killed the flower himself just to catch me at all the trademark violations.

He wouldn't have done that, would he?

Not Frank. We were old pals. He would have warned me first. Besides, I was small fish compared with the others he chased. And he preferred a homicide investigation to all others.

Then the number appeared on the screen, and my stomach churned even more. The flower *was* ours. Ours, and lost, and turning up dead in a hotel room rented by Davis Drew.

It just didn't add up. If Drew wanted to murder his wife, why not do it in their home? Or hire someone?

Or why didn't he simply divorce her? It would ruin her reputation, not his. He could go back to being a multi-media mogul with no soul, and she would have to explain how her religion failed them both.

I shut down that program and opened the indoctrination program. The flower had been given a standard chip, and had been set on minimal communication. She couldn't even have registered at the Hurrah by herself.

Finally, I called up the security tape of Gerda giving the

flower instructions on finding the apartment. It was, as Gerda said, standard. And the flower had nodded as if she understood.

She had been an amazingly good likeness of Shardeen. Aged to perfection, clothing exact, even the nail polish its garish combination of purple, green and gold spangles. Someone had found her a rip-off gold cross, the kind that little Catholic girls used to wear after their confirmation, and that Shardeen still wore in the hollow of her neck, and the masquerade was perfect.

As long as the flower didn't open her mouth.

I reopened the pix. No gold cross, no nail polish. The cross could have been removed, along with the clothing. I would have to check.

I let the computer disappear into its hiding place, and reset the security protocol. Then I swiveled my chair, and used the regular computer to view the autopsy once more. The flower had been brought in wearing a linen pantsuit, no make-up, and no shoes.

Curiouser and curiouser.

I leaned back in my chair. There were too many players. That thought kept coming back to me. If Davis Drew murdered his wife, he would lose everything. If he murdered a flower to make a point, he would still lose everything. Flowers were considered human under the law, but it took something extreme to prosecute a flower case.

This was extreme.

And even if he'd done it to make a point about the tabloids' use of flowers, he was being silly. He owned more tabloids than any other mogul outside of England. He had to have his own flower business, fully funded and with the same silly rules as ours.

Flowers.

Frank was right. The key was in flowers, but I wasn't sure yet how.

Flowers, and the last Hurrah.

I had some suspicions, things I knew Frank wouldn't think of. He never cross-checked cases, especially if there wasn't a body involved. He also wouldn't check when Shardeen was due in New York, and he'd try to ask Drew himself what kind of relationship he had with his wife.

I knew Drew'd lie. Hell, if I were married to Shardeen, I'd lie. But facts rarely did. Real facts, the kind a good data person could uncover.

I sent e-mail to Research, requesting three pieces of information: how many people, if any, got stomach flu the week that the flower died; how many appearances Shardeen made that same week; and when was the last time Davis Drew spent some quality time with his wife.

I told them I wanted the answers within ten minutes.

I got them within five.

Davis Drew never spent quality time with his wife. They didn't even live in the same house. Theirs, it seemed, was a perfect marriage on the surface with some unusual gaps underneath. They appeared in public together, yes; they had children together, yes; and they gave interviews filled with anecdotes about their undying love, yes.

But.

No one else remembered the incidents portrayed in the anecdotes. No one ever saw them together outside the public eye. No pix of the happy couple at home or on some nude beach or frolicking contentedly with the kids.

In fact, the kids had a house—and presumably a nanny— all their own.

Heads were going to roll in Celebrity. This was better

than some concocted story about a flower Shardeen and a lover in some hotel room. This was *real*.

Although convincing the non-tabloid press of that would be really, really interesting. Sometimes we paid, big-time, for our so-called reporting techniques.

As to the second question, Research flagged its own findings. The return e-mail said:

> Here's what we got, boss. Double and triple checked. Still seems strange. Got to be a glitch in the system some- where. We'll see if we can find it.

And then they gave me a list of Shardeen's personal ap- pearances in the week the flower died:

138 church services all on a single Sunday morning, all in small rural churches without much attendant publicity; 29 special church appearances throughout the week, usually in the evening; a five-day recording session at her Nashville studios; a concert in Central Park; and a religious revival, done as a favor for Rufus G. Falwell, whose family had been in the revival business for more than sixty years. No one snubbed the Reverend Rufus G.

Along with the listing were the dates, times and places. Only the really public events did not conflict with anything. The night of the religious revival, Shardeen had nothing else scheduled, and the same with the afternoon in Central Park.

I printed out the figures. I wanted them in my hand.

I didn't like what I was thinking.

If there was anything I knew, it was flowers. They could be programmed with a shtick, just like anything else. If they were supposed to be part of a pix, they would get one kind of programming. If they were supposed to sing, and repeat a few words from the Bible, they could do that too. Evergreens especially could learn a particular program and stick with it.

I sent a question back to Research before turning to their third answer to my original e-mail.

Does Shardeen get paid an appearance fee?

Then I opened the third piece of e-mail.

Seventeen personal physicians made house calls at the Hurrah in the last two weeks of the flower's life; two-dozen conference attendees got food poisoning after the banquet supper; and three penthouse clients were hospitalized with severe stomach ailments. Research had more numbers, but the rest were speculation. These 44 incidents were directly tied to the Hurrah.

Someone had been putting designer poison in the food that came out of the Hurrah's kitchens. It wasn't in the e-mail, but it was obvious.

I printed up that letter too.

Then I paged Frank, my stomach jumping with excitement. He answered immediately—or rather one of his junior officers did, saying Frank was nearly done with Davis Drew and would come to my office when he finished.

I hoped Frank had as good a session as I did.

My computer pinged.

Research had sent the last piece of information.

And I felt like a reporter again.

When Frank arrived, I was redoing *Gossip Hourly*'s budget. I was using figures from the real budget and the hidden budget so that I could get the work done. Money that went into flower production and storage; evergreen production and storage; reporter's fees; research; web space; overhead. The amounts were staggering, and the subscriptions had leveled. About five years ago, the folks who logged on every day, every hour, remained about the same. Sure we got the occasional blip from the spectacular story, but we got fewer and fewer of those.

We needed a change.

I was about to break into *The Star*'s monthly budget report when my door opened and Frank came in unannounced. He closed the door behind him. His color was up, his eyes were too bright. He was annoyed.

"Davis Drew had fifteen lawyers who all disagreed," he snapped before I could ask a single question. "They spent the entire meeting arguing about whether Drew could talk on the record, then ended the whole thing after I had him state his name and occupation."

"Got another meeting set up?" I asked, knowing I was playing with fire.

"Of course, and if they try this horseshit again, I'm gonna to get all fifteen of them lawyers for hampering a police investigation."

"Can you do that?"

"I sure as hell can try."

I suppressed a smile. One thing I had learned in all the years of my business: avoid people as sources as much as possible.

"Well, I did have some luck," I said. I waved a hand expansively. "Sit down."

Frank did, with a grunt and a moan. The man needed a vacation. Hell, I needed a vacation, although I wouldn't know what to do with one.

"I got three separate things for you," I said, "and I want your permission to let us break the stories."

"Fine," he said. "When the time comes."

"When the time comes," I said. Then I did smile. "And I want you to give *Gossip Hourly* credit for helping you solve the case."

His eyes narrowed. "Only if I can talk about your flower practices too."

"You'll open us up for lawsuits," I said, no longer worried about them. Amazing how a half hour can change your life.

"You'll get enough profit to cover the losses," he said.

"Deal," I said.

He narrowed his eyes. He knew I capitulated too easily. Slowly he folded his beefy hands over his chest. "You ain't exactly ingratiating yourself to me. I had a hard day."

I nodded. "First, the Hurrah. There's been some trouble in the old Trump empire, hasn't there? Some jockeying for position?"

"Rumors of some stock manipulation scheme," Frank said. "Something about devaluing the company so it can get bought out."

"And the crown jewel of Trump New York is?"

"The Hurrah," Frank said.

I slipped him the hard copy, the one with all the illness numbers.

He stared at it for a moment. "Where'd you get this?"

"Our guys in Research know how to use a computer." I didn't tell him that we had access, legal and illegal, to nearly every database in the country, and a good half of the developed world.

"No longer looks like a flower murder, does it?" I said.

"Yeah, but you'd think Drew's people would know this," Frank mumbled. "He probably had a touch of the poison himself."

"But he was hiding something else," I said. I slipped him the second hard copy.

"Is this a joke?" he said, looking at Shardeen's appearances.

I shook my head. "And she gets paid a fee for each one."

"Flowers," he whispered.

"Manufactured, I'll wager, by Davis Drew's own flower-making enterprise."

"How'd you know he's got one?" Frank asked.

"What made you think we do?" I countered.

He grinned. A wide, toothy look that was the reason I liked him even though we'd been at odds for a long, long time. "You're quick."

"And Drew likes to make a buck."

"So there's no Shardeen?"

"Don't go daffy on me now, Frank," I said. "Flowers are *clones*. There has to be a Shardeen. And you'll know where she was if you look at that schedule closely enough."

He peered at it. "Recording studio session."

"Right," I said. "Plus the concert in the park, plus Rufus G's revival."

"Everyone else got a flower."

"Yup."

Frank frowned at me. "I still don't get it," he said. "If he had flowers, he knew what one was. He didn't need to bring your flower to his room."

I leaned back in my chair, and put my feet on the desk. Frank's face grew redder. "Think about it, Frank. Our flower was lost."

"And Drew thought she was one of his? Ain't there no way to check that sorta thing?"

I wasn't going to answer that, not for all the companionship in the world. "Flowers are illegal, Frank. Would

207

someone like Drew leave a trail?"

"Guess not," Frank said, but he sounded unconvinced. Hell, I was unconvinced on that part. The only thing I could figure was that Drew brought the flower back to his room so that he could check her number, and get her off the street before someone found her. When he realized that her number wasn't one of his, then he had to figure out what to do with her.

By then, she was probably quite ill from eating the poison in room service food, and he didn't dare take her to a hospital.

Frank was mulling over the information. Three separate incidences that formed one case. He shook his head, and stood. "Gotta hand it to you," he said. "If this stuff checks out, you're one brilliant guy. We'd never have found this on our own."

I put my hands behind my head, waiting.

"And a deal's a deal," Frank said. "I want some time to double-check this stuff, but go ahead and break the stories. Be prepared for flak and lawsuits on your flowers."

I smiled. "I'm prepared."

He shook his head. "You're one strange guy, Colin."

I shrugged. "I know," I said.

Everyone remembers the stories. The poisoning at the Hurrah, which resulted in hundreds of arrests, from the execs who masterminded the plan to the kitchen staff who carried it out. Arrests, lawsuits, famous people, and the closing of a hotel—it would have been enough right there, but it wasn't.

We published the story on the death of the flower, complete with autopsy report and morgue pix. Our researchers found Drew's flower facility (which, thankfully, wasn't ours) and the ensuing uproar was even better than we'd hoped. The Christian community treated Shardeen like a devil, numbers of related ministries toppled, and cries of hypocrisy filled the land.

Some of those cries, of course, were directed at us. But we managed to put a nice spin on the flower story, showing how well we treated ours, and vowing not to use flowers ever again.

And we don't use flowers. At least, not technically. We have a few evergreens—it's tough to get any kind of pix of the president these days—but now we rely mostly on reported stories. I had to let the bulk of my staff go, the Gerdas and Jacques of the world, people who could write and manage three screens of info at one time, but who couldn't think and make the kind of connections I made.

Now research runs *Gossip Hourly*. We've bulked up our staff with folks who know how to investigate databases, how to ferret out information, how to read autopsy reports in seconds, and we're the hottest publication to hit since the turn of the century when the first vocal, vid, and written mag downloaded in less than six seconds. The articles we've been running still fit the new legal standard—they are "true to the best of our knowledge." Subscriptions are up, and so are profits now that we no longer have much of our cash tied up on flower support.

It's the best situation I could hope for all around.

And flowers. Those changes were long in coming, and of course, *Gossip Hourly* takes much of the credit, however undeserved. The Senate Hearings are nearly done, and it's becoming clearer that the regulations on cloning will become more stringent. Enforcement and prosecution will go up. Of course, the black flower market will merely get more clever, but that's a story for the future. Right now, we have waaay too much current stuff to report.

Like the use of flowers by celebrities for appearance fees, fan stroking, and other strange activities. Like the way politicians can fundraise all over their home state, and never leave their estates.

When we got hit with our first trademark violation suit related to the use of celebrity flowers in the aftermath of this case, our attorney used my argument: how do we know who violated the trademark? The flower existed. Maybe it was even created by the celebrity. There is no proof that *Gossip Hourly* created the clones or even knew that the flower was a clone at all.

We didn't even have to pay court costs in that case. I doubt we'll have to pay them in any of the pending cases either.

And me, I haven't had to go in for ulcer capping at all this year. The doc says the changes I've made in my lifestyle agree with me. I guess. It's more fun reporting the news than it is making it up. And more creative too. What people really do with their lives is a hell of a lot more unbelievable than anything we could invent.

Our rising subscription base proves it.

Maybe someday I'll even assign someone to stories of flower exploitation. It'd have to be an idealistic cub, someone who didn't know about *Gossip Hourly*'s flower history. And I'd have to figure out what to do with the evergreens, something I'm not willing to do yet.

The only downside about all of this is that I don't see Frank much. He became famous during the resolution of the Davis Drew flower murder, and he spends a lot of his time dodging the press. With all the changes in trademark infringement, and our decreased use of flowers, he has nothing to harass me with.

210

He'll come up with something, I'm sure. As soon as the press lays off him.

Kinda nice to have the tables turned for once. Real nice, actually. Especially since I didn't need a flower to do it.

Amazing how life can change in the space of a day, an hour, a minute.

You'd think I'd know that, given the business I'm in.

But every now and then, I have to learn the lesson again.

The One That Got Away

It happened at the Thursday night blackjack tournament, and we were miffed. Not because it happened, but because of *when* it happened. And to get to that will take a bit of explaining, both about the tournament and about us.

There are about ten of us, and we call ourselves the Tuesday/Thursday regulars because we never miss a tournament. The local Native American casino—the Spirit Winds—held an open tournament every Tuesday and Thursday. Anyone could play if he put up twenty bucks, and if he won, he got a share of the pot. The pot consisted of the buy-in fees, and the buy-back fees plus another hundred added by the casino. The casino made no money on the tournament. The game was a freebie designed to get people into the casino—and it got me there twice a week.

Me, and nine others. There were more regulars than us, of course, but we were the ones who never skipped a week. I was a pretty good player—I'd made a living counting cards in the mid-seventies—and I'd swear that Tigo Jones had professional card-playing experience as well. Five more of the regulars played basic strategy, and the rest, well, they relied upon luck or God or their moods to supply their strategy. It worked for them every once in a while.

In blackjack, you learn to honor luck.

The good players just try to minimize it. They try to rely on skill. But luck can win out, in the end, if you're not careful.

On most nights, the pot's only worth about two hundred to the winner, a hundred to second place, and fifty to third, with four dinner comps to sop the folks who made it to the final round. What that means is that there's good money in this for me and Tigo because we place every four tournaments we play. A few regulars are losing money each time they play, and about five—those basic strategy guys—are giving their gambling fund an occasional shot in the arm.

It's all in good fun, and we've become a family of sorts—the kind of family that barflies make or old ladies make when they work on church social after church social. We look after each other, and we gossip about each other, and we tolerate each other, whether we like each other or not.

We also know who's crazy and who isn't, and, except for Joey, the kid who is pissing his inheritance away twenty dollars at a time, no one who shows up for the blackjack tournaments at Spirit Winds is crazy.

Or, at least, that's what we hope.

That night, I noticed a few strange things before I even made it to Spirit Winds. For one thing, the ocean was so black it was impossible to see. Now, the ocean is never black. It reflects light—and even if the sky is completely dark, the ocean isn't because it's reflecting the light of nearby homes. In fact, I like the ocean on cloudy nights because it has a luminescence all its own, a glow that makes it look alive from within.

The second strange thing was that there was no wind. None. Zero, zip, zilch. We usually have a breeze in Seavy Village and often have more than that. The ocean again. It is a major part of our lives.

And the final strange thing was the power outage that swept through the neighborhoods like anxious fingers pinching out candles. I didn't know about that until later—the casino has back-up generators—and if I had known, well, it would have made no difference.

I would have been at the tournament anyway.

I have nothing better to do.

You see, I call myself retired, but really what I am is hiding out. I'm good enough to play in big tournaments, but when Spirit Winds holds its semi-annual $10,000 tournament, I'm conveniently out of town. That way, I don't have to fill out a 1099, and I don't have to show three pieces of ID, and all the correct tax information. Because I don't have three valid pieces of ID, and I haven't filed taxes since 1978, the year I fled Nevada with the wrong kind of folks at my heels. I moved too fast to get any fake ID, and so I lived off cash for far too long. By the time I had settled down, I didn't know anybody in that business any more. The government had closed the loopholes making fake IDs simple for anyone with half a brain, and I really didn't want to put fingers out to the criminal element, since it was the criminal element I'd been running from.

I confessed to a local banker with hippie sympathies, let him think I had been underground since my college activist days, and had him set me up a checking account. It's amazing what a man can do with a checking account—the lies he can tell to get him a real life in a small town.

But it couldn't get me a driver's license, nor could it get me a credit card. I still use cash much of the time, and a lot of that cash comes from my safety deposit box in the afore-mentioned bank. The gambling at the small casino is just incidental. I figure I'm old enough now that no one would recognize me and my problem is so out of date that the folks who were looking for me are either dead or in prison. But I have learned to be cautious by nature. I don't rub anyone the wrong way.

And I never, ever call attention to myself.

The tournament was big that night, bigger than it had ever been. Later I learned the reason: the power outage. The casino was packed on a Thursday because much of Seavy Village had lost their lights, their heat, and their cable. I had been in the casino since mid-afternoon. I'd been on a roll at one of the regular tables, parlaying my lucky hundred-dollar chip into six thousand. Normally that puts you in tax declaration territory, but I would get five hundred on one table, then pocket it, and move to the next. I was hot that afternoon, and it felt good.

Lucky streaks are important. Knowing how to maximize them is even more important, and that's what I was doing. Perfecting the old skills.

When I reached six grand, my brain shut off, and I decided to replenish it with food. I had a solitary dinner at the buffet, and then wandered to the tournament tables.

There were a lot of unfamiliar faces around the table, and I was burdened with a small fortune in chips, stuck in my pockets and my fanny pack. I couldn't take anything to the car because I didn't have one, and I also didn't have time to walk home. I'd been in that situation before, and I'd learned not to be too friendly. The last time I'd told one of the regulars about my run and a pit boss overheard. I had to spend a good fifteen minutes making a show of losing the money at various tables.

Normally the pit bosses don't tell on me. They tolerate me and Tigo and the other local professionals. It's the out-of-towners they kick out of the casino. Oregonians and their dislike of "foreigners." Gotta love 'em.

That night, though I wasn't taking any chances. I leaned against one of the slot machines and smoked a cigarette, adding to the thick, slightly bluish air already growing around the tables. The casino is new and modern—no tokens for slots, only cash and cards—high ceilings, good traffic flow. The place feels more like a spa than a casino, especially the casinos of my heyday. I still miss the chink-chink of tokens as they clink out of the machines. I'm not sure I'll ever get used to those electronic beeps. But not even the modern recycling system was taking care of the cigarette smoke. In a blue-collar town like Seavy Village, card players get nervous when more than $50 is on the line.

That night, forty players had signed up for the tournament, and the pot tipped a grand for the first time since the casino opened.

I'll leave out the detailed descriptions of the rounds, although I can recite all of it, every card, every bet, from the first round, the semi-final round, and the buy-back round. I know by what percentage Tigo beat the odds when he doubled down on eighteen and got a three. I know the exact moment luck abandoned Cherise and it wasn't when she drew a twenty to the dealer's twenty-one. I even know that I made a small mistake on the twenty-ninth hand, and if the cards hadn't gone my way, I would have been out—deservedly so—and it would have peeved me to no end.

I rarely make mistakes.

I can't afford it.

No. I won't say much about the game except that tempers flared early, even among the regulars, because of the amount of money on the table. And people left angry when they were eliminated because everyone could taste their share of the pot.

When it came to the final hand, only the players and the regulars were left.

Tigo and I were on the table, of course, along with the idiot Joey whose luck was running better than usual, and Smoky Butler who was a dealer at another casino on the other side of the coast range. The rest of the players weren't regulars. Two were bad betters and even worse strategists who managed to get the right cards at the right time, and the other one was a black-haired woman who'd caught all of our attention.

She looked like she should be in Monte Carlo, not Seavy Village, Oregon. She wore a black cocktail dress cut in a modified V that revealed more cleavage than I had seen in years. Her hair was pulled into a chignon and over it she wore a cloe hat complete with small veil. Her lips were dark red, and she smoked a cigarette through a cigarette holder.

And she wasn't lucky.

She was good.

Almost as good as me.

The cards were running hot and cold that night, and our pal Joey's luck ran out first. He was off the table in five hands. Then we lost the first of the two bad betters. The second was holding in, but not worth our time. He was out by the eleventh hand.

The rest of us, though. The rest of us had a game.

For our buy-in, the casino gives us $500 in tournament chips (which you can't carry to the real tables) per game. The winner, of course, is the person with the most chips after fifteen hands.

By end of the eleventh hand, I had fifteen hundred eighty-five dollars in phony chips.

Tigo had fifteen hundred seventy-five.

Smoky Butler had fifteen hundred and fifty.

And the woman, well, she had two thousand even.

For the first time since I'd left Nevada, I was in a blackjack game where everyone knew how to play. That meant they knew how to draw cards, they knew how to bet, and they knew strategy.

I damned near licked my lips and rubbed my hands together in glee. Instead, I crouched over my chips as if I were protecting them from prying eyes.

We all put out our bets.

The lady put out a hundred.

Smoky put out a hundred and fifty.

Tigo a hundred and twenty-five.

And me, a hundred and fifteen.

Then Rosco, the dealer, began the hand. I was first base (a revolving position), and he gave me an ace of clubs.

Followed by an ace of diamonds for Tigo, an ace of spades for Smoky, and an ace of hearts for the lady.

"They should be playing poker," someone said from behind me.

Rosco gave himself a three of hearts. Then he reached toward the shue for my next card.

At that moment, the lights went out. The place was pitch black except for several small red dots made by the tips of a hundred cigarettes. I fell across my cards and chips, and Rosco yelled, "Freeze!" to the tournament players. The pit bosses were yelling and the dealers were shouting orders, and some old lady near the slots was wailing at the top of her lungs.

All the time, I kept thinking that this shouldn't be happening. It couldn't be happening. The casino had generators. They should have kicked in. (At the time, I didn't know they'd already kicked in, which meant that they shouldn't have gone off—at least, not all at once.)

Then the lights came back up, or I thought they did, until I realized that the overhead lights in the casino were white, not green. Everyone looked as if they were peering at each other through a fish tank. Even the mystery lady looked green. She was holding her cigarette holder over her chips, and glaring at us all angrily, as if we had caused the problem.

The pit bosses were looking mighty scared. I don't know how much money they had to protect, in chips mostly because the cash disappeared into slots beneath the tables, but I knew it was a lot. And there were more civilians in the casino than pit bosses. Security guards had stationed themselves near the casino banks, and other employees had fanned themselves around the room.

I had never seen anything like it, but it made sense. The casino had to have a drill policy for all types of emergencies.

The place was hot and smoky and everything was green. I kept my hands over my chips and scanned for the source of the light.

As I did, a wind came up. First it licked my hair—or what's left of it—and then it cleared the smoke. At first, I thought the air recycling system had turned back on. Then I realized something greater was happening here.

The source of the green lights were small dervishes the size of my coffee saucers at home. They looked like the alien spaceship out of *E.T.*, only shrunk down into toy specials for MacDonalds' Happy Meals. Except they worked. Their top was a dark cone, and their base was a rotating series of lights, all various shades of green.

And there must have been thousands of them in that small space. Maybe even millions of them.

They hovered over various tables, avoided the slot machines, and disappeared into the back. The poker room was filled with them. I could see them from my vantage points, lined up like tiny aircraft carriers facing a city, the poker players backing against the wall, hands up.

Five crafts found their places over our table, and a sixth placed itself above the dealer. The woman pulled a small pistol from her handbag, and a pit boss immediately grabbed it from her—firearms are illegal on Indian land. He pointed it, wobbling for a moment, at one of the little crafts, then Rosco said, "If you shoot one and it explodes and we get that green goo all over us and we die, you're going to regret that."

"He'll regret it more if the bullet hits one of us," Smoky said.

"It could ricochet," Tigo added.

The pit boss let the weapon fall to his side. The woman glared at him.

"I wouldn't have missed," she said, as if she blamed him for taking away her opportunity.

The little crafts were above us, whirling and creating the breeze. Rosco had his hand on the money slot. So, it seemed, did every other dealer in the place. We all stared at the things.

"What are they?" Tigo whispered.

I took the question as rhetorical, and apparently everyone else did too because no one answered him.

One of the pit bosses was on the phone, talking with the 911 dispatch. He was whispering loudly, so loudly he may as well have been shouting: "No, really, I'm not kidding. Please . . ."

Aside from the whirs, the soft mumbles of scared patrons, and the wailing woman, the casino was eerily quiet.

No electronic beeps and buzzes, no blaring music, no tinkling chords of winning slots. The silence unnerved me more than anything.

"What do they want?" Tigo whispered.

"Ask them," Smoky snapped.

"I feel like I'm in a James Bond movie," the woman said, and that started a ripple of panic through the pit bosses. They apparently hadn't thought of the things as high-tech theft devices.

"If you were in a James Bond movie, my dear," I said, "you'd have better lighting." No one looked good in that ugly green. Not even the most beautiful woman in the place.

Then, as if on cue, green lights flared out of the bottom of the tiny crafts. I backed away from the table, chips forgotten. So did everyone else. Rosco let go of his hold on the money slot, and one of the pit bosses screamed at him but—I noted—did not make a move toward the money, the table or any of the lights.

The lights hit the table and I expected to see big burning holes appear. I was ready to run for cover—all of this going through my mind in the half second it took, mind you—when I realized what was going on.

The cards rose off the surface, whirling and twirling as if they were in a tornado. For a moment, the entire casino was filled with swirling cards. It looked like an elaborate fan dance, or as if green sea gulls were swarming the beach or like an electronic kaleidoscope performance designed especially for us.

Then one by one the cards slid into the crafts through a slot in the sides. They made a slight ca-thunk! as they entered. Then the green tractor lights—what else could they be called?—went out, and the little green ships whirled away.

The doormen and the folks in the parking lot at the time all say the little ships sped out the doors and into a larger ship that had been hovering over the ocean. A number of green slots opened on it, letting the little ships through, and then they disappeared into the night.

The ocean, which had been dark, regained its luminesence, and slowly the lights flickered on all over town.

At least, that's what the outdoor folks said.

Inside, it was chaos. People started shouting and screaming, and that wailing woman continued. A few people stampeded toward the door, and one relatively fit young man got trampled just enough to later attempt a suit against the casino.

Then the lights came back on. The slot machines groaned as they started up, then beeped through their start-up protocol. The slot players, the video poker players, and the keno players all continued with their games except for a few sensible folks who decided to call it a night and left.

I have no idea what happened inside the poker room, but at the tournament table, we counted our chips. The pit bosses put the game on hold as they made sure the money was fine.

It soon became clear the only thing missing from the casino were the cards.

All of them.

Including the decks stored in the back rooms, and the discards waiting to be trucked off the place, and even the little souvenir cards in the gift shop.

Gone.

All gone.

The pit boss who had called 911 was off the phone, saying the police were going to arrive soon, but I suspected it would take them some time. If, as people were saying, things were a mess all over town, it would take the police a while to get anywhere.

"We still have money on the table," Smoky said.

"And a game to finish," Tigo said.

"How do you propose we do that with no cards?" Rosco asked.

"We know what was dealt," the woman said

"But we don't know the order in the rest of the shue," I said.

"We're going to shuffle a new shue and start over," Rosco said, "just as soon as we get cards."

"We need the other three players," Tigo said. I glanced around me. Joe was standing behind me as he usually did after he got knocked out of a tournament, but the others were nowhere to be seen.

"We're going to have to put this game on hold until the cops arrive anyway," the pit boss said.

"Until we get cards," Rosco added.

"Besides, everyone'll have to report what they saw," Smoky said.

At that point, the woman and I both stood up. "I think my luck has just run out," the woman said.

"Mine, too," I said.

We left the table and headed toward the door.

"Hey!" Tigo said behind us. "We can't replay the game without you guys!"

"I think the game is forfeit," the woman said.

"Yeah, have the casino put the pot in for next week," I said, knowing they never would.

Then she and I walked through the casino, side by side. The conversations were strangely muted, only a few people discussing what they saw. As we stepped outside, we ran into chaos, cars cramming the parking lot, attendants staring at the sky, a warm bath of light all over the town.

A familiar bath of light.

I had missed it more than I realized.

I turned to her. "There's a nice coffee place about a block from here. Care for a walk?"

"I'd love it," she said.

And we had a nice cup of coffee, and a nice evening, and a nice night, and an even better morning. I never learned her name and she never learned mine, but we both knew that we had left the casino for the exact same reason.

We didn't need to see the police.

Or the media.

Or anyone else, for that matter.

"What do you think they wanted with the cards?" she asked long around midnight.

"I don't know," I said. "Maybe they use bigger shues than we do."

And a little later, I said, "That, by far, has to be the strangest thing I ever saw in a casino."

"Really?" she responded. "I've seen stranger."

But she never elaborated and I didn't ask her to.

Some stories are better kept close to the vest.

You see, that isn't the strangest thing I'd ever seen in a casino either.

But it's the only one I'll admit too.

And I only do that because I'm a regular and it's a shared group experience. A bit of local legend—the one game that never finished, the pot that got away.

Well away. The casino had to shut down both the poker and blackjack tables for two days while it ordered cards from all over the country. During that time, regulars gave interviews on every show from *CNN* to *Hard Copy*. Except for me.

I laid low for a while even after my lady left. Laid low and watched the skies.

And wondered—

What would have happened on the thirteenth hand if we had all blackjacked on the twelfth?

What would have happened then?

Results

Do it now, do it later. Do it when you're twenty-five, do it when you're forty-five. Each choice involves risk. Each choice involves an element of chance. That's what her parents fail to understand. They don't realize that the world she faces is different from the one they knew.

Jess stands, feet apart, in the subway car. It's half full, but all the seats are taken, and she holds the metal bar. She loves this antique method of travel in a city that hasn't updated itself in any real way for nearly a hundred years. New York, she heard a colleague say, is becoming America's first European city, a lot of people in a small space, history crammed against the future, land buried so deep no one remembers what grass looks like.

She loves it here. The past mingling with the future. Making the present bright.

Her parents, stuck in Des Moines, surrounded by grass, just don't understand.

She leans her head against the metal bar. It's cool against her scalp. The clickity-clack of the cars along the old track is somehow comforting.

She should have called her folks last night. They paged her three separate times after the test. But she wanted to wait until she had results, until she had something new to say instead of going over the same old arguments. She's twenty-five, old enough to make her own choices. Old enough to make her own mistakes.

Her parents thought the testing was mistake number one. It certainly was expensive enough, but the doctor said he advised it for any couple about to get married. If they're genetically incompatible, he'd said, they have the choice of terminating the relationship, planning for an expensive future, or tying tubes—practicing irreversible infertility, as one of her friends called it.

Options. That's what her parents don't get. It's all about options.

And results.

Her stomach flutters. She wonders why tests are always a production, why now, in the days of instant communication, results must wait a day, a week, sometimes a month. The doctor said that while communication might be instantaneous, science is not. She wonders if that's true, but doesn't really know.

The train stops at Times Square. She gets off, walks away from the smell of exhaust, a smell that will remain on her clothing all day. As she emerges from the tunnel, the city assaults her: sunlight thin as it trickles between the buildings, cars honking, people yelling, a jackhammer rat-a-tat-tatting two blocks away.

Her mother asks, *How can you raise a child there? There are no lawns, no quiet places,* and Jess says, *There are plays and museums and concerts.* And her mother says, *How're you going to afford that, honey?*

A little boy on a leash stops in front of Jess, and she nearly topples over him. He's blond and curly-haired, with enormous blue eyes that twinkle as he investigates a spot of gum on the sidewalk. New Yorkers form a path around him, like a river diverted by a stone, but she glances over her shoulder as she passes, sees the young man who is his caretaker, a black-haired, blue-eyed man, who does not have the look of wealth. A nanny perhaps? Or a lucky man, a man whose genetic code needed no tampering at all.

She wants to turn around, go to the man, ask, *Did you choose the right options or did you wait and see what nature would provide? Did you trust the process?* As if there is still a process to trust.

She lets herself into a side door, an unmarked rusted metal door that has been on Broadway since time immemorial. She goes through back hallways that lead to the box office of a theater whose name has changed ten times in the last five years, each name with the claim of authenticity.

At the end of her hallway, the box office. Hot and squalid, air-conditioning fifty years old and inefficient. She puts on small headphones so that she can hear her phone conversations without interrupting anyone else. She actually works on an ancient keyboard, the office computer plugged into a dozen services from the venerable TicketMaster to the brand new E-SEAT. It is her job to take the calls requiring her to deny someone's pleasure, helping the angry, the frustrated, or the very wealthy find the right ticket to the right show and then, promptly at 5:00, go to the box office itself and do the same thing in person, hand out tickets ordered by mail, soothe the customers who arrive on the wrong night, and press a small button beneath the shelf to get the manager who will discreetly lead those who get angry onto the street.

The job pays very little and she only has it because human beings still expect to find, beyond e-mail and the digitized voices, a human face, a real person which, as her parents used to say, is becoming increasingly rare.

229

Her fiancé Bryan's job is marginally better. He is a short-order cook in a restaurant near the George Washington Bridge. He gets home as she's leaving for work. They only have evenings together.

She puts on her headphones, hands shaking, the day already seeming longer than it should. Results, she knows, could come today, tomorrow, or next week.

Results.

What are you going to do with them? Her father asked. *What if there's nothing catastrophic? What if you're somewhat compatible? Then what will you decide? Will you base your entire future on a set of numbers, on percentages that have no meaning?*

She had no answer for him when he first asked the question, and she has none now. She goes through her morning's backlog, checks to see if she must return calls, and finds no personal messages. Then she deliberately fills her mind with times for this season's remake of *Fiddler on the Roof*, the latest Oscar Wilde revival, the newest—and probably last—play by Mamet, the one that deals, unsurprisingly, with the indignities of manly old age.

By the time the call comes, she has put the test out of her mind and is surprised to hear Bryan's voice. He knows that personal calls are forbidden, so he speaks fast:

"The results are in. Meet you at our special place at one."

"How bad are they?" she asks, voice breathless. She hasn't realized until now how shallowly she's been breathing, how much she has invested in this single moment, in knowing what the future will bring.

But he does not answer her. In deference to her work—and how much they need her paycheck—he has already hung up.

She takes another deep breath, feels the air go in and out of her lungs. Only once before has she been this conscious of her body, and that was when the lab tech pricked her finger—painless, the woman had promised, but a prick was a prick, sharp and sudden and a little bit invasive. Jess watched the blood well, a dark, rich, red, and she wondered what secrets it would reveal.

Now she'll know.

Bryan already knows.

And he is going to make her wait two hours before he tells.

Their place is Washington Square Park. She used to work in the neighborhood, and went there for lunch, sometimes a dog or a knish from a vendor, sometimes a sandwich bought at a nearby deli, sometimes a banana brought from home. What she ate then wasn't important, it was the brief moment outdoors, even if it meant sitting in a park more concrete than grass with trees that were spindly because of the dirt in the air.

Bryan worked nearby too, and they sometimes sat on the same bench. They never talked, not until some tourist—coincidentally from Iowa, like they both were—couldn't figure out how to use her new camera and desperately wanted a picture to e-mail to her uncle Syd.

They still laugh about that. *Technology,* Bryan says, *is what brought us together.*

Technology, Jess always adds, *that most people don't understand.*

Now they are facing another side of technology. One she is sure will tell her if the life she wants is something she can have.

She almost splurges and takes a cab, but at the last moment, she remembers how many more expenses there could be. The subway is old. It creaks and groans and her friend Joan swears it'll one day just fall apart, but it gets Jess to the park with time to spare.

She does not buy lunch. She knows she will not be able to eat. She sits on their bench and waits for Bryan who is uncharacteristically late.

He has chosen this place for its symmetry. Symmetry is important to Bryan. It is, in his mind, an element of perfection. Only she cannot guess exactly what the symmetry is.

Are they here because they will decide what their child will be? Or are they here because they will commiserate together, knowing that to bring a child into this world will either be too costly or too dreadful?

She does not like the waiting. Fortunately she told her boss she might be late. He knows that this is an important moment for her, and he understands.

The park is full of children: in strollers, in parents' arms, running around the benches. These are not the perfect children she usually sees. They have bad skin, mismatched features, eyes that are slightly crossed. They are not perfect. There is no intelligence in their faces.

These are the children of the poor, the desperate, those who will not listen to their doctors or cannot afford one. Those who believe that they must go through with a pregnancy no matter what. Those who cannot afford in-the-womb enhancements. These are the children who will be, in the-not-too-distant future, A Burden On Society.

Maybe that is why Bryan chose this place. To remind her about the costs of making the wrong choice.

She sees him emerge from the subway, head down. He is balding ever so slightly, just a lighter spot at the crown of his head. He used to joke before they got the test that he will make certain none of his children will go bald.

He hasn't made that joke in weeks.

He makes his way to the bench without a second glance at the children. When he reaches the bench, he does not touch her.

Instead, he hands her his palmtop. On it is an e-mail already opened. She skips the salutation and the signature, reads the body instead.

Percentages fill her brain. She glances at the high ones first, expecting something awful—a high chance of spina bifida or Alzheimer's Disease. Instead she sees none of that. The high percentages are silly: 97 percent chance of child having blond hair. 96 percent chance of child having brown eyes. 98 percent chance of child being tall.

It is in the middle percentages that the problems strike: 47 percent chance of having an IQ above 120. 36 percent chance of having artistic talent, acting talent, musical talent. 24 percent chance of having strong athletic ability.

Mediocre. The test results show that their child will be mediocre. At best.

She scrolls through the e-mail, searches for anything positive, anything that will negate this bizarre news. She sees instead the layman's explanation of how the figures are arrived at. Her IQ, lower than Bryan's, brings down the total score. His physical abilities mismatch with hers; her talents do not go with his. They are genetically incompatible. Already they are, before her first pregnancy, failures as parents.

She does not raise her head. She doesn't want to see the children playing across from her, screaming, laughing, not knowing that, in some undefinable future moment, their poverty will catch up with them and hold them back.

Their parents' decision to bring them into the world will

make them Burdens that no one else can measure.

What you don't understand, honey, her father said when she told him of the test, *is that there is more to children than statistics.*

I remember your first real smile, her mother added. *Whenever I'm sad, I think of that.*

Sometimes, her father said, *the best accomplishments are small ones.*

Bryan takes the palmtop from her hand. He puts a finger under her chin, looks into her eyes. His are brown, just like hers. They both have blue-eyed great-grandparents, hence the small percentage chance of a blue-eyed child.

"Maybe we should just go home," she says. "Forget the museums and the parks. Our parents will love a grandchild, any grandchild—"

He puts his finger over her lips. His skin smells of lemon polish and garlic.

"It won't work," he says softly. "We aren't the right choices for each other. You need someone who'll add to your scores. So do I."

She inclines her head back so that his finger no longer touches her mouth. "Let's think about it."

"No. I want a child I can be proud of. I don't want—" he grimaces at the baby in the stroller beyond, the baby with ears too big for his tiny face "—something I'll always regret."

Besides, her father said. *Statistics are just that, statistics. They're not proof. What if they're wrong?*

They can't be wrong, Daddy.

All right, he says, *but sometimes people beat the odds.*

"Maybe we should try," she says.

He puts the palmtop in his pocket. "I was afraid of this. I was worried that you wouldn't believe the results. We can't afford a lot of enhancements, Jess. We have to go with our combinations. Maybe if we were rich—"

"We can wait," she says. "You'll get a better job. So will I. Then we can try."

He shakes his head. "Don't you remember what the doctor said? Your eggs will deteriorate with time. We'll have to have more enhancements rather than less."

Her eggs and his sperm. Deterioration isn't just a female thing. But she doesn't say that. She knows him too well. He has made up his mind, and has done it without her.

"You can do what you've always wanted," he says. "You can act now instead of work box office. You can become someone."

Someone who can pay for a child who will be perfect. A child she wants to share with Bryan who will, by then, be gone.

"It's all about chances," she says. "Risk. Maybe we should just do it the old-fashioned way. Our parents did."

He nods, but doesn't look at her. She flushes. Suddenly she realizes how he read the report. The failures are not his. They are hers. The way her body combines with his will produce a result he will be ashamed of. Whenever he looks in his child's brown eyes, he will always see this report. 47 percent chance of IQ above 120. And if the child is not as intelligent as Bryan wants, he will blame her.

He will always blame her.

No matter how many museums she goes to, or how often their child smiles. No matter how much simple joy that young life will bring them, Bryan will always see the failure.

He gets up, kisses her on her crown where she—and all the people she has descended from—have a full shock of hair, and makes his way through the crowd.

She sits on their bench, knowing now what the symmetry

235

he sought was. It is over. Sure, they will divide possessions, figure out who inherits the apartment, maybe even sleep together for old times sake. But the future, the bright shining future, is gone.

She sits on the bench for the rest of the hour, watching the children, searching for their parents. Women sit on other benches, occasionally look toward the playing children, smile, and continue their conversations. The smiles are warm ones, contented ones, as if the children's high spirits are infectious.

What would their results have looked like? 98 percent chance of brown hair? 75 percent chance of gray eyes?

Nowhere on that form was an area for percentage chance of bringing joy. Nowhere was there a space for all the years of laughter, now denied.

She has choices of her own to make. All of them involving risk. All of them involving a world that has changed even beyond her understanding.

This morning she thought it irresponsible to have a child without knowing the risks. But she hadn't known the greatest risk of all. The risk of believing the statistics, reading too much into the numbers.

Perfection is not possible.

Would Bryan have been satisfied with a 53 percent chance of an IQ above 120? She never thought to ask.

Until an hour ago, she hadn't even known the answer for herself.

Reflections of Life and Death

"No," Sarah's mother said, her voice barely more than a whisper around the tubes. "You can't. They kill people in there."

Sarah held her mother's good hand—the one without the IV. Small chips dotted her mother's face and body, each scanning vital signs. It made her mother look as if she had chickenpox.

The doctor was watching Sarah. The doctor was a thin thirtyish woman with nut-brown eyes, and light brown skin. Her hair, a delicate blonde, was shoulder length and covered with a nearly invisible clean net so no strands fell free.

"Sarah?" the doctor said, and it made Sarah wonder how a woman ten years younger than herself managed to sound make one word sound so condescending.

"Sarah—" her mother said again. "You can't."

"You can't go home," Sarah said.

"But you could take me."

Sarah closed her eyes. One more thing. It had taken all of her strength to get to the hospital each day before visiting hours closed. She had lost a day of work to be here this afternoon. Her secretarial job was rare, precious, and difficult. It also only paid a quarter of what she really needed. Besides, the children were doubled up in one room in her two-bedroom apartment. If her mother came to stay, someone would have to sleep on the couch.

Her mother's hand clutched, the bones cutting off the circulation in her fingers. Sarah opened her eyes. Her mother's skin was chalk-white; her lips almost blue.

"Please," she said.

"You didn't take Gram," Sarah said, and then bit her tongue.

"I don't think you need me any longer," the doctor said. "Page me, Sarah, when you reach a decision."

"It's not her decision to make," her mother said.

"What do you want to do, Mrs. Chomley?" the doctor asked, addressing Sarah's mother for the first time.

"I want to go home," her mother said.

"That's not possible," the doctor said.

"Then I want to go with Sarah."

The doctor looked at Sarah. Sarah looked away. How come the doctor, who ignored her mother, used a respectful title when she finally addressed her?

"Do you have other family?" the doctor asked.

"No," Sarah said.

"Then it looks, my dear," the doctor said, "as if it's up to you."

1985: Gram's backyard. Icicles hanging off winter trees, sleet making the air a grayish mist. The streetlights burned white, and the cold was so deep Sarah could see her breath.

She couldn't move in her snowsuit and mittens. Gram sat beside her on the ice-crusted snow. They were going to make angels, but Gram had started crying. Sarah had never seen Gram cry.

"I don't see nothing burning," Sarah said, looking skyward. She'd seen the images all day. The happy astronauts waving as they carried their cases into the shuttle. The liftoff, and then the speck, exploding in the sky. She knew that when she threw something in the air, it came down. The higher she threw it, the longer it took. And Gram had said the shuttle was really high when it blew up.

"You won't, hon," Gram said. She had her arms wrapped around her knees. The tears made her eyelashes clump together. "The pieces have landed already. Far away. In Florida."

"Floor-e-da," Sarah repeated. "How come are you crying? Did you know them people?"

Gram shook her head. Then she tilted it back. "You can't even see the moon tonight," she said.

"There's a man in the moon," Sarah said.

"No, honey," Gram said. "But once upon a time, there was a man *on* the moon."

"Did you know him?" Sarah asked.

"No," Gram said. "But it sure felt as if I did."

The Martin Luther Extended Care Facility covered one city block near the old Dane County airport terminal. Sarah remembered when the entire area had been fields that were filled with the richest brown dirt she had ever seen. The MLECF was a new facility for middle- to low-income elderly. It covered the city block in small buildings, each stacked on top of each other, making the place a maze. The brochure said the design maximized available space. Sarah thought it maximized confusion.

It had been decades since she had been in a place like this. Not since she was a teenager, when nursing homes were still called nursing homes, and the places smelled of pee and antiseptic. MLECF smelled like roses. Nanotech hadn't met the technological promises made by its proponents in the early nineties, but it had achieved a sort of olfactory victory: Perfume companies had discovered a way to make good odors eat bad ones. It was an expensive, but satisfying service, one that made life in the late '20s much more bearable than life in the '90s.

The hospital had given her a twenty-four hour reprieve. It was not charity: the reprieve was required by law to anyone who requested it. It snapped all the social services into action. A social worker had been waiting for her by the front door of MLECF.

The tour was scripted: she saw the rehab rooms, the private suites, the entertainment center, and the kitchen. Mobile residents could cook their own meals on small counters in special suites. The place was as lovely as its brochure, but she knew this part of the facility was designed to put her at ease.

Except she wasn't. She had seen no elderly.

"Where is everyone?" she asked the social worker when he brought her back to the front desk. He was a small man with graying hair and long, fashionable sideburns. His hands were the smallest thing about him—child's hands really—soft and square and delicate.

"Privacy laws," he said. "We're not allowed to let outsiders see the residents without their permission."

"So when I visit my mother, will I be able to go to her room?" she asked.

"If you sign non-disclosure forms."

"And if I were to sign them today?" she asked. "Could I see the rest of the facility?"

His smile was small, tolerant, distant. "We don't have short-term forms," he said.

"I'm not making a short-term decision," she said. "This is my mother's life."

His gaze darted to her, then, and he sighed. "Come to my office, Ms. Chomley," he said. He went around the front desk through a narrow corridor and into a small cubicle with no windows. His desk was built into the wall, the computer screen larger than normal and rather old. Its component parts hummed, something she associated with the computers of her childhood.

He sat in the chair behind the desk, and she took the only other one, a wire seat with an arched back. It was not made for comfort. She perched on the edge of it, waiting for him to go on.

"Your mother was diagnosed with old age, am I right?" he asked.

"They said you didn't need to know," she said, "not unless I decided."

He shrugged. "It's logical. People with hope of recovery don't come here," he said.

"But you have rehabilitation rooms," she said. "What are they for then?"

He folded his small hands and rested them on the desktop. "They are for the handful of people who come here after surgeries, long illnesses or comas. Not for people diagnosed as old."

"Then why do old people come here?" she asked.

"Make their last years as comfortable as possible," he said.

"Is that possible here?" she asked. "In one room?"

"One eighth of a room, Ms. Chomley," he said. "We don't have private rooms."

"But the suites—"

"Are for rehabilitation patients." He tugged on his sideburn, leaned forward, and whispered, "Do you love your mother, Ms. Chomley?"

241

"Of course," she said automatically, even though she wasn't sure it was true.

"Then take her home," he whispered. "Take her home."

1998: Hazlet's gym. A private club, converted from a row of seventies apartments by a local developer, designed for his tenants, but later opened to paying memberships. Nights and afternoons belonged to the students. Mornings from 5:00 a.m. belonged to the seniors.

"Gram," Sarah said, holding a five-pound weight against her chest. "I don't need this. I jog."

"Women need strength," Gram said. She was wearing gray sweats and had her long gray hair tied back with a red scarf. She was on her back, pressing thirty-five pounds, another elderly woman spotting her as she worked. "Jogging keeps the weight down, but it doesn't give you strength."

"I had self-defense in school," Sarah said.

"I'm not talking self-defense," Gram said. "I'm talking strength. To carry a box, to lift a carton. To be independent."

Sarah laughed. "I am independent," she said.

"Now," Gram said. "Wait fifty years. Independence is something you won't take for granted then."

The pizza box was lukewarm by the time Sarah got it to the apartment. The heating chip had burned out a mile away from home, leaving the pizza inside to cool. She pulled the apartment door open, tossed the box on the counter, and threw her coat over a chair.

Janie, her oldest, was studying, squinting at her palmtop. She wasn't supposed to use such a small screen, but Sarah couldn't afford anything larger. She knew it meant upgraded lenses for Janie's bad eyes, but the lenses were in the future. The computer expense was part of the present.

Her son, Keith, whom her daughters had nicknamed Scooter, was taking apart the motorized car she had given him for Christmas. The car had cost half a week's salary; she hoped he could reassemble it. He was humming along to a radio chip, the telltale chord—required of all in-ear objects—trailing down the side of his head like an errant strand of hair.

Trina, her youngest, was already in the kitchen, standing on a stool as she begged the cereal cabinet to release its lock. She hadn't figured out the new code yet. It would only be a matter of days. She generally figured out cupboard codes by day five.

"I called," Sarah said. "I told you I'd be late."

"House screen's out," Scooter said.

"Yeah," Trina said. "He took out the sound chip for his car."

Sarah suppressed a sigh. "Scoot," she said. "We don't own the house screens. Why didn't you use your radio chip?"

"Cause I need that," he said. He stretched out one bare foot, scraping car parts against the hard wood floor.

"Well, see what you can do with the heater on this box," she said. "I don't want to pay for microwave time if I can help it."

"It burn out again?" Janie asked, setting her palmtop aside. "You gotta stop going there."

"I gotta stop ordering the special," Sarah said. "They always put it in the oldest boxes."

Scooter put the car parts beside the baseboard, then got up, brushed himself off, and came into the kitchen. He slid the box off the counter, and stuck a finger in the cardboard. Sarah pulled Trina off her chair and set her on the floor.

"Guys," she said. "I have a question. Can we make room for your grandmother here?"

"I thought you didn't like her," Janie said.

"Yeah," Scooter said. "Why should we make room for her when she didn't make room for her mother?"

"Does she know the cupboard codes?" Trina asked.

Sarah bit her lower lip. She hadn't realized she had put those thoughts in her children's brains. "I went to that center today. The social worker advised me to bring her home."

"Why?" Janie set her palm top on the end table.

"Shut it off, please," Sarah said, and Janie did. Behind her, cardboard ripped and Scooter cursed. Sarah ignored it.

"Why are you supposed to bring her home?" Janie asked again.

"Because she'd be in a room with eight others," Sarah said. "Because it's no place to spend the rest of your life."

"What do you care?" Scooter asked. "She never did anything for you."

Sarah sat down. She was shaking. "She raised me," Sarah said.

"Yeah, but she didn't want to," Trina said. Sarah looked at her daughter. She didn't remember telling Trina why her mother had left Sarah with Gram at various points in her life.

"You always said she was too busy living her life to care about someone else's," Scooter said.

"She's my mother," Sarah said, feeling defensive.

"So?" Janie asked. "That doesn't mean you have to take care of her."

"I know," Sarah said, and sighed.

2003: Her mother's living room. Sarah was standing; her

mother was sitting on the white, pink, and blue couch bought at an auction the year before.

"I'll take care of her, Mom. Instead of paying some home, give me room, board and some pocket change. That way she can stay home."

Her mother, small and delicate, still wore her hair long. It reached the middle of her back, a gray and black wave as chaotic as her mother could be. The black hairs were straight. The gray was coming in curly.

"Have you ever watched anyone die of cancer?" her mother asked.

"No, but—"

"I have. When I was married to Jack." Jack. Husband number two. The rich one. The one who died on her, and left all his money to his son, a man two years older than Sarah's mother. Jack had achieved perfection before he died. The men after that had no hope of catching up. "I did volunteer work at the hospital."

As if Sarah didn't know. Her mother was proud of the volunteer work, prouder of that than of her paid work. The volunteer work meant she had time on her hands, time to give away. The paid work—done to support her daughter from her ill-advised, rebound of a third marriage—never measured up.

"They used to have fans on in the cancer ward to keep the stink down." Her mother wrinkled her small nose as if she could still smell the memory.

"Mom, that was in the seventies."

"It hasn't gotten any prettier," her mother said. "And you don't have the stamina for it. Better that Gram goes where people can take care of her. Better to let her die with dignity, on clean comfortable sheets, in a clean comfortable room."

"Shouldn't she have her family with her?"

"She'll have her family with her," her mother said, staring past Sarah at something on the street. "We'll visit her every day."

"I'm going to take care of her," Sarah said.

Her mother shook her head. "It's your choice," her mother said. "It's not something I would do."

"I know," Sarah said. "You always did what was convenient for you."

"Not fair, Sarah."

"But true," Sarah said.

Sarah clutched the entrance documents in her right hand. As she entered her mother's hospital room, her fingers tightened, crumpling the pages. Her mother was asleep. The skin stretched across her tiny face, revealing the angles and hollows. Through the translucent surface, Sarah thought she could actually see bone.

—*Her strength is failing,* the first doctor had said. *The pneumonia was just a stage. We can cure the stages, but they will continue. We can stop any disease she gets except the one that's going to kill her. She's got old age. No one recovers from that.*

—*Old age isn't a disease,* Sarah said.

—*Oh, but it is,* the doctor said. *For a reason we don't understand, the cells fail to regenerate. Or they regenerate improperly. We can stimulate regeneration, but only in certain parts of the body. We can't touch the brain cells. And no matter what we do, some parts always fail. The heart muscle atrophies. It's as if total degeneration is built into the system. Your mother's degeneration has started. We can do nothing to end it except—end it.*

—*She's not that bad, is she?*

The doctor shrugged.—*I've been secondary approving physician on cases less advanced than hers. Once it reaches this stage, the future is certain. Death.*

—*The future is certain now,* Sarah said. *You'll die. I'll die.*

The doctor shook his head. *That's not certain. There is research in Sweden that shows degeneration can be prevented.*

—*Then why can't we use that treatment on Mother?*

The doctor's look was withering.

—*Because she can't afford it?* Sarah asked.

The doctor took a step back, as if Sarah's tone startled him.—*Because it's experimental. And even if it weren't, she's not a candidate. Degeneration is advanced in her. The Swedish treatments begin before the internal organs show advanced signs of wear. For some, that's age twenty. For others, that's forty-five. For no one is it seventy. No one at all.*

—*So you're saying kill her,* Sarah said.

The doctor didn't meet her gaze. *What's more humane? Letting her die now, with all her faculties in place, or waiting until she shuts down, part by part?*

—*Isn't that what death is?* Sarah asked.

—*Death,* the doctor had said as if he were quoting a textbook, *is the cessation of life.*

"Mom?" Sarah said. She sat beside the bed, and put the papers in her lap. "Mom, wake up. It's me."

Her mother's eyes opened. They were yellowish, bloodshot, exhausted. "Sarah?" she whispered.

Sarah nodded. "I brought papers here from the extended care center."

"Papers?" Her mother's voice was stronger now. She dug her hands into the mattress and pushed herself up. "What kind of papers?"

"Entrance agreements. They have the regular agreements there on computer. I told them you weren't linked here."

Her mother frowned. "Have you read them?"

"Yes," she said. "They seem fine. All they ask is that you agree to the rules of the center."

"And what are those rules?" her mother asked.

"They're listed in the regular document," Sarah said.

Her mother crossed her arms over her sunken chest. "I won't sign," she said.

"If you don't sign, you can't go," Sarah said. "The hospital has the legal right to put you on the street."

"I'll go home," her mother said.

"Mom." Sarah had been dreading this moment. "They rented your apartment. I had to put your stuff in storage."

"I pay my bills," her mother said.

"No, Mom," Sarah said. "Your weekly allowance has been coming here, for the deductible."

"You didn't pay my rent?"

"I can't afford *my* rent."

"But you can afford storage."

"It's cheaper than rent," Sarah said.

Her mother's lower lip trembled. "They'll kill me in that center."

"People die there, yes, Mom, but the officials don't kill anyone."

"Read the forms," her mother said.

"Mom, they have to have ways of dealing with the critically ill."

"I'm not critically ill," her mother said.

"Your doctor says you're dying," Sarah said.

"My doctor's wrong." Sarah's mother raised her chin, a slight gesture of defiance.

"That's denial, Mom."

"No, Sarah," her mother said. "I'm alive, and I like breathing. And I'm not afraid of what the future holds. I want to see each phase through, the way God intended."

Sarah shook her head. Her mother didn't understand. She couldn't. If she did, she wouldn't want to die, bit by bit, piece by piece. "Gram—"

"Your grandmother was a coward," her mother said.

"Gram was thinking of us," Sarah said.

Her mother's eyes narrowed. "Was she? Was she really?"

2003: Gram's house. An EMS truck was parked in the driveway. Sarah's mother stood in front of the door, arms crossed. Her hair was falling out of its ponytail and her right cheek was streaked with blood.

Sarah parked her car across the street, and ran to her mother. Her mother held out one blood-stained hand.

"You can't go in," her mother said.

"But you called—"

"I did," her mother said. "Before I knew. Gram's in the truck."

"Then she's all right?" Sarah started for it, but her mother grabbed her arm.

"No," her mother said, her voice oddly calm.

"I want to see her."

"*No,*" her mother said.

"What happened?" Sarah asked, panic eating at the edges of her stomach.

"She used your grandfather's handgun. She always said she would. Dramatic to the end." Her mother shook her head slightly, as if she couldn't quite believe it. "She called to say good-bye, and not to worry. That's when I called you. That's when I came here. The neighbors heard the shots. They'd already called 911."

"But she's all right," Sarah said.

Her mother's eyes met Sarah's. "She's gone."

Sarah frowned. "But I told her I'd take care of her. Yesterday. I told her I'd be here, and we'd get through it."

Her mother blinked hard and wiped at her nose. "Your grandmother said to tell you that she didn't want you to waste your life."

"But I wanted to help," Sarah said.

"I know." Her mother put her arm around Sarah, not noticing as the blood on her hand stained Sarah's white sleeve. "But you can't any more. And now we have to get through this. Together."

Sarah sat at her desk and scanned the documents the social worker had e-mailed her from MLECF. Her hand was shaking as she scrolled, her brain overloading from the legalese.

She would have found nothing if the social worker hadn't highlighted two sections for her.

1. Patient grants MLECF power of attorney in all matters pertaining to health.

and

50. Patient agrees to allow doctors and social workers to determine, in tandem, when resources allotted exceed gains returned.

She printed up both and handed them to her cubicle mate, Lars. He scanned them. "So?" he asked.

"What do they mean to you?" she asked.

"They mean the facility has the right to put a patient to sleep if they can no longer afford treatment."

"That's legal?"

"Sure," he said. "Has been for as long as I can remember."

"And it doesn't shock you?" she asked.

"Why should it?" he said. "These places have been doing it for years."

"I didn't realize," Sarah said.

"Not many people do," Lars said. "It's just an efficient way of dealing with a burden on society." He handed the hard copy back to her. "Why'd you ask?"

"For my mother," she said.

"Oh," Lars answered, and had the grace to flush.

1990: Spring thaw, Lake Wingra. First meeting of the Wingra Seniors' Polar Bear Club. Sarah wore her down jacket, unzipped, and a pair of fleece-lined boots. Her mittens dangled from strings, and the sweater her mother had made her wear that morning was too hot. But her face was cold. An icy mist was falling, making it feel as if the air were spitting.

Near the water's edge, four old men wearing rubber boots stomped away the last of the ice. A doctor stood beside the men, shaking his head as he watched.

Gram was beside Sarah. She wore a heavy carcoat over her sweats. In her arms, she clutched a fluffy towel, still warm from the dryer.

"You're nuts, Gram," Sarah said.

"I'm living, baby doll," Gram said. She handed Sarah the towel, then peeled off her carcoat, and her sweatshirt, revealing a one-piece suit underneath.

"That water's cold, Gram. What if you get a heart attack? What if you get sick?" Sarah lowered her voice. "What if you die?"

"Then I'll go out happy," Gram said. She shucked off her shoes and her sweatpants. Sarah took those too.

"Life's one big adventure, Sarah. You gotta live it the best way you can," Gram said, and ran for the frigid water.

Sarah stood at the door of her mother's hospital room

and watched her mother sleep.

Old age.

It was going to kill her, and no matter what the doctor said, it would probably kill all of them eventually.

It didn't matter how you died, Gram used to say. What mattered was how you lived.

And how had she lived these last few years? Like her mother. Selfish and focused and angry at the hand life had dealt her. Ever since Greg left—

Greg. She hadn't let herself think his name since he walked out, leaving her with three children and an apartment she couldn't afford on her own. No one had one-caretaker apartments any more, and she had been struggling against that for years, angry at Greg, angry at the world.

Not proud of herself like Gram would have been.

Proud for beating the system.

Sarah swallowed. "Mom?" She came closer to the bed. "Mom, wake up."

Her mother smiled. The dots on her cheeks moved as she did. "I was awake. I was watching you."

Sarah started. She hadn't expected the same scrutiny she was giving her mother.

"Children grow away from you, you know," her mother said.

"I know," Sarah said. She'd been watching hers do that every day.

"From the minute they leave the womb, they're not yours any more. They're strangers."

Sarah approached her mother. "Are we strangers, Mom?"

Tears floated in her mother's eyes.

She touched her mother's arm. She had lived inside this body once. It had been her first home. How could she let someone else discard it, as if it had never been? "I'm going to bring you to my place," Sarah said.

Her mother blinked, but her cheeks remained dry. "I'm not going to be noble like your grandmother was."

Sarah smiled. It was against her mother's nature to be noble. She squeezed her mother's arm. Gram's suicide had been awful.

"Nobility's overrated," Sarah said.

1985: Gram's backyard. Sarah put her pudgy arms around her Gram's neck and wiped her tears with one grimy mitten. "How come you're crying for the people in that shuttle if you didn't know them?" she asked.

Gram shook her head, then buried her face in Sarah's hair. "I don't know," she said. "Sometimes lives and dreams are so mixed up together, and you don't realize it until it's too late."

Gram was holding her too tight. Sarah squirmed. Gram let go. Sarah sat on Gram's knee.

Gram smiled at her. "You don't know what I'm talking about, do you?"

Sarah shook her head. Sometimes big people said all kinds of stuff she didn't understand.

"It's okay," Gram said. "You'll figure it out soon enough."

The hide-a-bed cost half a month's salary, but Sarah figured she could afford it, with her mother's allowance going toward rent. The living room was crammed with knick-knacks Sarah had once hoped she would never have to live with again. Her mother's heavy, ancient television set with its curved screen sat in the hallway, waiting to be carried to the back bedroom. The bedroom had been Sarah's. From that night on, it would be her mother's.

And, surprisingly, Sarah didn't mind. This was the chance she had missed with Gram. This was the chance she needed with her own mother. Too many people watched life's beginning and shied away from its end.

"I still don't get it," Janie said as she carried in the last box from storage. "Why doesn't she get her own apartment?"

"They don't make new leases with people over seventy, stupid," Scooter said. He was rummaging through the previous box, seeing if there were any old chips. Sarah reached into the box beside her and brought out an old attachable house sound system. She handed it to Scooter. He squealed with delight and looked for the chip.

"I don't see why she has to come here," Janie said again.

"Because I asked her," Sarah said.

"You don't even like her, Mom," Trina said. She was bouncing on the hide-a-bed, testing its springs.

Sarah took Trina's arm, and gently stopped her bouncing. Trina let her, almost as if she had been expecting it. After three children, Sarah knew how to parent.

But her mother had only had one. Sarah had been an accident, unplanned. Sarah's children were planned, but being raised the same way. By one woman alone.

"I don't know her any more," Sarah said. "I don't know if I like her or not."

"Then why bring her here?" Janie asked, sitting beside Trina.

Sarah looked at her daughters, and wondered how they would feel after their grandmother was gone.

When their own mother was dying.

The law said they weren't responsible, any more than she was.

"I'm bringing her here," Sarah said, "because life's an adventure."

She had forgotten that. All these years, she'd forgotten it. It had taken her mother, of all people, to remind her.

"An adventure?" Janie asked, as if she had never heard that before.

"An adventure," Sarah said. "I'd just forgotten, until now."

Present

Mason Evers sat on the edge of the bed, expecting another failure. He hadn't even taken off his tie.

Roxy had made her intentions clear. She had rolled up the television screen, turned down the bedroom lights, and changed the wall colors to a light, but sexy red. She had put satin sheets on the bed, and turned down the coverlet. On the bedside table, she'd placed a magnum of champagne and the crystal goblets they'd gotten for their last wedding anniversary. Right now, she was in the bathroom, preparing her entrance.

He wished he hadn't called out her name as he walked into the bedroom, heard her husky response as she asked him to wait. He'd followed the trail of clothing she'd left like breadcrumbs from the front door, his stomach churning as he picked up each piece—the silk blouse, the bra, the stockings, the panties.

Part of him worried for her—this littering of clothes had never happened before—and part of him worried for him. Not that he was afraid he'd find her with someone else. Roxy was nothing if not loyal. But he really didn't want to go in that bedroom, not with her expectations up, especially if they'd been up all day.

He sighed and flopped backwards on the bed. It was his

thirtieth birthday. Thirty years old, and a complete and total failure.

During his lunch appointment, his shrink had tried to convince him otherwise. His job, linking hospital operating rooms with each other for virtual surgery, was going very well. He didn't have to travel as much as he used to, and people had become quite accepting of the technology. The virtual operation—having the surgeon in one location and the patient in another—was no longer the wave of the future. It was the here and now, and he'd helped to bring that about.

But it didn't satisfy him.

He had good friends, a strong family, and an eleven-year-old marriage, which he was convinced would end in the next year. His shrink believed otherwise, but Mason knew that sooner or later, Roxy would get tired of him and his problems.

The bathroom door opened and Roxy swept into the room. She was wearing a diaphanous nightgown, so thin that it barely qualified as clothing, and it revealed every inch of her body. Her breasts were fuller than they had been when he first touched them in the backseat of his parents' car all those years ago, but her waist was still thin, her stomach still flat, and her legs as perfect as they ever were.

A wave of desire ran through him and he willed it away. *The mind could control everything,* the shrink had told him. Only Mason's mind didn't seem to control anything.

He closed his eyes, but the desire didn't fade. Amazing that the girl who had attracted him when they were both sixteen still attracted him now. That was, the shrink said, part of the problem. Mason's attraction to her had formed during his sexual development, and his response was a young man's response.

Control was what he needed. Not the drugs he'd tried (which left him fuzzy and uninterested), not the various tantric techniques the sex clinic had tried to teach, not even the weird virtual devices his company made as a sideline.

He had control in every other area of his life. The doctors said there was nothing physically wrong with him. He would eventually outgrow this, or so they assured him. Or he could learn to outthink it.

Yeah. Right.

"Mason." Roxy sat beside him on the bed. "Sit up, honey. I have a present for you."

He didn't want to sit up. He didn't want to move. He squeezed his eyes even tighter.

"Mason." The bed moved as she lay down beside him. She knew better than to touch him so soon. "Please, honey."

"Rox," he said. "I don't think this'll be such a good present this year."

"It's not what you think."

"Rox, I'm not in the mood."

She shifted her weight slightly, rolling closer to him. He could feel her warmth. "You are in the mood. I can tell."

He was always in the mood around her—at least, physically. But not mentally. Not now. "I don't want to struggle, not on this birthday. Turning thirty's difficult enough without being reminded about my inadequacies."

"Trust me, Mase," she said. "I have a little something that's going to make this birthday a whole lot of fun."

Something rattled above him. He opened his eyes as a bell went off, saw Roxy holding a square box the size of a grapefruit, wrapped in white paper and tied with a gold ribbon.

Only Roxy wasn't smiling. "Damn," she said. "How the

259

hell did I do that? This wasn't exactly how I—"

The bathroom door opened and Roxy swept into the room. She was wearing a diaphanous nightgown, so thin that it barely qualified as clothing. He found himself staring at her and got so aroused that he was dizzy.

"Son of a bitch." Roxy was staring at the small white box in her hand. "I did not plan things this way."

She strode toward the bed and sat beside him. He couldn't help himself. He reached for her.

She slapped his hand away. "If we don't do this right, you're gonna hate this. Damn."

He was still dizzy and confused, his hand stinging from her slap. Still, he reached for the single ribbon tied loosely around her neck. The ribbon held the nightgown in place. So much for control. All pretext of control had disappeared when she came out of the bathroom, looking just like he had imagined she would when he had stretched out on the bed and closed his eyes.

Never before had his wife so matched one of his fantasies. It was incredibly erotic.

She pushed his hand away.

"Mason," she snapped. "You have to concentrate."

"I don't concentrate well at moments like this," he said, loosening his tie. He didn't think he could get this aroused any more. He thought he had analyzed the entire problem to death, that only his body responded—much more quickly than he wanted it too. His mind had been teaching him to avoid all sexual situations.

He leaned in to kiss her, and she shook that small gold-ribboned package at him.

"Mason," she said. "You have to help me with this."

A bell went off.

She rolled her eyes. "I can't believe I did it again."

"What?" he asked, feeling slightly irritated. He'd have to tell her that he'd been fantasizing about her a moment before she walked through the door.

"Well," she said. "You see—"

The bathroom door opened and Roxy swept into the room. She was wearing a diaphanous nightgown, so thin that it barely qualified as clothing, and for some reason he was still laying on his back. He remembered loosening his tie, but it was tight around his neck.

"Oh, this is going to get old real quick," Roxy said.

Mason sat up. He wasn't aroused at all. He was a little dizzy though. But she did look beautiful, the way that gown held just enough of her in shadow so that he had to imagine the rest.

She leaned against the bathroom door. "Mason, we have to talk."

"You're not dressed for talking," he said, distracted in spite of himself.

"I hadn't planned on talking," she said. "But things have gotten out of control."

"Not yet." He stood up and walked toward her. He took the box out of her hand and kissed her. He'd been wanting to do that since—

He pulled away and frowned at her. "What the hell is going on here?"

She raised her eyebrows and gave him her impatient look. "That's what I've been trying to tell you. We've got a problem."

He liked the way she was pressed up against him. The material of her gown was so thin that he could feel her warmth through it.

The arousal was back. But how could it be back if it hadn't been there in the first place?

Was he drunk? He glanced at the champagne. Nope. The bottle was still closed.

"Mason," she said, putting her hands between them. "Give me that box."

He had forgotten he was holding it. "What is it?"

"Don't shake it," she said, taking it from him as if it were going to break at any moment. She slipped away from him, and pulled the box open. "This is going all wrong."

"Oh, no, babe," he said. "It's weird, but I'm kinda enjoying it."

She frowned at him, and tipped the open box toward him. "Look in here."

He sighed. Anything to please his wife. He peered inside the box. Inside, he saw a gold egg-shaped device. It looked like a Faberge Egg, only without the elaborate scrollwork.

"What is it?"

"A time machine." She sounded panicked.

"A what?" he asked.

"It's not functioning right." She ran a hand through her hair. "I must have set it off when I waved the package at you. I didn't mean to start it for a while. After all, I figured we had—"

The bathroom door opened and Roxy swept into the room. She was wearing a diaphanous nightgown and even though he'd seen it three times before, the look of her bathed in light, half her body in shadow, turned him on.

Mason sat up. "This has happened before."

"Of course it has." She leaned against the door and set the package down. The box was closed. "That's the beauty of the thing."

"What thing?" He wanted to touch her, but he didn't get off the bed. Although he did take off his tie.

"Haven't you been reading up on this?"

"No," he said.

"Time travel is impossible."

"Huh?" he asked. "You just said that was a time machine. Not to mention we've been going through the same five minutes for maybe 20 minutes now."

She sighed. "What I mean is, they found out that time travel like in the movies is impossible. You can only go back about five minutes, and then you loop for a while, and then time goes on. This is a novelty item. An expensive novelty item, but a novelty item all the same."

He frowned at her. "Then why did you get it?"

"Think, Mason," she said. "We clocked you at six minutes. If I turned this machine on at the right time, we'd get fifty minutes of love-making without yoga or breathing exercises."

He stared at her, his mouth open. "But I'm six minutes on a good day."

She grinned. "I know. But with this thing, you go back in time. Your body resets."

He felt a little overwhelmed. And he was still having trouble concentrating. His wife, after all, was naked under that see-through gown.

He made himself focus. "But—"

The bathroom door opened and Roxy banged into the room. This time she didn't even try to be sexy as she slammed the door behind her. She set the box down.

"But what?" she asked, sounding very annoyed.

He was a bit disconcerted too, lying on his back, his damned tie too tight—again. But he wasn't aroused. He wouldn't be aroused until he really looked at her.

Which he did. He couldn't help himself. She was so beautiful. How lucky was he to have such a beautiful wife?

"But what?" she asked again, using that tone she always used when she was about to get angry.

But? What had he been about to say? Oh, yeah. "But your body would reset too."

She nodded, her mouth a thin line. "That's why I wanted to time this perfectly. But I screwed it up. I had the machine set so that all I had to do was touch it at the exact right moment, and apparently I made it too touchy. And now we're in the middle of this thing, and *I don't know how to shut it off.*"

He recognized that tone of frustration. He loosened his tie and got up. "Give me the machine."

"It's also reset," she said. "One wrong shake and it'll go off again."

"Was that the bell I heard?" he asked.

"Yes," she said.

"So it's running twice."

"Yes," she said.

"Two loops?"

"Yes," she said.

"What does that mean?" he asked.

"I don't know," she said.

He picked up the box very carefully and tugged at the bow. It came loose in his fingers. He could see his wife's hip over the edge of the box. Her skin looked peachy, thanks to the effect of the gown. He loved that curve there, the way it—

The bathroom door slammed open. Roxy tugged the lid off the box and handed it to Mason. She was close enough to touch, and he did, running his hand along her arm.

She pulled away. "Let's solve this first."

He sighed and peered in the box. "Instructions?"

"Against the side." She caught his hand. "Better let me. My fingers are smaller."

She removed a slip of paper and handed it to him. The instructions were calligraphed on the page, making it hard to read. A novelty item. A curiosity. Not meant to be used so much as admired.

He squinted, read, and frowned.

"What?" she asked, sitting next to him.

"There are ten loops," he said, "every time you try this thing. Ten loops and no way to shut it off."

She put a hand against her forehead and closed her eyes. He remembered that posture from college. It happened whenever she got stumped by a math problem.

The posture also made her left breast rise slightly. He stared at it.

"Okay," she said. "I hit it twice. So does that mean we're going to have twenty loops or twelve?"

"Twelve?" His concentration was fading. He had to touch her.

"The ten from the first time, and then the ten from the second, which started in the second loop—I mean, the first real loop, so nine would be overlapping."

He took the box out of her hand and set it on the floor. He made certain his movements were deliberate so that he didn't make the machine go off again.

"I have no idea," he said as he—

The bathroom door slammed open and Roxy stomped out. "Did it say in those damn instructions why I go back to the bathroom and not the bed? I shook the box at you on the bed."

She was getting very angry. Her color had risen, making her skin flush from her cheeks all the way down to her chest.

Mason stood and took off his tie in a single movement. "It said something about a two-minute delay."

She let out an exasperated sigh. "I have to stop skimming instructions."

He was already across the room. He took the box out of her hand, reached around her, and set the box inside the bathroom where neither of them could kick it.

"What are you doing?" she asked.

He untied the ribbon holding her gown together, and pulled her against him. He was aroused, but his body was a little bit behind him for the very first time in his life.

"You were wrong, you know." He kissed her. She tasted very good.

"Wrong?" she asked against his mouth.

He nodded. "I don't reset."

She pulled away ever so slightly. "Oh, honey, I'm sorry. I thought—"

He caught her mouth, silenced her with his own, letting the kiss linger. She—

The bathroom door slammed open and Roxy ran out, untying her gown, letting it fall off of her. She must have set the box down before she came out because it wasn't in her hands as she dove onto the bed.

"We have to get this timing down," she said, reaching for his tie.

"See?" He smiled at her.

"What?"

"You don't reset either."

She shook her head at him. "I'm afraid I did."

"Your body resets," he said softly, "but not your mind. And the mind, the shrinks tell me, is all that matters."

"Oh," she said and then her eyebrows went up as she understood. "Oh."

He leaned forward and kissed her like he hadn't kissed her since they were dating. For once, he had time.

"I figure," he said after a moment, "that we have at least five more loops, if we don't waste them. And maybe as many as thirteen."

"Thirteen?" Her eyes sparkled.

"Maybe."

Then she frowned. "But we have to take off our clothes every time."

"Just mine," he said, grinning. This was the best birthday present she had ever given him. "Just mine."

Without End

The sun, high in the hot August afternoon, sent short shadows across the neatly trimmed grass. A small clump of people huddled in a semicircle, close but not touching. The coffin, in the center, sat on a platform covering the empty hole.

Dylan placed a rose on the black lacquer surface, and stepped back. A moment, frozen in time and space.

A hand clutched his shoulder. Firm grip, meant as reassurance. He turned. Ross nodded to him, mouth a thin line.

"She was a good woman," Ross whispered.

Dylan nodded. The minister was speaking, but he didn't care about the words, even though the rest of the group strained forward.

"She would have found this silly," Dylan said, and then stopped. Ross's expression had changed from one of sympathy to something else—confusion? Disapproval? Dylan didn't know, and didn't really want to find out. Outside he was calm. Inside he felt fragile, as if his entire body was formed of the thinnest crystal. One wrong look, a movement, a shadow on the grass, would shatter him into a thousand pieces.

A thousand pieces. Shards, scattered on the kitchen floor. Geneva, crouched over them, like a cat about to pounce. *Look, Dylan,* she said. *To us, a glass shattered forever. But to the universe, possibilities. A thousand possibilities.*

He stared at the black box. He could picture Geneva inside as she had looked the night before: black hair cascading on the satin; skin too white; eyes closed in imitation sleep. Geneva had never been so still.

He wondered what she would say if she stood beside him, her hand light on his arm, the summer sun kissing her hair.

For just a moment, trapped in space and time.

Stars twinkled over the ocean. Dylan stood on the damp sand, Geneva beside him, her hand wrapped in his and tucked in his pocket—the only warm thing on the chilly beach. Occasionally the wind would brush a strand of her hair across his face. She would push at her hair angrily, but he liked the touch, the faint shampoo smell of her.

She was staring at the waves, a frown touching the corners of her mouth. "Hear it?" she asked.

He listened and heard nothing except the pulse of the ocean, powerful, throbbing, a pulse that had more life than he did. "Hear what?"

"The waves."

In her pause, he listened to them crash against the sand, the heart of the pulse.

"It's so redundant," she said.

"What is?" He turned, his attention fully on her. She looked like a clothed Venus, rising out of the sand, hair wrapped around her, eyes sparkling with unearthly light.

"Sound is a wave, a wave is sound. We stand here and listen to nature's redundance and call it beautiful."

He leaned into her, feeling her solidness, her warmth. "It is beautiful."

She grinned at him. "It's inspiring," she said, and pulled

270

her hand out of his pocket. She walked down to the edge where the Pacific met the Oregon coast. He didn't move, but watched her instead, wishing he could paint. She looked so powerful standing there, one small woman facing an ocean, against a backdrop of stars.

He went through her papers for the university, separating them into piles with equations and piles without. The cat sat on the piles without, watching the proceeding with a solemnness that suited the occasion.

Dylan's knowledge of physics and astronomy came from Geneva. He had had three semesters in college, a series called Physics for Poets (hardly any equations), and by the time he met her, most of his knowledge was out of date.

If you knew so little about women, Geneva once said, *I'd be explaining to you what my clitoris is.*

His specialty was philosophy, not so much of the religious type, even though he could get lost in the Middle Ages monkish romanticism, but more a political strip: Descartes, Locke, Hegel, and John Stuart Mill. He liked to ponder unanswerable questions. He had met Geneva that way—one afternoon, wind off the lake, Wisconsin in the summer, sitting on the Union Terrace, soaking up the rays and pretending to study. Only he wasn't even pretending, he was arguing basic freshman philosophy: if a tree falls in the forest, and no one hears it, does it made a sound? Geneva had been passing at the time—all legs and tan and too big glasses on a too small nose.

Of course, she said, *because it makes a disturbance and the disturbance makes a wave, and that wave is sound.*

He didn't remember what he said in response. Something intriguing enough to make her sit and argue until the sunset turned the lake golden, and the mosquitos had driven the other students away.

From that moment on, he and Geneva always talked that way. The philosophy of physics. The physics of philosophy. He got the education without the equations and she, she felt free enough to explore the imaginative side of her science—the tiny particles no one could see, the unified theories, the strings binding the universe.

There's something out there, Dylan, she would say, *and it's more than we are.*

He knew that, as he held her papers, in her sunlit office just past their den. In her crabbed writing, on those dot-matrix computer sheets, was the secret to something.

If he could touch that, he could touch her. And if he could touch her, he might be able to hold her.

Forever.

The campus bar was full of people impossibly young. Dylan grabbed his frosty mug of beer and sat across from Ross, watching the people intermingle. A different university, a different time. Now the students wore their hair short, and the professors wore theirs long. Dylan sipped, let the foam catch him full on his upper lip, and let the sound of co-mingled voices and too loud music wash over him.

"I worry about you," Ross said. His beer was dark and warm. Its color matched the tweed blend of his blazer. "You've locked yourself up in that house, and haven't gone anywhere in weeks. You don't have to get her papers in order before the end of the term, Dylan. The department just wants them on file."

Dylan shook his head. He wasn't always working. Sometimes he wandered from room to room, touching her clothes, the small sculpture she had brought back from Africa, the pieces of Inuit-carved whale bone they had found

272

in Alaska. "I'll get it done," he said.

"That's not the point." Ross pushed his beer aside, ignoring it as a bit of foam slopped out. He leaned forward, and would probably have touched Dylan's arm if Dylan had been the kind of man who permitted it. "She's dead, Dylan. She's gone. She was a spectacular woman, but now you have to get used to living without her."

Dylan stared at Ross's hand, outstretched on the scarred wooden table. "But what if she isn't really dead? I can feel her sometimes, Ross, as close to me as you are."

"That's part of grieving," Ross said. "You're in the habit of feeling her presence. It's like a ghost limb. You know it was there; you know what it felt like, and you can't believe it's gone."

"No." Dylan's fingers were frozen to the side of the mug. He pulled them away. "She was working on space-time equations, did you know that?"

Ross removed his hand from the tabletop, the odd expression—the one Dylan had seen at the funeral—back on his face. "Of course I knew that. We have to report on her research twice a term."

"She said she was close to something. That we thought about time wrong. That we were looking for beginnings and endings, and they weren't important—and possibly not even probable. She said we were limited by the way we think, Ross."

"It's not a new area," Ross said. A cocktail waitress went by, her tray loaded with heavy beer mugs. Patrons ducked and slipped into each other to stay out of her way. "We've been exploring space-time since Einstein. Geneva was going over very old ground. The department was going to re-examine her position if she hadn't taken a new angle this term."

"Her angle was new." Dylan wiped his hands on his jeans. "It was new from the beginning. She said the problem was not in the physical world, but in the way our minds understood it. She said—"

"I know what she said." Ross's voice was gentle. "It's not physics, Dylan. It's philosophy."

Dylan's entire body tensed. "I didn't change her, Ross. She was thinking this way when we met, when she was an undergraduate. She said that our limitations limited the way we looked at the universe, and she's right. You know she's right."

"We already know about space-time," Ross said. "About the lack of beginnings and the lack of endings. We know all that—"

"But we still think in linear terms. If we truly understood relativity, time would be all encompassing. We would experience everything at once."

"Dylan," Ross said, his voice soft. "Linear times keeps us sane."

"No," Dylan said. "That's why ancient maps had dragons on them, and why no one believed that the world was round. Why Galileo got imprisoned for showing the universe didn't work the way the church wanted it to. You all got upset at her because she was showing you that your minds were as narrow as the ancients', that you have your theories of everything and think you can understand it all, when you don't take into account your own beings. She is doing physics, Ross. You're just too blind to see it."

Dylan stood up. The conversation around him had stopped, and the short-haired, too-young students were staring at him. Ross was looking at his hands.

Dylan waited, breathing heavily, a pressure inside his chest that he had never felt before. Ross finally looked up, his round face empty of all emotion. "The anger," he said. "It's part of grieving too."

They first tried it in her dorm room, shutters closed on the only window, lights off so that the posters of Einstein were hidden, so that only the glow-in-the-dark stars on the ceiling remained. They crowded, side by side, on her narrow bed, after removing their clothes in the dark. He could smell her musk, feel the warmth of her, but as he leaned into her body, she moved away.

"We can't touch," she said. "Defeats the purpose."

So they lay there, staring up at the bright pink and green stars. And she began speaking softly, her voice no more than a murmur in his ear.

She told him what she liked to do with him, how he tasted, how soft his mouth was, how sensitive his ear. She worked her way down his body, never touching him, only talking to him, until he thought he could wait no longer. And then she was on top of him, wet already, nipples hard, and within a few seconds, they had worked their way to mutual orgasm—the best he had ever had.

She rolled back beside him, and sighed. "Intellectual foreplay," she said. "It really works."

Ghost limb. From the moment Ross mentioned it, Dylan felt not one but dozens of ghost limbs throughout the house. Here, in the bedroom, done in designer pink by the previous owner (*all we need is a big bow on the bed, and it'll be perfect—for eight-year-old girls,* Geneva said). Something they were going to remodel when the money allowed. The small side room, well heated, well lit, filled with boxes and scraps of Christmas wrapping: he saw babies in there. First the little boy, cherubic face puckered in sleep. Then a little

275

girl, all wide-eyed and exploring, Geneva in the raw. Future ghosts, possibilities lopped off with the branch that was Geneva.

One night he woke in the dark, confident that he had just missed her. Her scent lingered; the energy of her presence electrified the space. He knew, just a moment before, that she had been there—Geneva, alive, bright, and dancing with ideas.

He got up and went into the living room. The cat followed him, sleepy and dazed. Together they stared out the wide living room window at the street. A long streetlight illuminated a patch of concrete. The light's reflection made the neighboring homes look gray and indistinct. Ghost homes, full of possibilities.

The cat got bored and leapt from the sill, but when Dylan closed his eyes, he could still see her, outlined in red shadow against his eyelids. Even though she was alive, moving, and breathing, the cat too left ghosts.

It flashed across his mind, then, the possibility—and as quickly as it appeared, it was gone. But he knew it was there. He knew he would find it, and then he would no longer be alone, among the ghosts.

"Dammit. The little shit!" Geneva's voice rose on the last syllable, so Dylan knew she wasn't upset, just inconvenienced. He came out of his office to find her standing by the front door, hands against her hips. "Cat's out," she said.

He glanced out the door. The cat sat on the porch huddled against the rain, acting as if the world had betrayed her by getting her wet. He picked her up and carried her inside, closing the door with his foot.

Geneva reached beyond him and locked the bolt.

"There's no need," he said. "Door's closed."

Geneva grinned at him. He dropped the cat and she scampered into the living room, pausing at the end of the couch to clean the vile wetness off her fur.

"Little shit," Geneva said again. She was staring at the cat fondly. "She figured out the door. I came out here in time to see her grasp the knob in both paws and turn."

"Cats can't do that," he said.

"No. *Dogs* can't. Cats think differently." She kissed him lightly on the nose. "Imagine, being trapped by your mental abilities. A cat can get out of a man-made trap. A dog can't."

Then she smiled as if she had solved the riddle of the universe, went back into her office, and closed the door.

He had chalk on his hands. Facing all those clean, bright students, he felt rumpled and old. Most of them sat before him because his elective brought them three credits. Only a handful liked to grasp the elemental questions as much as he did. He rubbed his hands together, saw chalk motes drift in the fluorescent light.

"The Deists believed in a clockmaker god," he said, leaning against the metal lip of the blackboard. "A god who invented the world, then sat back and watched it play, like a great ticking clock. Jefferson believed in Deism. Some say that was why he became a great political philosopher—he believed that God no longer intervened in his creation, so the creation had to govern itself."

Dylan paused, remembering Geneva's face when he had discussed this with her, so many years ago. None of the students had her sharpness, her quick fascination with things of the mind. He waited for someone to raise a hand, to ask why those who believed in God the clockmaker didn't believe in predetermination, but no one asked. He couldn't go into his long explanation without prompting, and he didn't feel like prompting himself.

He waved a hand, almost said, "Never mind," but didn't. "Read chapters thirteen and fourteen," he said to those blank faces, "and write me a paper about the contradictions in Deistic philosophy."

"By tomorrow?" someone asked.

"Four pages," he said tiredly. "I'm letting you out early." They looked at him as if he had betrayed them. "You can do four pages. It's not the great American novel."

He grabbed his books and let himself out of the room. The hallway was quiet. It smelled faintly of processed air, and looked cleaner than it did when filled with students. Down the stairs, he heard a door slam. A moment later, a woman appeared on the staircase.

She was tiny, blonde, her hair wrapped around her skull like a turban. When she looked up, he recognized her. Hollings, from psychology.

"What are you pondering so seriously?" she asked.

He studied her for a minute, then decided to answer truthfully. "If God were a watchmaker, like the Deists believed, and if he abandoned his watch, which they did not believe, wouldn't that leave a vacuum? Wouldn't that vacuum have to be filled?"

Her mouth opened slightly, revealing an even row of perfect white teeth. Then she closed it again. "A watchmaker makes a watch and gives it to someone else. Presumably the watch owner maintains the watch."

"That assumes a lot of watches—and a lot of watchmakers."

"Indeed it does." She smiled and walked away.

He watched her go, wondering if the exchange had happened or if he had imagined it. He thought no one besides Geneva would engage in flip philosophies.

Perhaps he was wrong.

Perhaps he had been wrong about a lot of things.

They lay on their backs on the public dock. Below them, Devil's Lake lapped at the wood, trying to reach them. In the distance, they could hear the ocean, shushing its way to shore. The Oregon night was cool, not cold, and they used each other for warmth.

Above them, in the Perseids, meteors showered at the rate of one per minute. Dylan oooed his appreciation, but Geneva remained unusually silent. She snuggled closer and slipped her hand in his. It was thinner than it used to be. He could feel the delicate bones in her palm.

"I wonder," she said, "if that's going on inside of me."

He tensed. She didn't talk about the cancer much, and when she did, it often presaged a deep depression. "You wonder if what's going on inside of you?"

"If somewhere, deep down, two tiny beings are lying on the equivalent of a dock on the equivalent of a lake, watching cells die."

"We're watching history," he said. "The cells are dying inside you now."

"But who knows how long it takes the message to reach those two tiny beings on the lake equivalent? If the sun died now, we wouldn't know for another eight minutes. So to us, the sun would still be alive, even though it was dead."

Her words sent a shudder through him. He imagined himself, talking to her, listening to her response, even though she was already dead.

"We think about it wrong, you know," she said, breaking into his reverie. She was alive and breathing, and snuggled against him. He would know when she died.

"Think about what wrong?"

"Time. We act as if it moves in a linear fashion, straight from here on as if nothing would change. But our memories change. The fact that we have memories means that time is not linear. String theory postulates twenty-five dimensions, and we can barely handle the three we see. We're like cats and dogs and doors."

"And if we could think in time that wasn't linear, how would it be?"

He could feel her shrug, sharp shoulder bones moving against his ribcage. "I don't know. Maybe we would experience everything at once. All our life, from birth to death, would be in our minds at the same time. Only we wouldn't look at it as a line. We look at it like a pond, full of everything, full of us."

Her words washed over him like a wave, like tiny particles he could barely feel. "Geneva." He kept his voice quiet, like the lapping of the water against the dock. "What are you saying?"

She sat up then, blocking his view of the meteor showers, her face more alive than it had been in weeks. "I'm saying don't mourn for me. Mourning is a function of linear time."

"Geneva," he said with a resolution he didn't feel. "You're not going to die."

"Exactly," she said, and rested her head on his chest.

He pulled open the heavy oak doors and went inside. The chancel smelled vaguely of candle wax and pine branches, even though it wasn't Christmas. A red carpet ran down the aisles between the heavy brown pews. The altar stood at the front like a small fortress. He hadn't been inside a church since he was a teenager, and inside this one now, he felt small, as if that former self remained, waiting for a moment like this.

A ghost limb.

He smiled just a little, half afraid that the minister would find him, and order him out. He sat in a back pew and stared at the altar, hoping the words would come back to him. He ran through the rituals in his mind. Standing up for the opening hymn, watching the choir process, listening to the readings, singing more hymns, and then the offering—and the music.

> . . . as it was in the beginning
> is now and ever shall be
> world without end.
> Amen.
> Amen.

World without end. He picked up a hymnal, stuck in the back of the pew, and thumbed through it. They listed the Doxology, but not the year it was written, nor the text it was written from. Surely it didn't have the meaning that he interpreted. When it came to the church, the hymn probably meant life ever after. Not time without end. Not beginnings without endings, endings without beginnings. Not non-linear time.

He stood. He had never been in this church before, of that he was certain. So the ghost limb he brought with him applied to the Presbyterian church in Wisconsin, the one in which he was raised, where they too sang the Doxology, where a red carpet ran down the aisle, where the altar rose like a fortress.

Then a memory came, as clear and fresh as a drop of

spring water. He couldn't have been more than eight, sitting beside his father on Christmas Eve, listening to the way that God had sent His only son to earth, to have Him die for our sins.

And why, Dylan asked, *if God had a son, why didn't God have a father?*

Because God is the father, his father replied. And no matter how much probing Dylan did, he couldn't get at a better answer.

The beginnings of a philosopher—the search for the deeper meanings. Not being satisfied with the pat, the quick, the easy answer. That path had led him away from the church, away, even, from God, and into Geneva, whom he felt understood the mysteries of the universe.

He wouldn't find Geneva here. She felt that the church destroyed thought. He didn't know why he had come looking in the first place.

Bare feet on the deck, cat behind her, hat tipped down over her eyes. Geneva wasn't moving. Geneva, frozen in sunlight.

"How'd it go?" he asked.

The cat leapt off the chair, rubbed her soft fur against his legs, demanding attention. He crouched and scratched her back, all the while watching Geneva.

"They imprisoned Copernicus," she said, not moving. "Newton too. They kicked Einstein out of Germany, and made Socrates drink hemlock."

"It didn't go well, then," he said, sitting on the deck chair beside her.

She tilted her hat up, revealing her green eyes. They shone in the sun. "Depends on your point of view. If they accepted me, I probably wasn't on enough of an edge."

He didn't know how to respond. He was secretly relieved that she hadn't gotten the post-doc. MIT was an excellent school, and an even better research facility, but she would have been in Boston, and he would have been in Oregon. Together only on breaks and during term's end.

"Did you ever think of working on your theories on your own time?" he asked.

"And give those stupid committees the pap that they want?" She sat up then, and whipped her hat off her head, letting her black hair cascade around her shoulders. "You ever think of becoming a Baptist?"

"Geneva, it's not the same."

"It is too the same. People become arbiters of thought. In your area, the church still holds. In mine, it's the universities. This is an accepted area of research. That is not. Scientists are children, Dylan, little precious children, who look at the world as if it is brand new—because it is brand new to them. And they ask silly questions, and expect cosmic answers, and when the answers don't come, they go searching. And if they can't ask the silly questions, if they get slapped every time they do, their searches get smaller, their discoveries get smaller, and the world becomes a ridiculous, narrow place."

She plopped her hat back on her head, swung her tanned legs off the deck chair and stood up. "I can make you come without even touching you. Just the power of our minds, working together. Imagine if the right combination of minds, working together, break through the boundaries that hold us in our place in the universe. We might be able to see the Big Bang at the same moment we see the universe's end. We might be able to see the moment of our birth, this moment, and every other moment of our lives. We would live differently. We would be different—more than human, maybe even better than human."

Her cheeks were flushed. He wanted to touch her, but he knew better.

"It's steam engine time, that's all it is," she said. "A handful of minds, working together, change our perception of the world. Does a tree falling unobserved in the forest make a sound? Only if we believe that a tree is a tree, the ground is the ground, and a sound a vibration. Only if we believe together."

"And someone who doesn't believe gets denied a post-doc," he said.

"It's the twentieth century equivalent of being forced to drink hemlock," she said, and flounced into the house.

He hadn't turned on a light yet. Dylan sat in the dark, watching the fuzzy grayness slip over the entire living room. The cat slept on a corner of the couch. Geneva's papers were piled on the coffee table, on the end tables, in the corner. He had been sitting in the dark too much, thinking perhaps that was when her ghost would arrive.

A light flipped on in the kitchen and he jumped.

"Jesus Christ, don't you use lights anymore?"

Ross. Ross had let himself in the back door. Dylan took a deep breath to ease the pounding of his heart. He reached up and flicked on a table lamp.

"In here," he said.

Ross came through the dining room door, and stared at the living room. The cat curled into a tighter ball, hiding her eyes from the light.

"We need to get you out of here," he said. "How about a movie?"

Dylan shook his head. He didn't need distractions now. He felt like he was very close. Her papers held little illuminating, but his memories—they were like a jigsaw puzzle, leaving gaps, creating bits of a picture. As if she had given him the answer out of order, and he had to piece it together. Alone.

"Okay," Ross said, slumping into the sofa. "How about a beer?"

The cat sat up and looked at Ross, then jumped off the couch. Dylan wished he could be as rude.

"I want to be alone right now," he said.

"You've been alone since the end of August. Lock yourself up in here long enough, and you'll never get over her."

"I don't want to get over her," Dylan said.

Ross shrugged. "Wrong choice of words. You got your own life, and the last thing Geneva would have done was to want you to stop living because of her."

"I'm still living," Dylan said. "I'm still thinking."

"Not good enough." Ross stood, grabbed Dylan's coat off the back of a chair, and held it out.

Dylan looked at it and sighed. Then he rubbed a hand over his face. "Sit down," he said.

Ross sat, still holding Dylan's coat. He rested on the edge of the couch, as if he were about to jump up at any point.

"When Geneva and I went to Alaska, some friends of ours took us to a glacier. We went up in the mountains, saw this fantastic lake, filled with icebergs, and at the edge of the lake, the tip of the glacier. A boat took us right there, and we could see geologic history being made."

"I remember," Ross said. His tone was dry—*get to the point, Dylan*—and he clutched the coat tighter. "You told me when you got back."

"But I didn't tell you about the exhibit. One of those museum things, where they showed you how the glacier has traveled in the last hundred years or so. It receded so much that the point where we stood at the edge of the lake had been glacier only 150 years before. That sucker was moving fast. Geneva stayed inside, where it was warm, but I went back out, and put my feet where that glacier had been a hundred years ago. And if I closed my eyes, I could feel it. I knew what it was like in the past; it was as if it was still there, only half a step away, and I could get to it, if I took the right step."

Ross leaned back on the couch, the coat covering him like a blanket. "When Gary died," he said, "I used to go in his bedroom and pick up one of those models he worked so hard on. And if I held it just right, at the right time of night, I could feel his little warm hand under mine. Dinah would just watch me, she wouldn't say anything, and I used to think she was jealous—Gary shows up for Ross, but not me kinda thing. But she was worried about losing me too. She was afraid I would never come out of it. I still miss him, Dylan. I see another man with a six-year-old boy and it knocks the wind out of me. But I survived, and I moved on, and we have Linny now, and she's precious too."

"You're telling me this is another phase?"

"No." Ross was twisting the coat sleeve in his hands. "I'm telling you I finally know how she felt. Dylan, give yourself a chance to heal. Geneva will always be part of your past, but not part of your future."

"What makes you so sure," Dylan asked, "that they're all that different?"

Geneva rested on her stomach, knees bent, feet crossed at the ankles. She held a blade of grass between her fingers, and occasionally she would blow on it, trying to make a sound. The summer sun was hot, and the humidity was high. Wisconsin in the summer. Dylan couldn't wait to leave.

"Did you know that Mormons marry not just for life, but for all eternity?"

"You saying we should incorporate that into our vows?" Dylan rolled on his back, feeling the grass tickle his shoulders.

"I wonder if we won't be doing that already." She put her thumbs to her mouth, a blade of grass stretched between them. As she blew, it made a weak raspberry sound. "I mean, if you look at an event like you look at a pebble falling into a pond, the action will create ripples that will stretch out from the pebble. Each event has its own ripple, independent of another ripple—"

"Unless they collide," Dylan said with a leer.

"Unless they collide," she repeated, ignoring his meaning. "But who is to say that once a pebble gets dropped, you can't go back to the same spot and watch it get dropped over and over again. You can in videotape, why not in life?"

"Because life doesn't have rewind and fast forward," he said.

"Who says? Time is just perception, Dylan."

He rolled to his side, kissed her bare shoulder, and draped an arm across her back. From his perspective, the blade of grass between her fingers looked ragged and damp. "So you're saying you might perceive that you're marrying me for eternity, and I might perceive that I'm marrying you for Wednesday. So I could turn around and marry someone else for Thursday—"

"Only if you get a divorce first." She threw away the blade of grass. "Legalities, remember? Other people's perceptions."

"—and you would still think you're married to me forever, right?"

"I think I heard about a court case like that," she said, leaning her head into him. Her hair smelled of the sun. He kissed her crown.

She turned, so that she was pressed flush against him, warm skin against his. "But when you say you'll love me for eternity, you mean it, right?"

He leaned in, his face almost touching hers. He couldn't imagine life without her. "When I say I'll love you forever," he said, "I mean it with all my heart."

The dean's office was on the second floor of Erskine Hall, where the senior professors resided. Dylan used to aspire to walking that staircase every day. Then he would have had tenure, been able to stay in Oregon until he retired. He used to imagine that he and Geneva would buy a beach house. They would work in the city, then drive the hour to the beach each weekend. They would sit outside, on a piece of driftwood, staring at the point where the sky met the ocean. Geneva would contemplate the universe, and Dylan would contemplate her.

Dreams. Even dreams were ghost limbs. Moments, frozen in time and space.

He walked down the narrow corridors, past the rows of crammed offices, filled with too many books and stacks of student papers. The dean's office was a little larger, and it had a reception area, usually staffed by upperclassmen. This time, though, the receptionist was gone.

He knocked on the gray metal door. "Nick?"

"Come on in, Dylan, and close the door."

Dylan did as he was asked, and sat on the ancient upholstered chair in front of Nick's desk. Students probably felt like they'd walked in hell's anteroom when they came here. Everything was decorated early '70s, in browns and burnt orange.

Nick was a white-haired man in his late fifties, face florid with too much food and stress. "I'm sorry about Geneva," he said. "She had spirit. I never expected to outlive someone like her."

Dylan made himself smile. "My mother said she was like a flare, brief but beautiful."

"You don't believe that," Nick said.

Dylan took a deep breath. "You didn't call me in here to talk about Geneva."

"Actually, I did. Indirectly." Nick stood up, and shoved his hands in his pockets, stretching out his pants like a clown's, and making his potbelly poof out. Geneva used to call him Chuckles when he did that, a comment made all the better by the fact that the gesture meant Nick was going to say something difficult. "Word is that you've been acting a bit erratic lately. Letting classes out early, missing meetings, spouting spontaneous philosophy in the halls."

"Doesn't sound like the crime of the century," Dylan said, then bit his lip. Defensive. He couldn't get defensive.

"No, and it's not even all that unusual—except for you, Dylan. You were always consistent and quiet. I'm not saying you're doing anything wrong, but your wife just died. I wanted you to take the term off, but you insisted on working, and I'm not sure that was such a good idea."

Dylan stared at him for a moment, uncertain how to respond.

It begins with little complaints, Geneva once told him. *Maybe your clothes are a little unusual, or you don't conduct class according to the right methods. Then, one day, you wake up and find you've been imprisoned for your beliefs.*

289

He opened his mouth, closed it again, and thought. The classes meant nothing this term. The students, merely full-sized reminders of how much time had passed since he had sat in their chairs, since he had met Geneva.

"You're right," he said. "I think I should take a leave of absence, maybe come back next fall term."

Nick turned, pulled his hands out of his pockets, and frowned. Obviously he hadn't expected Dylan to acquiesce so easily. "Sure it won't leave you alone too much?"

Dylan smiled and shrugged. "I'm not sure I'm really alone now," he said.

Toward the end, she had shrunk to half her size, her skin so translucent he could see her veins. The hospital room had deep blue walls, a bed with restraints on it, and a television perched in the corner. The restraints were down, the television off, and the window open, casting sunlight against the awful blue.

Dylan sat beside the bed every day, from the moment visiting hours began until the moment they ended. At noon on August 23rd, she opened her eyes and found his. Her gaze was clear for the first time in three days, for the first time since he had brought her to the hospital.

"Dylan?" Her voice was no more than a rasp.

He took her too-small hand. It no longer fit just right in his. "I'm here, Geneva."

"You know those two tiny beings on the lake equivalent?" Each word was an effort. He leaned forward so that he could hear her. Her grip was tight in his. "I think in about eight minutes, they're going to see a supernova."

She closed her eyes. He couldn't hear her breathing. He pushed the nurse call button, once, twice, then three times.

The grip in his hand tightened. Geneva was looking at

him, a small smile on her face. "Don't mourn, Dylan," she said. "Forever, remember?"

"I remember," he said, but by that time, she had loosened her grip on his hand. The nurses came in, with their equipment and needles, pushing him aside. He watched as they checked her, as they looked under her closed eyelids, and felt for her pulse. One of them turned to him, and shook her head. He shoved his hands in his pockets and walked out of the room, a much poorer man than he had been when he entered.

On All Hallow's Eve, he packed his car to the light of the single streetlight. During the afternoon, he had taken the cat over to Ross's, explaining that he was going on a short trip, and wasn't sure when he would be back. He waited until dark, packed the car, and headed west.

He had awakened with the idea, the jigsaw puzzle complete in his mind. He knew how to find her, and how they could be together, forever, as she had said. As he drove over the Coast Range, the puzzle became clearer; the answer seemed right. Steam engine time, she had said. But who would have thought that a philosophy professor would be the first to ride the rails?

Geneva had. She knew that philosophers were used to broad concepts of the mind.

He pulled into the public beach at Lincoln City, grabbed a blanket and a cooler from the back of the car, and walked to the loose sand. He was careful to sit on a driftwood log, untouched by high tide.

Geneva called the point where the sea met the sky infinity. In the dark, it seemed even more vast than it did in the day. He put the blanket on the sand, set the cooler to the side, and leaned on the driftwood log.

He managed to arrive on the dark side of the moon. The night sky was full of stars, points of light, points of history. To their friends, these stars could be dead, but to him, they lived, and twinkled, and smiled for one last show. His mind could grasp each point of light, see it for what it was, and for its pattern, feel the backdrop of blackness against it and beyond.

The ocean spoke to him in its constant roar, and beneath it, he heard Geneva's voice talking about sound and waves, waves and sound. *Inspiring,* she had said, and so it was.

The edge of the universe was just beyond his imagination. The whole universe was within his grasp. He didn't want to see the big bang or the end of everything. He didn't want to see all of time, nor all of time and space. Only those points of light that were Geneva, from her birth to her death and back again. He wanted to hold all of those points in his mind at the same time, to be lying with her on the dock at the same time he sat here alone, to be holding her hand in the hospital while they played at intellectual foreplay in her dorm. He wanted his mind to be like the sky, holding history, the future, and infinity at the same time.

Geneva.

She was out there, in time and space, each moment of her existence a moment for him to hold.

He cast his mind into the inky blackness—

—and felt the barriers break.